DEFENDING HILLSBOROUGH

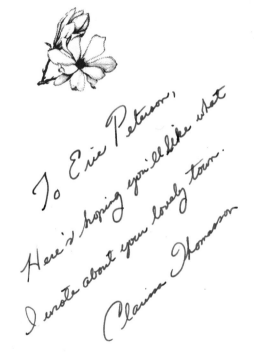

To Eric Peterson,
Here's hoping you'll like what
I wrote about your lovely town.

Claire Thomason

DEFENDING HILLSBOROUGH

Clarissa Thomasson

RTP
RESEARCH TRIANGLE PUBLISHING

Published by
Research Triangle Publishing, Inc.
PO Box 1130
Fuquay-Varina, NC 27526

ISBN 1-884570-85-2

Cover Design by Kathy Holbrook

Library of Congress Catalog Card Number: 98-66826

⊗ The paper used in this publication meets the minimum requirements of the
American National Standard for Information Sciences—Permanence of Paper
for Printed Library Materials, ANSI Z39,48-1984.

Printed in the United States of America
10 9 8 7 6 5 4 3 2 1

This book is dedicated to my mother, Dorothea Camfield, the real Sarah's great granddaughter, and to the memory of my great-aunt, Octavia Perry, the daughter and namesake of Sarah and Henry's youngest daughter. It was through the tales of these two remarkable women and visits with them to Henry's inn in Hillsborough, North Carolina, that I first learned of Sarah's courage and became interested in her true story.

I'd like to thank my talented editor, Lane DeGregory, for her many hours spent with my manuscript and her excellent suggestions for making the text flow. Many thanks also to my supportive husband, Neill Thomasson, who has allowed me to realize my own "dream."

For everything, there is a season,
and a time for every matter under heaven:

A time to be born, and a time to die;
A time to plant, and a time to pluck up what is planted;

A time to kill, and a time to heal;
A time to break down, and a time to build up;

A time to weep, and a time to laugh;
A time to mourn, and a time to dance;

A time to cast away stones, and a time to gather stones together;
A time to embrace, and a time to refrain from embracing;

A time to seek, and a time to lose;
A time to keep, and a time to cast away;

A time to rend, and a time to sew;
A time to keep silence, and a time to speak;

A time to love, and a time to hate;
A time for war, and a time for peace.

Ecclesiastes 3:1-8
Revised Standard Bible

Prologue
April 1865

THERE'S NOTHING TO DO now but wait," Sarah sighed as she looked around the small room one more time. "Am I being a traitor to my homeland in trying to save Henry's dream?" she asked herself as she patted the large Confederate flag, folded on the table. But she knew the answer. She had known it since that first day more than twenty years ago when Henry had confided his dream to her—as he had to no one else, including his twin brother.

"One day, Sarah Holeman," he had said to her, "I'm going to own the Tavern House. I'll serve the best meals in Hillsborough and provide the best lodging to be found in this part of the state." And he had done just that, with Sarah by his side. It had taken half a lifetime of planning and sacrifice, but they had finally realized his dream. He had changed the name to the Orange Hotel, and it had become known throughout North Carolina as one of the foremost inns of its time.

Now, she knew, she could not let his dream die. She owed that much—and so much more—to her beloved Henry, who had died in her arms that winter day only two months ago—a victim of this cruel and senseless war.

The Yankees had killed his flesh. But she swore she'd lose her own life before she'd let them kill his dream. For, as long as it survived, she could feel Henry's presence in every rocker on the wide, white veranda, in every balustrade on the curved, wooden staircase, in every guest room, and especially in the family's own west wing of the inn. She smiled at the daguerreotype on the sideboard in front of her. The tall, blond, dashing Confederate officer with the gray eyes that smiled back at her looked no older than he had more than twenty years ago when she had first known their lives would be intertwined.

"Better hide that picture, Miss Sarah. It wouldn't do for a Yankee to see a Confederate uniform in here!" her servant Tom whispered from behind her. The forty-year-old man with his kind eyes and infectious grin had been with Sarah all her married life and had been a mainstay for the whole family in the dark days after Henry's death. He stood in the doorway now, dressed as a field hand for the part he was to play in their plan.

"Oh, Tom, you startled me so!" Sarah gasped, turning with her hand to the lace front of her somber, black dress. "I suppose you're right, and I must hide this flag as well. We've come so far. We mustn't slip up on a single detail now," she sighed, laying the picture face down on top of the folded flag.

"Now sit right here, Miss Sarah, and don't worry your pretty head anymore. I'll hide these in the stable. Won't be no Yankees messin' 'round there when they see there ain't no horses. I set 'em free as you said to. At least no Yankee's going to ride them out of Hillsborough. An' you can bet no Yankee's going to find them gals in the attic neither!" Tom said proudly.

"Thank you, Tom. I couldn't have gotten this far without you and Lucy. Are the girls really all right? I worry about them the most. Lord, Tom, when I think of what could happen...."

"Don't even think it, Miss Sarah. Just let them 'Bummers' touch one hair on those babies' heads, and they'll have me to reckon with!" Tom replied.

"No, Tom, I can't let you take that chance. Remember, as we rehearsed, you and Lucy must appear as they will expect. We must all seem to be helpless victims of the war. We cannot show any strength or resistance if our plan is to work. They will just as soon shoot us if we give them any trouble. Now, how did you leave the girls? Do you think Mary Frances will listen for once? I declare, Tom, she's so headstrong sometimes," Sarah replied, taking a seat before the fireplace.

"My Mary Frances is going to do all right. She's got the other young 'uns in tow. Those young gals is all settled in the attic as snug as four bugs in a rug with a whole box o' food stuffs Lucy packed for 'em. They can outlast any Yankee visit. An' the Yankees ain't never goin' to find 'em," Tom grinned again, pulling a trowel from behind his back. "I removed the molding from the attic door and papered right over it. They'll never know what's behin' that closet wall!

"You just keep an eye on Lucy and them babies and play your part, Miss Sarah, an' we'll outsmart them ruffians. You'll see. Now, I'd better get these out of sight before we hear them drums," Tom said, picking up the photo and flag and heading for the back door.

"Are you sure they're still coming, Tom? Could the people you saw have been mistaken?" Sarah asked.

"Sure as shootin', Miss Sarah. I heard it with my own ears from those retreatin' Rebs down by the depot, south of town. They said General Sherman is marching right through Hillsborough on his way to Richmond. They tracked him to Raleigh yesterday, chasin' after General Johnston. He's doin' the same as he did in Georgia: killin', lootin', and burnin'.

"But we're goin' to put a stumblin' block in that path, Miss Sarah. You wait and see," he called, popping the battered hat he had resurrected for the occasion on his head and ducking out the door.

Sarah rose from the bench and walked to the window to watch Tom leave.   Pulling back the sheer, lace curtain, she watched as the little girls in the yard ran to him squealing and asking for piggyback rides. Petting each head in turn, Tom shook his finger at them—a signal for "Not now, but I'll be back." Then, flashing his familiar grin, he walked to the stable with the flag and photo.

Lucy stood beside the old magnolia in the courtyard, smiling tremulously at Tom as he passed. Sarah's heart went out to the quiet, loyal housekeeper and nurse who had given her whole life to this family since coming to live with Sarah and Henry when she was only seventeen. It was clear Lucy was frightened to death, but she would not falter, Sarah knew.

Noticing Sarah watching from the window, Lucy squared her shoulders, patted her dark hair into place under her scarf, and waved toward the window with a forced smile. Only her liquid, brown eyes showed her fear.

"They'll be all right," Sarah thought. "Oh, what would I do without Tom and Lucy?" For it had been Lucy's idea to bury the family valuables behind the inn—under the magnolia tree. To cover any signs of recent digging, she had set little Octavia's pram under the tree and had given Pattie and Annie tin spoons to dig with. The children's efforts had quickly labeled the place a playground.

Fearing the little girls would make too much noise and give their older sisters away if they were hidden with them, Lucy had also proposed that they play as usual in the inn's old, brick courtyard. If life seemed normal to them, perhaps it would to the invading Yankees as well. Frightened though she was, Lucy had promised to stay with the children at all costs. So far, there had been no reports of Sherman's men harming children. And, if they burned the inn, the children would be safe outside.

The risk was great for her older daughters, walled into the attic. And Sarah shuddered to think she might have made a mistake. It was common knowledge, however, what the "Bummers" had done to thousands of women they had encountered on their march. Better to risk being burned alive than to endure the indignities and suffering those men could inflict on innocent girls.

"Lord, it's got to work," Sarah prayed, holding the gold cross, which was her only jewelry besides her wedding ring. "Please, God, save us. Let them come, and let this be over. The waiting is too difficult."

The sunlight filtering through the lace curtains on the front door of the inn threw patterns on the faded, flowered rug by the desk. Sarah noticed how the sunlight picked up the gleam in the oak floors she had polished week after week and highlighted the dark, paneled walls and the curved staircase, which led from the lobby to the guest rooms upstairs. This was her home and her family's only refuge. The thought of losing it was too painful to bear.

Turning her head to one side, she listened for flapping on the flagpole over the front veranda and assured herself once more that everything was ready for her expected "visitors" from the North. The clock in the courthouse at the end of King Street chimed two. Feeling restless, Sarah walked to the front door to look out, hoping—and yet fearing—to see the Yankee soldiers approach down King Street.

Glancing right toward Churton Street, the main road from Raleigh, she saw no signs of life. "Of course, not," she thought resignedly. "Any person who was able to has already gotten out of town. I should have, too, if I'd had an ounce of brains in my head. Henry would have insisted on it," she mused, remembering how protective he had been of her and his girls. "But he would have stayed to save his inn. Since he's gone and cannot defend it, I must do it for him."

Looking toward town, Sarah felt a tight knot in her stomach. By nightfall, all the buildings and homes might be only ashes with more than a hundred years of history destroyed—as it had been in Atlanta and all the other towns through which Sherman's army had marched.

At the end of King Street, where it joined Churton, stood the county courthouse. Sarah remembered with fondness how proud everyone in town had been at the dedication twenty years ago of the beautiful, new Grecian structure with its red bricks and white, columned portico. The town clock on the steeple was reported to have come from England in 1769 as a gift from a representative of King George III. It had been housed previously in St. Matthew's Church and later in the Market House tower. Townspeople had told their time by it since Colonial days.

The old cemetery—the final resting place of the town fathers and that courageous group of men known as the "Regulators," who had been among the first colonists to resist British rule—lay across the street from the courthouse. Sarah pictured the wide, stone steps and the two marble headstones just beyond the gate—beneath which Henry and their baby daughter Rebecca now lay. "At least, they are at peace," Sarah told herself.

On the corner of King and Churton Streets, diagonally across from the inn, Sarah could make out the familiar flat-roofed building with the whitewashed bricks that housed the Hillsborough Improvement Company, the company Henry had owned with his brothers, Alfred and Cave. The windows were dark and shuttered against the strong afternoon sun.

The whole town—usually so full of life—was now totally deserted, Sarah realized as she stared across the street at the old, red brick Masonic Lodge with its peeling, white columns. She could smile now as she remembered how indignant she had become at having to face the roomful of men after she had glimpsed their sacred ceremonial items. It seemed so long ago now—and so inconsequential.

Beyond the lodge and stretching down King Street for two more blocks stood the homes of some of the town's wealthiest and most influential families. The wide, grassy lawns were dotted with early spring bulbs and sheltered by spreading oaks covered in pale-green canopies. Moss-covered brick walks led to white, wooden homes with spacious verandas and wide, double doors—now uselessly bolted against the expected tide of destruction.

"So many dreams to go up in smoke," Sarah thought, wiping her streaming eyes with a lace handkerchief. "So many memories...."

"But I mustn't dwell on what might happen," she decided, settling on the green, brocade settee for the interminable wait. In an effort to forget, she fixed her eyes on the magnolia tree in the courtyard, where two of her youngest daughters were climbing under Lucy's watchful eyes. Suddenly, another sunny April day and another magnolia entered her thoughts to block the unbearable worry for a time. She smiled as she remembered.

Chapter One
April 1843

FROM HER VANTAGE POINT high in the magnolia tree outside the second-floor windows, Sarah looked over the rolling hills of her father's plantation. It was her favorite time of year, for April always seemed to bring God close enough to touch in each fragile new leaf and newly-sprung flower.

She watched as Buck, the aging gray mule, plodded up yet another hill, dragging the rusty plow and Jeremiah, the elderly farm hand, with him. Jeremiah paused a moment to lift his battered straw hat and wipe his forehead with the wide sleeve of his large, white shirt.

Drinking in the smell of the newly-turned Carolina red dirt, Sarah suddenly sneezed. "Heavens, I mustn't do that too often, or I'll fall off this limb," she laughed, grabbing at a branch above her. "And what a pretty picture that would be!"

Smiling at the thought, Sarah again buried her head in the book in her lap. She was reading Jane Austen's *Pride and Prejudice* and had set a goal of two more chapters before supper.

Suddenly, the sound of buggy wheels on the gravel drive roused her. Craning her neck to look through the still-bare branches of the dogwood trees, Sarah saw a sleek, black horse approach, drawing a large, black buggy.

Seated in the buggy were two gentlemen, dressed for calling in gray jackets and tall, black hats. The buggy slowed near the door, then disappeared as the corner of the house cut off Sarah's line of vision. "Father did say he had some business to attend to this afternoon," Sarah mused. "I suppose they're part of it. Well, I won't have to worry about being spotted by Father for a while," she smiled, continuing her reading.

As Sarah paused to turn a page, she heard a twig crack below her. Grasping her wide, lavender skirt in her hand, she pulled it aside to see beneath her. As she shifted position, however, she lost her hold on the book and gasped as the treasured pages brushed several limbs before landing in the dirt below.

"Were you trying to smash my hat, or did you have other motives in mind, like knocking my head off?" came a voice from just below her.

"Oh, my goodness. I'm sorry!" Sarah called, trying in vain to see the voice's owner. "I didn't know anyone was there. I hope I haven't hurt you or ruined your hat," she added, struggling to keep her balance on the limb.

A booming laugh erupted directly below her. "I believe I've never seen a young lady in such a swirl of fabric. Actually, I've never seen a young lady in a magnolia tree either, come to think of it. But it's a rather delightful sight!"

"I beg your pardon, Sir. A true gentleman would not only not view a lady from beneath, he would most assuredly not laugh at her," Sarah retorted, incensed.

"I beg your pardon, Ma'am, for being so uncouth. But, may I remind you, a proper young lady would also not be perched in the branches of a magnolia tree above a gentleman's head!" the voice replied.

"Oh, bother, keep your voice down, or the whole household will hear. Then I would really be in for it. Why, if anyone ever guessed where I do my reading. . . .," Sarah whispered, annoyed at the intrusion. She'd had her whole afternoon planned out. And it hadn't included an uninvited guest. Why, if her secret got out. . . She wasn't sure whether she'd prefer her mother's wrath or her father's stern disapproval. Neither was a comforting thought.

"I could remedy that possibility," the young man continued, amused. "If you can inch your way down that branch, I could lift you to the ground. And I promise, as a gentleman, never to divulge your secret."

"Gentleman" was certainly not the title Sarah would have used for the uncouth young man who had ruined her afternoon. But, under the circumstances, she couldn't continue to hold a conversation from the branches of a tree. . . "You'll have to promise to shut your eyes and keep them shut until I'm down the branch," she ordered at last, gathering her skirts in her hand and beginning to slide forward.

"You have my word on it," came from below.

"All right, you can open your eyes now and help me down before someone comes," Sarah called at last, looking around as she neared the end of the branch.

As she spotted the intruder, however, her face turned crimson. The tall, blond young man with the laughing, gray eyes was Henry Calvin Stroud. His sister Tibitha had been a class behind her at the Burwell School for Young Ladies, and she had seen him and his twin brother at church.

Advancing toward her, Henry reached his hands out to grasp her waist firmly. He lifted her gently, whirled her lightly through the air, and set her on the pale-green lawn beside the tree. Then, smiling, he waited for her reaction.

Sarah felt a thrill of excitement at the whole proceeding. Realizing it was highly improper for a gentleman to touch a lady so familiarly, however, she turned her head to avoid meeting his eyes and busied herself in smoothing her skirt. "I suppose I should thank you, Sir, for helping me down," she scoffed at last. "Although, if you hadn't startled me into dropping my book, I would still be reading quietly and wouldn't have needed your help. As it is, I suppose you'll tell your tale to all your friends at the Tavern House, and I'll soon become the laughing stock of Hillsborough society." She winced inwardly at the thought of the tale reaching her mother's ears.

Removing his hat with a sweeping bow, Henry grinned. "Your servant, Miss Holeman! I assure you, our secret will go no further than the boughs of this tree. But I, instead, should thank you for making this one of the most interesting afternoons of my life. And here I was, prepared to be bored for hours while Cave and your father discussed business," he added, turning to pick up Sarah's book from the grass. "Interesting reading?" he inquired, looking at the cover. "I'm not familiar with the author."

"She's well known in England," Sarah replied. "But I'm sure this wouldn't be required reading in a male academy."

"At least not in Hillsborough Academy," Henry laughed. "Since my brothers and I studied business, I'm afraid we missed some of the finer things of life. Perhaps you'd share some of your favorite books with me sometime."

"I'd be most happy to recommend some books to you, Mr. Stroud," Sarah replied, amused at the thought of one of the Stroud brothers reading a Jane Austen novel.

"'Henry,' please," Henry answered. "After all, I think we're more than casual acquaintances now. Don't you agree, Miss Holeman?" he asked, reaching for her hand.

"'Sarah,' then. And, yes, I guess you're right there," she smiled, her anger subsiding as she offering her hand as well. He *was* gorgeous, she thought as her eyes met his candid, gray gaze.

"Sarah, Sarah Holeman, where'd you go, child?" called a voice from above as Sarah jumped, disengaging her hand. "I declare. You worry me to death. I'm too old for this foolishness," the voice continued.

Putting his finger to his lips, Henry quickly ducked back against the house, while Sarah brushed off her skirts and tucked a curl under her bonnet. Then, trying to look nonchalant, she glanced up at the second floor window where her nurse Nana was leaning over the sill, hands planted firmly and her wide, wrinkled face peering from under her kerchief. "Here I am, Nana. It was such a lovely day I came outside to read," Sarah called innocently.

Hearing a chuckle nearby, she glared at Henry pointedly, then tossed her head to peer at Nana again.

"It's your mamma who wants you, child. You'd better find her. And, don't go leavin' this window open anymore while they're plowin' that field. You gonna have dust piles all over," Nana answered in a huff. Continuing to mutter, she slammed the window sash, putting an end to the conversation.

"I guess she told you!" Henry answered, returning to Sarah's side. "Never let a body have a bit of fun. But I imagine you've kept her hopping over the years," he added with a twinkle in his eyes.

"And what do you mean by that?" Sarah asked. Gorgeous or not, she wasn't about to let him stand there and. . .

"Oh, don't take affront. I just don't imagine there are many other girls in Orange County who read books in magnolia trees," he smiled. "But I apologize. I've spoiled your afternoon and divulged your hiding spot—when all I intended was a tour of your lovely rose garden," he added, affecting a squint as he turned one of the short, bare canes over in his hand. "So, if you'll excuse me. . ."

"Goodbye, kind Sir, and thank you for your gallantry," Sarah laughed at his antics. It really had been an unexpected and delightful encounter.

"It's always my pleasure to rescue damsels in distress, especially ones so beautiful," Henry added, noticing the trim waist, creamy complexion, and dark, raven-colored curls beneath her bonnet. For once in his life he was happy Cave had talked him into coming with him. And he wouldn't need any urging next time the Holeman house was on their agenda. "Please don't hesitate to call on me any time you need a dragon slain," Henry called, sauntering toward the drive.

≈ ≈ ≈

THE BEAUTY OF April in North Carolina was often obscured by days, or even weeks, of mists and squally rains. April 1843 was no exception. And Sarah felt restless at having been cooped up inside the house for two weeks.

As she opened her eyes to one weak ray of sunshine bravely trying to peep into her bedroom, Sarah ran to the window and threw back the drapes. "I never thought I'd see the sun again," she sighed, enjoying the warmth and envisioning a ride this afternoon.

"Miss Sarah, how many times have I told you not to go hangin' out the window in your nightdress? What's your mamma goin' to say? And it's past time you was dressin' for breakfast. You know how mad your daddy gets if you come late," Nana scolded, entering the room and heading for the armoire.

Slipping the corn-colored dress over Sarah's head and buttoning the tiny buttons up the back, the old nurse spun her charge around at last to look at her. "Why, ain't you as pretty as a picture?" she beamed. "You'll be the belle of Hillsborough yet."

"I'm not sure I want to be the belle of anything," Sarah sighed. "There are so many more important things in life. I wish you and Mother would not push me so."

"What's more important than gettin' a husband?" Nana questioned. "Lord, child, what's your daddy gonna do if you don't find a gentleman to help out on the plantation—what with only girls in the family and him not gettin' any younger?"

"Pooh! I could help him if he'd let me," Sarah scoffed. "I've watched Father run this plantation all my life. I declare, I don't know why everyone thinks women's heads are filled with fluff. I know the proper time to plant, the best time to harvest, the ideal weather conditions, and even the going price of tobacco. Yet, whenever I try to talk to Father, he tells me to go help Mother, as if I hadn't a brain in my head."

"But your daddy don't want his women to do men's work. No, child, you just stick to doin' what a girl's s'posed to do and don't give him no bother. Now scoot before you're late for breakfast," Nana scolded, giving Sarah a playful push toward the door.

Lifting the hoop of her new dress with one hand—to free her ankles—and grasping the shiny, mahogany balustrade with the other, Sarah rushed down the curving staircase to the entry hall below. She sighed as she reached the bottom without being detected. She was not sure whose wrath she feared more—her father's for being late for breakfast or Nana's for allowing her ankles to be seen. But there was no help for either infraction. Unless she appeared in the dining hall in the next thirty seconds, she knew her father's bellow would shake the very foundation of the plantation house.

Sarah swung her skirts through the dining room door, swept past the group already assembled, placed a kiss on her father's bald head, and slid into her seat beside him just as the clock began to chime eight. Ignoring her mother's disapproving glance from the other end of the table, Sarah chose instead to look at her father expectantly.

Waiting until the last chime had died away, Samuel Holeman placed his spectacles on his narrow nose and cleared his throat audibly. Then, turning piercing gray eyes to his wife and seven daughters, who all sat motionless at the long, mahogany table with hands in laps, he opened the leather-bound Bible in front of him.

With a quick glance toward the long bench near the kitchen door to be sure that each of the household servants also was present, he began to read loudly. The passage he had chosen for this morning was from the Old Testament in the Book of Ecclesiastes: Chapter 3, verses 1-8, which began: "For everything there is a season, and a time for every matter under heaven."

When the reading was over, Samuel Holeman led his household in "The Lord's Prayer" and concluded with his loud "Amen," at which the servants rose and quietly disappeared.

"Sarah, was that one of the Stroud boys who brought you home from the church social yesterday afternoon?" Samuel asked when the servants were out of earshot, turning to his eldest daughter as he passed her a basket of steaming biscuits.

"Yes, Father. It was Henry. It was raining, and he offered me a ride. He was picking up Tibitha also, so I didn't think it was improper," Sarah answered.

"Sarah, I have some reservations about those Stroud boys," her father began. "I've had lots of dealings with Cave and the Hillsborough Improvement Company he, Henry, and Alfred own. I can't say I'm very fond of Cave. He's rather shrewd, despite his age. I'm afraid if we don't look out, he'll soon have mills and factories churning out black smoke all over Orange County.

"While I don't know Henry well, I wonder how different two identical twins can be," he added, shaking his head. "You do understand my concern, don't you? You are of marriageable age, and it is my duty to help choose your future mate carefully. I'm a planter, and I'll need a son-in-law to take over the plantation—not cover it with machinery."

"Oh, Father, I'm not at all interested in getting married. And I'm sure Henry's not either. We're only friends. I don't see what harm there was in accepting a ride home from him. And you really should get to know Henry. I know he and Cave look identical. But they're not at all alike otherwise. You'd like Henry, if you got to know him. He's kind, considerate, and lots of fun. . .," Sarah began, stopping suddenly as she heard her sisters giggle.

"Girls!" Samuel corrected them. "Sarah and I are having an important conversation. I'll thank you to remain out of it. Look to them, Mrs. Holeman."

Jean Holeman, although kindly by nature, was a formidable figure to her family and servants alike. With her dark hair pulled into a severe bun at the nape of her neck and her piercing brown eyes, she had only to raise one eyebrow at the offending children to silence them.

"Mrs. Holeman," Samuel began when the children were subdued, "how well do you know the Strouds? I know you and Frances were schoolmates. But since her death have you seen much of her children?"

"I see the whole family at church, Frances's six and Mary's four children. Mary is devoted to them all. It's hard to be a mother to the older ones, however, when they're only a few years younger than she. Alfred and the twins, I believe, have rather raised themselves. But they seem like nice young men, very polite. And the twins do cut a dashing figure," Jean replied.

"Then you really don't mind that Henry brought me home?" Sarah asked, turning to her mother with a relieved sigh.

"I'd prefer that you attend any young man at only properly chaperoned events," her mother countered. "A young lady of your age and upbringing can't be too careful to avoid setting tongues wagging."

"Your mother is right, Sarah. If Henry Stroud wants to enjoy your company, let him speak with me, and I'll see that you are properly chaperoned," Samuel put in, wiping his mouth with his linen napkin and rising from the table.

Chapter Two
May 1843

May came to North Carolina with a rush of lush beauty known only to the deep South. Stately magnolia trees spread waxen branches over plantation homes and slave cottages alike, bathing nature in the waxy, white blossoms' heady perfume. Fragile pink camellias raised their faces to the returning sunshine, while lavender wisteria vines and snowy-white jasmine crept over creamy marble columns and tumbled over wooden tobacco barns with the same abandonment, lending their unforgettable fragrance to the early morning.

As Sarah followed her family out of the small Mars Hill Baptist Church, a few miles from Hillsborough, she was unaware of a slender, dashing young man hurrying down the path behind her until Henry took her elbow to help her across the road, which was still dotted with muddy, red puddles. "Your father has given permission for me to escort you into town to see Mrs. Nash's garden, Sarah," he began. "It's too beautiful a day to waste. Would you like to go?"

"Why, that's one of my favorite places. I'd love to go," Sarah answered, hoping her voice wouldn't betray her happiness. After their breakfast conversation, she hadn't been sure how her father would react to any further contact with Henry.

"Our carriage is just over here," Henry added, guiding her around a large puddle. "I hope you don't mind sharing it into Hillsborough. My sister Mary is going into town to visit a friend and needs my escort."

The younger girl was already in the carriage and smiled at Sarah as she approached. She was only two years younger than Sarah, but at eighteen and in her last year at The Burwell School for Young Ladies, she still seemed very much the insecure schoolgirl. She was tall and slender, like her brother. Instead of his wavy, blond hair with a touch of red from the sun, Mary's hair was corn-colored and straight and hung down her back beneath her bonnet. Sarah had not thought her pretty before, but now, as she reached for Sarah's hand, her eyes of cornflower blue shone with genuine warmth, which drew Sarah to her.

"I hope you don't mind my tagging along," Mary offered, replacing a strand of hair under her bonnet. "Henry thought your father might agree to allow you to go walking with him if I were with you. And I'm sure my friend will be happy to see me. We have a lot of plans to make for graduation, at any rate."

"I don't mind a bit," Sarah answered, sliding into the carriage beside Mary. "It will give us a chance to become better acquainted. And you're right. I'm sure my father never would have allowed me to accompany a man unescorted. Thank you for coming along."

Arriving in Hillsborough, Henry turned off the main street onto King Street and drew the carriage to a halt near the old Tavern House—a two-story, white, wooden inn with a spacious front porch and wide, second-story veranda. Nodding to several ladies and gentlemen who were clustered on the porch awaiting admission for the noon meal, he alighted to help Mary and Sarah from the carriage.

After adjusting her parasol, Mary planted a kiss on Henry's cheek and turned to Sarah. "He's my favorite brother," she replied. "Call for me when you're ready to go, Henry," she called over her shoulder before entering the cedar-shaded path to Margaret Lane.

Henry looped the reins over the hitching block beside the road and once again took Sarah's elbow to help her from the carriage and lead her toward the lane where Mary had just disappeared.

It was a glorious day, Sarah thought, enjoying the feel of Henry's hand on her arm. "How nice to feel solid cobblestones under my feet instead of that slick, red mud," she remarked, catching his eye and smiling. "I declare. Most of my favorite shoes have been ruined by the recent rains."

"That's exactly how General Cornwallis must have felt when he and his soldiers camped here," Henry smiled back. Gesturing toward the eighty-year-old Tavern House, he asked, "Did you know that he made the Tavern House his headquarters when he came through here in 1781 during the Revolution? He ruined so many pairs of boots that he ordered his soldiers to pave both King and Churton Streets so he could walk in comfort and safety.

"So we have Lord Cornwallis to thank for our streets as well as our freedom," Henry chuckled. "But come on. You didn't accompany me to hear a history lesson. You came to see the gardens, and I'm keeping you from them."

Tall cedars loomed over each side of the walk, offering a cool respite from the May heat. The walk and the gardens had been planted many years before by Mrs. Nash, wife of Chief Justice Francis Nash, when they had lived in the house on Margaret Lane. The marble benches in the gardens were now a favorite place for young and old alike.

Today, the rose garden was in a profusion of blooms. Deep-red roses entwined with pale-pink ones to form an arch over the entry. Inside, white and coral roses circled a marble bird-bath. "It's so beautiful here," Sarah remarked, taking a seat on a nearby bench. "I love Mrs. Nash's garden. I'd love to be able to look at it every day."

"I'll be able to do that myself someday," Henry remarked in an offhand manner. He had picked his time carefully, and her lead was just the opportunity he'd been hoping for. He paused as he waited for her response.

"What do you plan to do here, become the gardener? I've seen how much you know about roses," Sarah laughed.

"Sarah Holeman, don't laugh at me, or I won't tell you my dream. In fact, I think you just lost that privilege," Henry answered with a mock snort—crossing his arms and turning his face away to hide his disappointment. Perhaps he'd been mistaken. He'd so hoped she—of all people—would listen and understand his plans.

"I'm sorry, Henry," Sarah apologized, noticing the hurt on his face. "It's just that the image of you bending over the bare bushes in our garden was so humorous. . . Seriously, though, do tell me about your dream. I really want to hear it," she added, putting her hand on his arm.

"Well, since you asked nicely," Henry said, turning back, "I'll tell you. But you must promise not to tell anyone—most of all, my brother Cave." Maybe he'd made a mistake bringing up this whole idea, Henry thought. If Cave ever found out. . . Why, he'd never live down his ribbing. But he'd gone this far.

"I promise," Sarah answered, picking an imagined speck from her pink, lawn skirt and lowering her dark eyes as she waited expectantly. "Please tell me."

"Well, one day, Sarah Holeman, I'm going to own the old Tavern House," Henry began in a rush, afraid to look at her. Pointing to the kitchen of the large structure visible beyond the cedars, he went on. "You'll see. I'll serve the best meals in Hillsborough and provide the best lodging to be found in this part of the state. I've loved that old building since my father first took me in there. And I've learned everything there is to know about it. I think being an innkeeper would be the most fun imaginable. There, now what do you think of that?" he asked, turning to look deeply into her eyes. "I've never told anyone else about my dream."

"It's a wonderful plan, Henry," Sarah responded, returning his look. "But what about your father's plantation? With Alfred and Cave so interested in business, I rather thought you would become a planter. Who'll take over when he can no longer maintain it? I know my father already worries about a successor—what with having only girls and all."

"Father knows that Alfred, Cave, and I have no interest in the land," Henry sighed. He knew how much he and his brothers must have disappointed his father, although he had never let on. "We never have had, in spite of our headmaster's claim that"—and here he drew himself upward, thrust out his chest, and said in a low voice that mocked the headmaster— "the land is the greatest resource of the South and must be preserved."

"Goodness, I don't want to destroy the land," Henry explained. "But I also don't want to work it. And I don't want to have to own men to help me keep it up. I want to work for myself and earn my bread by my own hand. Is that so wrong?"

"I think it's a wonderful plan, Henry, and I know you'll succeed. I'll come to the Tavern House myself when you own it. I'll bring my whole family and give you lots of business," Sarah said, flippantly.

"Oh, I do envy you having a chance to do something worth-while with your life," she added seriously. "Why, everyone just tells me to learn to run a household when I do so want to do something more." It wasn't fair. Henry had the opportunity she would have treasured, and he was willing to throw it away. And her father wouldn't even consider giving her a chance to help him on the plantation.

"Running an inn is not too different from running a house-hold," Henry said, noticing the hurt in her eyes. Maybe she did understand after all, he smiled to himself. "I don't see why a woman couldn't do it. You'd probably be good at it, too. Tibitha says you were the smartest girl in your class."

"I can't see any reason either, except that my mother and father would die of embarrassment if I tried to do anything except sit with an embroidery frame in my lap," Sarah re-sponded sarcastically. "To quote my mother, 'It isn't seemly!'"

"Maybe we'll test that theory, Sarah Holeman," Henry whis-pered to himself as he rose. If he was to run the Tavern House, he'd need a partner. . . And Sarah just might be the second half of his dream. Lifting her gently by the hand, he spoke directly. "As much as I'm enjoying our conversation, it's time to collect Mary and take you home. I promised your father to have you back for dinner, and I do want him to trust me."

Seating Sarah in the carriage with a tip of his top-hat and a bow, Henry turned quickly and strode off in the direction of Margaret Lane. Sarah followed him with her eyes until he was out of sight. Then she turned to watch the bustle around her as townspeople milled about enjoying the lazy Sunday afternoon.

Realizing Henry had just turned the corner beyond the ce-dar-lined walk, Sarah did a double-take as he seemed to appear in front of the Tavern House. "But that's impossible," she thought. "He only just left. And he went in the opposite direction."

Suddenly, the truth dawned as Sarah realized she was looking not at Henry, but at his carbon copy, Hawkins Cave Stroud. He was as arresting in appearance as Henry with his wavy blond hair and Saxon good looks. But there was something about Cave that made Sarah uncomfortable. Hoping he would not see her seated in the carriage, she opened her parasol to place it between herself and his line of vision. As she did so, however, she knew she had been spotted.

Sauntering down the front steps of the Tavern House toward the carriage, Cave seemed, at first, to have eyes only for the horses. He stroked the fine, silky, black manes and spoke a few words in one animal's ear. Then, with a calculated turn and feigned look of surprise, he seemed to notice Sarah for the first time.

Taking off his hat, he executed a sweeping bow. "Miss Holeman, how pleased I am to see you. And, pray, what would you be doing sitting in the Stroud carriage by yourself? Don't tell me my brother is a big enough cad to leave you here alone and defenseless. Let me apologize for his lack of manners. I assure you my dear, departed mother taught him better at her knee."

"No need to apologize, Mr. Stroud," Sarah answered, lifting her chin, which she hoped would mask her uneasiness. "I'm hardly defenseless, nor do I need to be afraid to be alone on the main street of town when the whole community is out enjoying the day. Your brother has just gone to call for Mary, who has been visiting a friend. He was kind enough to see me to the carriage first. They should be along directly."

"Ah, but I can't leave such a beautiful damsel in distress, so I'll play the gentleman and keep you company until my brother arrives. Perhaps I may also beg a ride home, since Alfred left me at the Tavern House several hours ago to conclude some important business."

With a shrug of his shoulders and an exaggerated sigh he added, "How difficult it is to be always about my brothers' business while they, dapper rogues that they are, find time to be with the ladies." So saying, Cave swung himself up on the seat beside Sarah and placed his arm directly behind her. "Now, you must tell me where you have been and what you and that brother of mine have been up to," he whispered conspiratorially.

Sarah tried unsuccessfully to adjust her position while pretending to adjust her parasol, but the seat proved too narrow to move any further, and Cave showed no inclination to move even an inch.

Her fidgeting and unrest were apparent to Cave, who smiled to himself. Waiting for her to turn toward him, he asked, "And how is it Samuel allows his precious jewel to be alone in town with young Henry?"

"We didn't come alone, Mr. Stroud. Mary was with us. And my father gave permission for me to accompany them after church," Sarah answered curtly, tossing her curls as she peered down the lane—hoping for any sign of Henry and Mary.

"My, how formal we are, Miss Holeman. Do you call my brother 'Mr. Stroud' also?" Cave asked with a sly grin, which turned his eyes almost green. "Aha, I think not. We have had the same introduction through Tibitha, so please call me 'Cave' and allow me to come courting as well. I must warn you, however, I am not as slow to action as my brother. And I always get what I go after," he added with a roguish gleam in his eyes.

"I must speak to your father. I'm sure he's told you we have become very close with our business dealings. Yes, my dear," he added, watching for a reaction, "I'm becoming very well-known in this town and not just a little bit wealthy, I might add. I could provide for you quite well, I should think," he said, giving Sarah an appreciative glance from head to toe and causing her to blush to the roots of her hair.

Sarah was saved the embarrassment of a reply by Mary's voice. "Look, Henry, Cave is here, too. What a coincidence. I didn't know he was in town."

Turning, Sarah was quick to glimpse the anger in Henry's eyes. His fists were clenched at his side. But he said nothing as he handed Mary up to her seat.

"Well, Brother, aren't you glad to see me? The least you could do is thank me for saving you from a boring business meeting this morning so that you could spend time enjoying the flowers," Cave said with a smirk. "This little lady here," he added, nodding toward Sarah, "offered me a ride to save my boots from the mud. Alfred has not returned, and, having completed our business, I am in need of a ride home. Hope you don't mind, Old Man. There's room for four."

Mumbling a brief, "Of course," Henry turned to unhook the reins from the post, looking back uncomfortably at Cave and Sarah. He'd never expected his brother to be in town. As children the two had been inseparable—especially after their mother's death. And, being so identical in appearance, their teachers—and even their father—had usually considered them to be two halves of a whole. Henry had always loved having a ready-made playmate and confidant and had been more than willing to defer to Cave's interests and ideas. To Cave, however, every childhood game and accomplishment had immediately become a contest he had to win. Watching his brother now, Henry knew nothing had changed. He was afraid Sarah had become the new "prize."

What had been a delightful drive on the way to town turned out to be a nightmare for Sarah on the way back. Seated as she was next to Cave, she was acutely aware of his constant perusal of her and the smirk lurking behind his eyes—as if he were enjoying the obvious discomfort he was causing both Sarah and Henry.

After what seemed an eternity, they finally covered the three miles to Sarah's home and drew up in her drive. Before Cave could get untangled from the ladies' skirts, Henry jumped to the ground to help Sarah down. As Henry offered her his hand, Cave muttered a mild curse under his breath, smiled graciously at Sarah, and tipped his hat.

Barely acknowledging him, Sarah turned to Henry, who had remained silent the whole trip. When they were out of earshot, she began hesitantly, "Henry, I didn't actually offer Cave a ride. But since it was your carriage, I didn't think. . ."

"It's all right, Sarah, I don't blame you," Henry sighed. "I know my brother. After all, I've lived with him for twenty-two years. I'm sorry if he made you uncomfortable. Cave seems to think he has a way with the ladies, and sometimes he goes out of his way to prove his prowess. Next time, I'll check his plans more carefully."

Watching the three Strouds depart, Sarah leaned against the door frame. It had been a lovely morning, despite Cave's effort to ruin it. Her conversation with Henry had given her a glimpse of the inner man—and she liked what she saw. "And he did say, 'Next time,' didn't he?" she asked herself, whirling her skirts as she untied her bonnet and prepared to join her family for dinner.

CHAPTER THREE
August 1843

SUMMER BROUGHT A RUSH of activity to Hillsborough, not the least of which was Fair Day. Banners fluttered from rooftops and festooned the streets. Townspeople and planters both took a holiday and went to the town center, dressed in their finest. The roads were closed to all carriages, wagons, and horses so people could mill about freely, tasting the delicious offerings of kitchens throughout the county, judging the size and color of vegetables and fruits, and marveling at the stitching employed in countless needlework items.

On the outskirts of town, pens had been set up to house horses, cows, sheep, pigs, and chickens offered for judging as well as for sale. It was common to see herds of sheep being led through the main street to the judging ring and to hear the excited squeal of a youngster leading his first pony by the bridle toward his father's waiting wagon.

Sarah had been touring the exhibits with her mother, and the two had stopped to admire the beautiful quilt members of the Ladies Auxiliary had stitched. Intersecting circles covered the colorful front, and tiny, even stitches were evident through-out. "It was worth the work. Don't you agree?" Jean asked her daughter.

"It's lovely, Mother," Sarah answered, smiling and feign-ing interest, all the while searching the crowds for a familiar face. Suddenly, her wish was granted as she noticed an easily-recognizable, tall, blond gentleman striding toward her through the throng. Smoothing her wide, pink-and-white-striped skirt and throwing her matching parasol over her shoul-der, Sarah turned toward the figure in anticipation, watching his approach from under the brim of her large bonnet.

Her smile and expectant look alerted her mother, who also turned to look. Seeing the dapper figure approaching, Jean retreated to the next booth where she pretended to be in-terested in the crochet work displayed there, a slight smile on her lips.

Sarah stood where she was, one hand on the quilt rack to steady her racing nerves. As the figure drew closer, Sarah low-ered her eyes until she saw the polished boots, which had stopped right in front of her. Raising her eyes with undisguised eagerness, she saw to her chagrin that she was looking directly into Cave's smiling face.

"My dear Miss Sarah," Cave began, bowing, "your beauty should be awarded top prize at the fair. You far outshine ev-ery other lady here. I'd be delighted if you'd do me the honor of touring the exhibits with me. I'm sure your mother can do without you," he added, taking her elbow and propelling her away from the table.

Looking back for her mother's help, Sarah was dismayed to see that she had vanished. She, too, had been fooled by the twin. "I can't blame her," Sarah thought. "I was just as fooled as she. Now what am I to do? What if Henry should come looking for me?"

"Such a lovely day, and I'm famished!" Cave began, steering Sarah toward the food booths. "I've taken the liberty of ordering a picnic basket for us. We have only to pick it up and be on our way. Where would you like to eat, my dear?"

"Cave, I—I can't eat with you. I promised my parents. . ." Sarah was at a loss for words.

"Of course, you can," Cave countered, sensing her lie. "You're perfectly safe here at the fair. Why, your mother even saw me walking toward you and discreetly left us alone." So saying, he accepted the waiting basket and produced several bills to pay for it. Then, half pulling Sarah after him with his brisk stride, he walked to the outskirts of the fairgrounds toward a wide meadow of daisies and clover.

"What a perfect place for a picnic," Cave stated, placing the basket on the ground, clasping his arms above his head, and stretching. Removing his jacket and spreading it ceremoniously on the ground, he motioned for Sarah to be seated.

When she perceived that no help was coming, Sarah sighed and decided to make the best of the situation. After all, Cave could be her brother-in-law someday. It would not do to appear unfriendly. And the smells coming from the basket were definitely delectable.

She turned to him with a half-smile, determined to learn something about this brother. "How is it you aren't working today?" Sarah asked for an opener. "I was under the impression you worked seven days a week. In fact, you as much as told me that yourself."

"Then I believe you misunderstood me," Cave answered. "Oh, I do put in a lot of hours. It takes work to make a business succeed—something my two brothers would do well to learn. But I still find time to enjoy the finer things of life," he said with a searing look at Sarah, which made her blush to the roots of her hair. "You know, you're especially lovely when you blush," he smiled. "Come now, you must be hungry. Do eat something," he urged, beginning to unpack the basket.

Since it had been hours since breakfast, Sarah was ravenous and took little time in complying. They ate in silence for a few minutes until Sarah ventured to speak, "Tell me, Cave. . ."

"Much better," Cave interrupted. "I see we've dispensed with formalities. As you were saying. . ."

"It's just that I'm interested in the new company you and your brothers have begun. The Hillsborough Improvement Company, isn't it? What exactly do you do?" Sarah asked, determined to use the day to some advantage by finding out about Henry's business and allaying her father's fears for the town as well.

"Why, we do exactly what our name implies," Cave said. "We seek to handle all business that stands to better Hillsborough. Mostly we deal with real estate and the buying and selling of property in and around Orange County.

"At the moment, we're in the midst of a very important deal, which stands to benefit the area immensely. We're trying to purchase a tract of land between the Eno River and the proposed railroad. My brothers and I feel that with its view and proximity to the eventual rail line from Goldsboro and Raleigh, it should be perfect for a boarding school.

"I was meeting with the owner that day I ran into you by the Tavern House—a most pleasant and unexpected encounter, I might add," he said with a mock bow affected from a sitting position.

"How exciting!" Sarah exclaimed. "That seems like a wonderful addition to the town. I know there's a need for it with the long distances some of my classmates had to commute. It must give you a great deal of pleasure to see your ideas take shape." She was beginning to appreciate Cave's business head, if not his manners. And there was no way Father could find fault with Henry's company buying land for a school.

"It is exciting," he answered, truthfully. "But sometimes there do not seem to be enough hours in the day. And there are always those who disapprove—whatever the project."

"But I'm still curious as to why none of you Stroud males has had an interest in planting," Sarah stated. "My father has made his whole fortune off of our plantation. Your father also owns a very large plantation. I should have thought he would have groomed one of you to take over after him."

"Haven't you heard, Miss Holeman? The South is in dire straits. 'Old King Cotton's' crown is slipping and in danger of falling off. Four years ago, cotton brought twelve and seven tenths cents a pound on the New York market—quite a profit for the planter. And tobacco was just as lucrative, which is why your daddy and mine have done so well for themselves.

"Since that time, there has been a glut of both crops on the market, however, and the prices have fallen steadily. Today the planters receive only a little more than six cents a pound on cotton. With the cost of producing cotton at five cents a pound, they receive only a penny a pound for all their troubles. Add the fact that good field-hands now cost almost $1,000 each, and you have today's planter—blue-blood through and through, and likely to be bluer as the cold winter sets in with no money to see him through.

"No, my dear, agriculture is not the way of the future for the South. But old habits die hard. And the Southern planters, for the most part, refuse to do anything differently than their fathers did. They will all go down gasping and squeezing their last cotton boll, I'm afraid, in the not-too-distant future.

"The 'time to plant' has passed. For the South to survive, it must now be willing to 'pluck up what has been planted,' and to turn some of that abundant farm land into industries to bring us into the second half of the nineteenth century.

"What the South needs is economic independence. We need to learn from our northern brothers and begin some industry right here. Hillsborough would be a perfect place for a cotton mill to produce goods in the South from the cotton we grow. Instead, we continue to depend on the middle men in the North to give us back in usable form what we owned in the first place—charging us through the nose for the privilege.

"That, dear Sarah, is what our Hillsborough Improvement Company is all about. We're trying to find new ventures for Orange County that will tide our area over when the economic decline forces your daddy and mine into bankruptcy. Mark my words. That time is coming. When you get ready to place that little hand of yours into another's, place it into the hand of a businessman, not a planter, if you want security for yourself and your children.

"Now, enough of business. A head as pretty as yours is meant to be looked at, not bored with talk," Cave concluded with a smile, his eyes boring into Sarah's.

"But I'm enjoying our conversation. Business is so much more interesting than talking about stitches in a quilt. Please go on," she added, attempting to avoid his eyes, which were making her very uncomfortable. Besides, she sensed some truth in what Cave was saying and was anxious to talk to her father about it. He seemed to have misjudged Cave and Henry's company.

"But I've forgotten myself. Business is what I came out here to avoid today. So avoid it I will," Cave answered with a sideways smile. And he refused to say more.

Feeling more than a little self-conscious as the silence continued, Sarah tried to watch the people passing nearby. Try as she might, however, she could not avoid making eye contact with Cave as he continued smiling mischievously.

Suddenly, a voice called out, "Here she is—in the meadow." Sarah turned as her younger sister Susan broke from the crowd and ran toward her, sunbonnet bouncing behind her back and brown braids flying wide. "We've been looking all over for you," the gangly, young girl gasped, totally out of breath.

"We thought you'd run away," Julia piped up, appearing in Susan's wake with blond ringlets plastered to her tiny face by perspiration. "Father's ready to go. He's bought a new pony for me and wants to get it home out of the heat," she added proudly.

"Oh, Julia, I'm so glad you have finally gotten your pony," Sarah said, grabbing the smiling little girl as she approached and giving her a big hug.

"Want to see it?" Julia questioned eagerly. "Come on," she cried, pulling on Sarah's arm.

"Just a moment, Julia. We're forgetting our manners. First, I must introduce you and Susan. Cave, these are my sisters, Susan and Julia—in case you hadn't guessed. Girls, this is Mr. Stroud—Mr. Cave Stroud," Sarah added after a pause.

"But you look just like Henry. I-I thought that's who you were," Susan answered with an embarrassed stammer.

"That's all right, Susan," Cave answered. "Lots of people get us mixed up," he added, looking at Sarah with a raised eyebrow and a slight smile as he offered her his hand. "Sometimes it works to our advantage."

Gathering her skirts about her, Sarah accepted Cave's hand. "Thank you so much for the picnic," she smiled as she rose. "I also enjoyed our talk. I must speak with my father. I had no idea what problems he's been facing."

"Talk to him, Sarah. Goodness knows. I've tried to talk to all of them. But I suppose my boyish good looks prevent them from taking me seriously," he added, grinning and tipping his hat as Sarah ran off after her excited little sisters.

Watching her until she was out of sight, Cave turned to pick up his jacket and the empty basket. Smiling to himself as he made his way back through the crowd, he decided it definitely had paid to turn the office over to Henry for the day. "I must do it more often," he thought, "especially when Miss Sarah Holeman is about."

≈ ≈ ≈

THE YELLOW POPLAR leaves in the distant woods lent a striking contrast to the brown oak trees bordering the drive to the Holeman house. Bright-red dogwood leaves carpeted the ground, exposing the even brighter red berries clinging to their branches.

Sarah stood on the front steps, riding crop in hand. Shielding her eyes with her free hand, she looked beyond the rolling lawns to see the farm hands busily working each row—their hands flying as they pulled the yellowed tobacco leaves, wrapped them into bundles, and deposited them in the unending line of wooden wagons rolling to and from the tobacco barns. It had been a fine growing season. The yield was sure to be good. She'd heard her father say so just last evening.

"Fie on Mr. Cave Stroud and his dire predictions," she said to herself with a disdainful shrug, "I'll bet Father will become rich with this harvest. Then I'd like to see Cave's face!" Filled with righteous indignation at the presumptuous young man, Sarah stomped down the steps and headed toward the stables.

There she found Millie waiting for her. Stroking the warm, brown nose and cooing to her horse, Sarah found her anger subsiding. Being honest with herself, she knew it was not Cave's prediction of economic disaster which had prompted her anger, but his insistence on keeping Henry by his side in town— forever bent over some new transaction. It was as if Cave had planned it all. And Henry never seemed able to say "No."

The land deal by the Eno River had taken place, as Cave had predicted. But things were not going smoothly, Henry had told her on one of their rare Sunday afternoons together. The land was steeper than they had realized, and construction would be complicated. Moreover, no one had yet seen the same potential the Stroud men had envisioned. Entertaining prospective buyers took much of his time. And Henry had begged Sarah's forgiveness for his lack of attention.

Sarah had been saved the humiliation of a repeat meeting with Cave, however, because of his even greater involvement with the project. "Thank goodness for small favors!" Sarah said to herself. "I guess some good comes of every situation.

"Oh, well, I'll not think of the Stroud boys today. It's too beautiful a day to waste inside. Winter will come only too soon," she mused, leading Millie from the stable, mounting, and riding off for the woods.

Henry reined his large roan to a halt at the steps of the Holeman home. As he began to dismount, he caught a glimpse of a horse's rump disappearing into the trees with a cascade of dark curls flying behind. Touching his heels to the roan, he took off in pursuit.

It took only a few moments to draw up alongside Sarah on the path beside the creek. "Too beautiful a day to stay inside, I said to myself," Henry began.

"So did I," Sarah answered with a toss of her head, designed to show him she could entertain herself.

"Please don't be angry with me, Sarah," Henry begged. "It's just that there is so much work right now. And Cave keeps taking on new projects. I really do want to see you more. I've taken the afternoon off just to be with you. Won't you please be civil?"

Softening her gaze, Sarah nodded slowly. "I do understand, and I know your work's important. I'm sorry. I'm glad you're here. At least we can enjoy the afternoon. Where would you like to ride?"

"Somewhere my brother can't find me," he answered ruefully. Then an idea seemed to strike him. "Why not ride with me toward Caldwell Institute? Would you mind? I'd really like to refresh my mind on the layout of the school so we can suggest a proper layout on our river property to prospective buyers. It isn't too far for you, is it?"

"Not at all. It's a perfect day, and I've no other plans," Sarah responded quickly, turning Millie toward the creek to follow Henry across.

The shallow water eddied under the horse's feet as Sarah paused in midstream. "Oh, I do love the peace of the forest, don't you?" she sighed, looking upward at the towering green pines beside the creek and catching Henry's eye as he, too, stopped beside her. "It's as if time stands still in here and nothing can touch us. I know your company does a great service, Henry. But in your haste to see all of Orange County developed, will you please leave a tiny corner of it like this forever?"

"Orange County is one of the prettiest places on Earth. Its beauty is one of our greatest selling points," Henry smiled. "Rest assured. We don't want to see the county overdeveloped either. We'll save lots of forest-land for you and your children to ride through. I promise."

They rode on in silence for another mile or so, intent on keeping to the narrow, poorly-marked path, where their way was often blocked with fallen limbs and brambles. When at last they reached the road leading to Caldwell Institute, Henry drew in his reins and waited for Sarah to catch up. He turned, smiling as he watched her brush some stubborn brambles from her riding skirt. She was obviously hot and tired, but she had kept up with Henry's erratic gait without a word. He tried to imagine one of his sisters doing the same and laughed to himself.

Finding the road much wider than the forest path, the two were able to ride side-by-side to the edge of the institute grounds. At the entrance, however, Henry stopped to stare at an all-too-familiar buggy and the figure of Cave Stroud striding up the wide, white steps to the main building.

Hearing the approaching horses, Cave turned. Then, catching sight of Henry and Sarah, he began to run back down the steps toward them. Ignoring his brother, whose hand was outstretched in greeting, Cave hastened to Sarah's side to help her dismount and led Millie to the shade of a nearby tree.

"Henry," Cave commented, turning at last to acknowledge his brother, "you can't have all your faculties about you to bring Miss Holeman on such an exhausting ride in this heat."

Looking down at them sheepishly, Henry began, "I'm sorry, Sarah, I didn't realize how really long the ride was. I had no business making you ride so far in this heat. . . ."

"Henry Stroud," Sarah interrupted, "I asked to go on this ride, and I really enjoyed myself. I'm not as fragile as you and Cave would like to think. I can take care of myself," she continued, turning to follow Cave toward the administration building.

"I'm sure you can," Henry answered, smiling as he dismounted. "In fact, I'm more sure of that fact than anything else at this moment," he added to himself. "But I hope you never have to."

The tour of the institute was not very interesting to Sarah. But she smiled as each of her guides pointed out various aspects of the complex. Finally, as they approached the last building, Sarah sat down on the steps. "Henry, Cave, why not tour this building without me while I enjoy the roses?" she asked, pointing to an overgrown garden in the main quadrangle where deep-red blossoms competed with white, yellow, and pink ones.

"If you're sure. . .," Henry added, hesitantly. Then, watching Cave disappear inside, he turned and hurried up the steps.

In what seemed only minutes, Sarah heard the clattering of boots behind her. Turning, she saw Cave approaching. But Henry was nowhere to be seen. "We've really seen all we came to see. I hope we haven't bored you," Cave said, stopping beside her.

"Not at all," Sarah answered. "It's a beautiful place, especially the rose garden. I'd forgotten. I came here for a social years ago when I was in school."

"Maybe if things work out, my brothers and I will be helping to build an academy very much like it closer to Hillsborough in the near future," Cave answered. "Now, there are several things I need to discuss with Henry back at the office. And I'm sure you're not ready to take that exhausting ride back by yourself. So why don't we just tie your horse behind my buggy and let you ride home out of the sun?"

"Why, I couldn't. . .," Sarah began.

"I insist," Cave interrupted. "I need to send Henry ahead to the office to sign some papers, anyway. So I have time. It will only take a moment to tie up your horse."

Sarah looked up to see Henry emerging from the building, making notes on a paper in his hand as he walked. Glancing up at last, he noticed Cave with Millie. "Where are you going with Sarah's horse?" he asked.

"Sarah has accepted my offer to drive her home," Cave called, taking Millie's bridle. "Surely you can't expect her to repeat that ill-advised ride, can you? You go on ahead. There are several papers on your desk I would like you to read and sign before I get back. I'll see you at the office."

Covering the remaining steps to Sarah's side, Henry reached for her hands. "The least I can do is see you to the buggy, Milady," he said, attempting a smile to cover his anger. He'd so hoped to spend the afternoon with Sarah, and now. . .

"Henry, I-I didn't ask Cave for a ride. He took it for granted," Sarah stammered. "I enjoyed our outing and was looking forward to the return trip." She was hot, she had to admit. And the long ride to the institute had left her rather tired. But she'd endure twice the distance just to spend some time with Henry. Curse Cave. It was almost as if he were following Henry's every move.

"There'll be other times," Henry sighed as he helped Sarah into the buggy. "Cave is probably right. The weather has turned uncommonly warm, and you'll be much more comfortable out of the sun."

"You'll find all the papers in the folder on your desk. I'll be back in an hour or so," Cave called to his twin. "That should give you enough time to read them. We'll discuss them when I return."

THE WEDDING OF Tibitha Stroud and John Quackenbush was the event of the Christmas season. Besides being the eldest daughter of one of the most successful planters in the county, Tibitha was also lovely enough to arrest any male eye. She was tall and slender with dark-blue eyes and flaxen hair, which she wore caught up in ringlets on both sides of her face.

Her groom, John Quackenbush, was equally attractive, with dark hair and sideburns and honest, hazel eyes. As a lawyer in

Hillsborough, he was known to almost every resident and had been the secret fantasy of many a young woman at the Burwell School for Young Ladies, which was situated across the street from his office. The couple's popularity and the promise of a lavish plantation wedding insured that almost every invited guest would be on hand.

The Stroud home was breathtaking in itself. But today it shone as never before. The curving drive, outlined in small boxwood bushes, led visitors to the massively-columned front portico and double, mahogany doors, which were decorated with fragrant bayleaf wreaths. Drapes of greenery, caught up with massive, white ribbons, covered both the upper and lower verandas. Tall, white candles shone from each window.

A servant admitted Sarah and her parents into the grand foyer, which was also festooned with evergreen boughs. Branches of holly with deep-red berries befitting the season draped the large, curving staircase down which the bride would descend.

As they entered, the Holeman family was greeted by their hostess, Mary Stroud, Tibitha and Henry's stepmother. Mary, the diminutive second wife of Hawkins Stroud, was no more than thirty years old, with alert brown eyes, dark-brown hair, and a penchant for entertaining. Her fame as a gracious hostess was widespread. Today was no exception.

With a hug for each, the elegantly-groomed little woman led Sarah and her parents into the dining room where a sumptuous feast had been laid out on the banquet table—interspersed with dark-green magnolia leaves and a myriad of candles, which showered the room with wavering light. All manners of finger sandwiches, cookies, cakes, and nuts filled gleaming silver bowls. A crystal punch bowl and cups occupied each end of the table.

As Sarah took a small cup of punch, she felt a strange prickling on her neck and turned her head. Across the room, leaning leisurely against the breakfront, Cave stood in his gray coat with the long tails, slim trousers, and polished boots. He glanced coolly at Sarah and proceeded to peruse her—ignoring all the other guests.

Feeling her face turn red, Sarah drained her cup quickly, placed it on the sideboard, turned with a quick backward glance, and started for the door. She had no intention of subjecting herself to Cave's unsettling effects today—or any day, for that matter.

Suddenly, she felt her progress blocked. Before she could catch herself, she stumbled full force into Henry, who was just entering the room from the parlor. "Whoa," Henry laughed, catching her as she pitched forward. "Where were you going in such a hurry? Contrary to popular opinion, marriage is not contagious. So you are really quite safe here."

Overcome with embarrassment, Sarah stammered, "I—I guess I was in somewhat of a hurry. I'm sorry."

"No apology's necessary, Sarah. It has been my pleasure to have you fall into my arms not once, but twice. We must do it again," Henry chuckled, smiling to himself at the sneer on Cave's face.

"I sincerely hope not," Sarah answered, righting herself and smoothing her skirts.

"Now, I was just about to invite our guests to the parlor for the service. May I escort you to a seat?" Henry asked with a bow, extending his elbow.

The service was as beautiful as the preparations. At the mantle, John Quackenbush stood transfixed as the strains of the wedding march began and his bride began her descent down the curving marble staircase.

Tibitha was an ethereal vision in yards and yards of white satin. The gentlemen in the room left no doubt as to their opinion of John's choice as they followed the beautiful young woman down the stairs with their eyes.

Ending without a hitch, the ceremony was soon over. And the happy young couple stood in the foyer to greet their many guests. "Tibitha, you look lovely and so very happy," Sarah remarked, kissing her friend.

"I hope you'll be as happy, Sarah," Tibitha whispered. "I know one young man who hopes so, too," she added with a nod toward Henry before moving on to the next guest.

After the ceremony, the wide, glass doors of the dining room had been thrown open for guests to enjoy the gardens. Glad of the fresh air, Sarah took a cup of punch and sat down on a marble bench set against a tall boxwood hedge. Lifting her head to catch the weakened rays of the winter sun, she closed her eyes.

"Mark my words, gentlemen. We may be witnessing the death knell of the old South," said a voice behind the hedge. "With market prices falling every day, it's no wonder so many are moving westward."

"I fear you're right, Hawkins," said another voice Sarah recognized as her father's. "Cotton prices have fallen to half what they were four years ago. And tobacco is not far behind. It almost doesn't pay to plant the fields. Truthfully, I'm not sure I'll be able to feed and clothe my family by the end of next year if things do not improve."

Although she could not see the two men, Sarah envisioned the tall and formidable Hawkins Stroud with his piercing hazel eyes, bushy, sandy-blond hair, and clipped chin beard—which seemed to belie his barber's efforts to keep it in check. Sarah smiled as she thought of her own slight father with his pale, neatly-cropped sideburns and bald head holding his own with this bear of a man. But she remembered with pride that he usually did a very good job.

"Gentlemen, have you also considered the increased influence the abolitionists are having in Washington? I fear for the South if our way of life becomes unlawful. And they will not cease until they have reached that goal," added a voice she knew belonged to Cave.

"Many of us will take up arms before we allow that to happen, Son," Hawkins added slowly and deliberately. "The people of the North don't understand our need for people to run our plantations. We cannot allow them to push legislation that will ruin us economically."

"Father, you're beating a lame horse," Cave interrupted. "As I see it, the only way to save the South is to dispense with our old ideas. We need to look to industrialization to allow us to market our own manufactured goods and avoid the tariffs our brothers in the North are charging us."

"Now there I cannot agree with you," Samuel Holeman countered. "I have no intention of seeing our lovely countryside stripped bare to provide room for a factory. Nor will I allow my land to be so used."

"Then, Mr. Holeman," Cave added with bravado, "you'd best hope one of your lovely daughters secures a husband who will look kindly on you in your old age, for I fear financial ruin for someone with that attitude."

"Cave, you will hold your tongue in front of our guests!" Hawkins Stroud erupted angrily. "I'll not have you baiting Samuel."

"Mr. Holeman and I are quite clear on one another's positions, Father, and have aired our disagreements privately as well as publicly," Cave answered.

"Leave him be, Hawkins," Samuel sighed. "Young Cave is right. I know his position only too well. But I fear for our community if your other sons adopt his thinking and begin looking for industrial sites with that company of theirs."

"I assure you, Mr. Holeman, our company has only Hillsborough's best interests at heart. We would never support a project that would divide the town. I give you my word," said a voice Sarah recognized as Henry's.

"Enough said," Hawkins added with a note of relief. "Now, what do you say, Samuel, to a cheroot in my study? I've just married off my daughter and feel in need of a celebration. Will you join me?"

The voices drifted off as Sarah shivered—not from the weather, but from the words she had overheard.

CHAPTER FOUR
December 1844

OVER A YEAR HAD passed since Tibitha's wedding. Sarah stood in the main parlor helping her sister Susan drape evergreen boughs along the marble mantle, while keeping her eyes on her five younger sisters. It was a big task keeping them all in line while her mother directed activities for the Christmas Eve dinner.

At least Susan was being cooperative for a change, Sarah thought, looking at the fourteen-year-old with her unruly, brown braids and freckled nose. She knew Susan longed to be riding her pony on this crisp, sunny day. And Sarah was grateful she was not having to listen to her complaints.

Glancing across the room, she saw that Jane had the other four girls entertained with opening ornament boxes. As fast as she unwrapped an item, however, one of the little girls would grab it from her hand. Sarah's heart went out to the quiet, sincere, twelve-year-old, with her serious eyes and straight, brown hair. She knew how Jane disliked all noise and confusion—a state that seemed to be ever-present in the Holeman home.

Suddenly, nine-year-old Julia ran off with a china angel, her blond curls bouncing as she playfully held it away from her sisters. Eight-year-old Martha, to whom life was a serious venture, had just found a perfect spot for the angel. Now, seeing it disappear in Julia's hand, she took chase, her strawberry-blond curls forming a cloud around her head. Round and round the room the little girls ran until Julia took refuge behind Sarah's skirt and turned her eyes to the beautiful prize in her hand.

Choosing her moment carefully, Martha popped around to Sarah's side and grabbed for the angel. Julia squealed and jumped aside, only to trip on the raised hearth. Her feet tangled in Sarah's skirts, the angel flew from her hand, and a silvery tinkle sounded loudly as Julia howled in anguish. All eyes turned to the hearth where the angel lay in pieces.

"You're really going to get it now," Martha hooted, lording it over her sister, but secretly glad the angel had not been in her possession after all.

"Julia, are you hurt?" Sarah gasped, dropping the bough and falling to her knees beside Julia, who lay perilously close to the fire, emitting a series of shrieks.

"She's only upset at breaking the angel," Susan said as she, too, dropped her end of the bough and rushed to help. "Here, Julia. Let's get you away from the fire before you get scorched," she added, grasping the child beneath the arms and attempting to right her.

Julia, however, remained as floppy as a rag doll, continuing her tirade until, with Sarah's help, they finally managed to move her away from the hearth. Sarah seated herself on the settee and pulled the little girl into her lap. Her face and dress were covered with soot, and big tears made rivers down each cheek through the black ash. Julia's bottom lip was extended to twice its usual size as she gazed at the angel's tiny right wing, which still remained in her hand—devoid of both head and body. "It was my favorite!" she gasped between sobs.

"It was Mother's favorite, too," Jane added, as Julia, fearing a punishment, began to sob even harder.

In the midst of the confusion, a loud knock sounded at the double front doors, although no one could possibly have heard a buggy approach. Looking toward the entrance hall, Sarah saw Aaron hurrying to answer the knock.

"Girls, pick up these things, quickly!" Sarah admonished, noticing the disarray. "We seem to have company." Placing Julia firmly on the floor and straightening her skirt, Sarah started toward the front hall.

Hearing Henry's friendly greeting, Sarah stood transfixed a moment, wondering if she could dare to leave the girls to go for a ride with him. Before she reached the vestibule, however, she saw with dismay that Henry had not even noticed her and was walking off behind Aaron toward her father's study. "Men," she muttered angrily. "He probably doesn't even know it's Christmas Eve. And I'm sure Father has forgotten. All they ever think about is business."

With a dark scowl, Sarah reentered the parlor, sat down heavily on the settee, and let out an angry hiss. "Who wath at the do-ah?" three-year-old Harriett lisped. Receiving no answer, she crawled up on the settee and peered into Sarah's face, violet eyes wide.

Finally, Sarah reached out a hand to stroke her youngest sister's dark-brown ringlets. "It was only Henry," she said, smiling in spite of herself at the earnest little face with its rosy cheeks. "He came to talk business with Father."

"What a terrible turn of events," Susan mocked, flipping a braid over her shoulder. "And you thought he had come to see you—it being Christmas Eve."

"Don't listen to her, Sarah. She's just jealous because Father says she's still too young for a beau. How sad. You must be devastated," Jane put in.

Feeling her unhappiness, the other little girls gathered around Sarah. Martha fingered a gold star, and looked dejectedly toward the ground. Five-year-old Maria looked from Sarah to her other sisters, then averted her bright-blue eyes beneath her long, brown curls as she busied herself with trying unsuccessfully to tie a red-and-green-plaid ribbon around her waist.

Suddenly, a voice boomed from the doorway, "Well, this is a gloomy group if I've ever seen one! I should think everyone would be full of mirth and holiday cheer on Christmas Eve. Perhaps all you need is a little sweetening up."

Turning at the sound of his voice, all the girls at once screamed, "Henry!"

"Now, that's better!" Henry grinned, placing a box of chocolates in the center of the table. "But not too many before dinner," he cautioned. "I wouldn't want your mamma coming after me with a switch for ruining her big Christmas Eve dinner."

Tears vanished like mists before the sun, as, within seconds, six eager pairs of hands were groping in the box. Harriett popped two candies at a time into her mouth, and soon was drooling chocolate down her chin.

Henry began to laugh as Sarah quickly removed her pocket handkerchief and began to wipe at her face. "Hold still, Harriett. You've got chocolate all over!" Sarah chided. "Mother will be after us all if we get any on the furniture."

Leaving Harriett to Sarah, Henry turned to Susan. "I must say, Susan, you become lovelier each day. I shouldn't imagine it will be long before I cannot find a place to leave my buggy for those belonging to all your beaus."

Susan beamed at the compliment, but could not think of an appropriate response. Doing as she had seen Sarah do so many times, she simply lowered her lashes and looked at the floor as Henry continued. "Now, before any of them begin arriving, could I ask you to look after the decorating for an hour or so while I take Sarah for a drive?"

Finding her tongue at last, Susan asked hopefully, "Don't you want to stay and help us with the decorating?"

"If there's still decorating to do when we get back, I'll be more than happy to help," Henry smiled. "In the meantime, would you feel too imposed on to take over the reins here for a while?"

"Of course not," Susan responded, secretly proud of the trust he was placing in her.

"I do love this family of yours," Henry added, turning to Sarah. "Susan is now in charge, so will you get your wrap? I haven't long since my family will be eating before church. But I didn't want to pass the day without seeing you."

IT WAS A glorious afternoon with crisp air and a cloudless, blue sky. There had been a light snow the evening before, and small patches still remained beneath the trees and under the boxwood bushes. The sun's late rays caught the remaining crystals and turned them to diamonds as Henry and Sarah left the house.

Henry handed Sarah into his buggy and tucked the lap robe snugly around her. Climbing in himself, he clicked to the horse. The couple laughed self-consciously as the animal snorted in protest and blew puffs of steam into the icy air before moving forward.

They rode in silence until Henry turned the buggy into the drive of Caldwell Institute. Sarah looked at him, questioning. She had not been to the site since that October day over a year ago when she'd accompanied Henry and Cave on their tour.

"I've something to show you," Henry announced, drawing the buggy to a stop in front of the old rose garden and waiting until Sarah looked in the proper direction. There, frozen in full bloom, was one perfect red rose lifting its head proudly to the sun as if it were July.

"It's beautiful!" Sarah cried. "A Christmas rose."

"Cave and I were here this morning to check some things out while the boys are on vacation. When I saw the rose sparkling through the snow, I couldn't wait to bring you here. I remembered how you loved this garden," Henry smiled. He'd chosen the right spot.

"I'm glad you thought of me," Sarah added softly.

"Why, Sarah Holeman, don't you know—I think of you all the time," Henry answered, looking sincerely into her eyes.

They sat in silence for several moments, each looking over the neglected rose garden, and each unsure of what to say next. Finally, Sarah began, "You must have had important business to discuss with Father."

"Oh, yes. It was extremely important and couldn't wait," Henry answered solemnly.

"I've never known Father to work on Christmas Eve before," she mused. Then, as a sudden thought hit her, she turned to Henry, "It wasn't bad news, I hope!"

"I sincerely hope not," Henry answered. "That is—not yet. Sarah, my business with your father was this," he said, pulling a small box out of his coat pocket. Dropping to one knee before her in the buggy, he flipped open the top of the box to reveal a blinding sparkle as the sun's late rays hit the diamond inside. "Sarah Holeman, will you honor me by saying 'Yes' when I ask you to marry me?" he questioned.

Sarah's mouth dropped open, and her right hand flew to cover it as she remained speechless. She'd hoped. . . But she'd never dreamed it would be this soon.

"Sarah," Henry prompted, his eyes probing hers. He'd been so sure of her reaction when he'd purchased the ring. And her father had seemed so pleased. But perhaps he had been mistaken.

"Henry," Sarah began hesitantly, "I think you know how I feel about you. But I'm not sure you know what you will be getting into with me. I-I'm afraid I am a little bit headstrong at times—no, most of the time. I'm forever doing things people seem to think I have no business doing. But I can't seem to shut off my brain as women are supposed to do. God gave me a brain, and I intend to use it, so if you would prefer some dewy-eyed young thing at your side. . .," she paused. She had to warn him. After all, as much as she wanted Henry, she knew she could not change—for any man.

"That's the very reason I picked you," Henry answered, relieved. "I think it's the reason I love you so much. I love every moment I spend with you. I enjoy our discussions, and I value your advice. I don't want some vacuous female with a head full of clothes and parties. I want someone to share my life totally—to be my friend and partner, as well as my wife. I want you, Sarah, and I'll be proud of everything you do, if you'll only say 'Yes'!" he begged.

"Oh, yes, Henry Stroud, then I should be proud to marry you," Sarah answered, her face breaking into a smile. "It has just come as such a shock. I'm sorry."

"Don't ever be sorry, Sarah," Henry admonished quietly, taking her hand. Then, raising his voice, he cried loudly, "You have just made me the happiest man alive, and I want to tell the whole town."

"But could we wait to do that until I have told the rest of my family tonight?" Sarah asked. She knew, despite Henry's visit, her father would have waited for her to tell her mother. And she couldn't allow her to hear the news first from some friend at church. "I'd rather that they didn't hear it from someone else."

"Of course, Sarah, whatever you ask. Now, will you please remove this glove so that I can see if my guess at your size was correct?" Henry asked impatiently, sitting beside her again and removing the ring from the box.

"It's the most beautiful ring I've ever seen," Sarah sighed as Henry slipped the gold band onto her finger and she held it to the light. Speechless, the two watched in silence as the round, clear diamond caught the late afternoon sunlight and spread a rainbow onto the patch of snow surrounding the buggy.

"It's not as big as I would like," Henry began at last. "But my business has a ways to go yet. I brought you here today because so much of my—I mean 'our'—future depends on the new academy we hope to build. I want to offer you so much more than I can now."

"This ring is all I ever want," Sarah answered with tears in her eyes. Leaning toward him, she intended a kiss on the cheek—until Henry, pulling her to him, covered her mouth with his. Totally unprepared for the feelings Henry's kiss awakened in her, Sarah returned the kiss with equal ardor.

After several moments, Henry released his hold, his eyes searching Sarah's as she silently begged for more. "Now, that's a proper way to seal our agreement!" he smiled, forcing himself to let her go. "Although, if we continue like this, I'm afraid I may take you away with me this moment—creating the scandal of the year in Hillsborough.

"But since I would prefer your father's blessing to the barrel of his musket, I suppose we must allow the proper space for an engagement—and for all those preparations you ladies seem to feel necessary. Tell me, how do you feel about October for the wedding? Will that give you enough time? We should have our academy under way by then, and I should be ready for some time off."

"That's perfect. October's a lovely time," Sarah added, still shaken after the overwhelming kiss she had just received.

"I wanted to ask you now—at Christmas—because it is such a special time. I was afraid when your father hemmed and hawed so long it might be New Year's before I got his answer, though!" Henry smiled, remembering how much his knees had quaked as Aaron had ushered him into Samuel's study.

"He didn't give you a hard time, did he?" Sarah asked, concerned her father had offended Henry.

"Not really," Henry answered. "I think he likes me. . . In fact, I'm sure he does because he tried to warn me about you, too," he put in with a laugh. "But I'm still not sure about your mother. So, before I incur her wrath for bringing the chocolates and taking you away, I suppose I'd better get you back home."

≈ ≈ ≈

ALL TOO SOON, the long, dogwood-lined driveway came into view, and Henry reluctantly turned his horse into it. As they neared the house, Sarah pulled on her glove to avoid giving away her surprise too quickly, although she hated to cover up the glorious ring.

"Will I see you tonight at church?" Henry asked as he helped her from the buggy.

"Just try to avoid me, Henry Stroud," Sarah countered, squeezing his arm.

"If you've told your family by then, maybe we can announce our engagement to my family after the service," Henry said, planting a fleeting kiss on her cheek as they reached the front door. "By the time the midnight bells are ringing, I want to be able to cry out the news from the church steeple. I promise you, I can't wait much longer than that to tell the rest of the world."

A FULL ORANGE moon and a myriad of twinkling stars illuminated the evening, as the long unbroken line of horse-drawn carriages wound toward the little Mars Hill Baptist Church. Merrily-jingling bells kept time with the slow "clop-clop" of the horses' hooves, as buggies and carriages drew up in front. The horses stamped the ground, blowing out clouds of steam to show their impatience with the delay, as fathers and brothers searched for the best place to hand down their ladies to avoid the slushy ground.

The strains of "Oh, Little Town of Bethlehem" were drifting on the crisp December air as the Holeman family turned from Mars Hill Road onto the long, circular drive. The chatter among her sisters had been nonstop since Sarah had broken her news over dinner, and Sarah and her mother shared a smile as Martha and Maria sat behind them verbally designing the dresses they would wear as flower girls.

Craning her neck, Sarah tried to see if Henry and his family had arrived yet. To her delight, she saw the two Stroud carriages two spaces in front of them. Mary caught Sarah's eye and waved gaily, then turned to speak to one of her brothers. It was impossible for Sarah to guess if it was Henry or Cave, but seeing the backs of two blond heads, she knew Henry was here, and sat back to await her family's turn at the door.

As he finally pulled to the front steps, Samuel alighted to help his wife. Turning to Sarah, Jean squeezed her hand companionably before stepping down.

Smiling at her mother's joy over her announcement, Sarah gathered her cloak about her and slid across the seat to await her father's return. Raising her head, expecting to see her father, she was startled to see instead the piercing gray eyes of Cave Stroud in front of her, hand outstretched.

"Cave," she gasped, flustered. "I didn't see you come up!"

"You look lovely as always, Sarah," Cave said with a bow. "May I offer you some assistance? The snow is still muddy, and we wouldn't want to mar such a beautiful dress," he added with a long perusal of Sarah that took in every inch of her person from her deep-green velvet bonnet with the gold braid to the hem of her fashionable, green velvet dress with the voluminous hoop skirt, which filled the seat beside her.

Looking about furtively for Henry, Sarah took a few moments to react. When she finally caught sight of him, he was at the church steps, helping Mary to the door. She had no choice but to accept Cave's hand, and she smiled tentatively as she leaned toward him.

As she extended her hand, Cave's fingers came around her glove with a firm grip. Even after she had alighted on the ground, he refused to let go. Instead, he used his grip to steer Sarah toward the back of the carriage as the rest of her family exited the vehicle.

Placing his hand under her chin, Cave drew Sarah's face into the light. "Merry Christmas," he smiled. "I'd hoped to get by to see you today, but I had so much business to attend to. . . I do have a gift for you, however. Will you wait for me after church?"

"I'm sorry. I promised to meet Henry after the service," Sarah hedged, uncomfortable with the situation. She knew Cave did not yet know of her engagement, and she determined to stop him before allowing him to be embarrassed. Unable to speak the words, she slowly disengaged her hand from Cave's and began to pull off her glove.

Surprised at her abrupt action, Cave's eyes followed her movements as the light from the doorway caught the diamond on her finger. As the brilliant sparkle lit the snow around them, Cave turned questioning eyes to Sarah.

"I thought you should know," Sarah began hesitantly. "Henry wanted to tell you himself, but I asked him to wait to tell your family until I had told mine. I'm truly sorry now, Cave, that I didn't let him tell you sooner."

Grabbing Sarah's forearm, Cave swung her toward him as his eyes pierced hers. "How could you have done this, Sarah? How could you humiliate me like this? You knew how I felt. I thought I had made myself clear on numerous occasions," he blurted out. Then, seeing the fear in her eyes, he softened and loosened his grip. "It's not too late," he pleaded. "You can change your mind. Tell Henry you were mistaken. Give him back his ring, and I'll buy you one twice its size. I'll build you the finest house Hillsborough has ever seen. . ."

"But I'm not mistaken," Sarah interrupted. "I've enjoyed the outings we've had. Truly, I have. And I value all our discussions. But Henry has asked me to be his wife, and that's what I want as well. I'm sorry if I've hurt you, but can you try to understand and be happy for us? We'll all be family now, and I do so want us all to be happy. I wouldn't want to come between you and Henry. Please, Cave," she begged.

"Never, Sarah," Cave hissed under his breath. "I can never accept you choosing him over me. It isn't fair. Why, Henry would be nothing without me. And here I've been slaving every day to make our company a success while he spent his time wooing you away from me.

"You ask too much, Miss Holeman, to ask me to forgive and forget and to sit back and watch you tend his house and bear his children while I play always the dutiful brother-in-law and kind uncle. I cannot, and I will not accept it—ever. And,

I warn you, don't ever look to me for help when that husband of yours pulls you into one of his fantasies and leaves you and your children destitute. You'll live to rue this day, Sarah Holeman. Mark my words!" Cave sneered, releasing Sarah's arm and striding angrily away toward one of the Stroud carriages—in the opposite direction of the church.

Standing alone in front of the church, Sarah leaned against the carriage for support—her head reeling. She'd thought Cave's attentions were merely flirtations. She had never knowingly led him on. Or had she? She had wanted them all to be so happy. . . But now there seemed little chance of that. She was sure Henry had no idea of Cave's feelings. She knew he would never have knowingly hurt his twin. Should she say anything to him before he went home? But she had hurt Cave enough already. Better to leave him what little pride he still had.

As she shook her head to clear it, she saw a concerned Henry descending the steps. With arms outstretched, he approached and drew her into his arms. "What is it, Sarah? Are you ill?" he asked, his soft, gray eyes probing her dark ones. "I got concerned when I saw your family come in without you."

"I'm only chilled, I think," Sarah lied, for indeed she did feel very ill after the scene with Cave. "I should get inside. I can't seem to stop shivering."

Removing his coat, Henry placed it over Sarah's cloak and began leading her toward the lighted entrance. Propelling Sarah toward the stove, Henry put his arm around her shoulders and stood in silence with her until the uncontrollable shivers subsided. Then, carefully taking both coats, he hung them on the nearby rack.

"Thank you, Henry," she said at last. "I'm warmer now. I'd better go before my family misses me. I'll see you after the service," she answered, slipping from his arm and making her way down the aisle to take her place beside her father.

Leaning over to share his hymnal with his eldest daughter, Samuel turned a quizzical gaze on Sarah. Receiving no response, he turned back to the page in front of him, but not before noticing Henry slip quietly into his family's pew beside Mary. A sly smile creased his lips as he looked around quickly to see if anyone else had noticed the two latest arrivals.

Cave's disappearance did not go unnoticed. Several times during the service, Sarah saw Mary and Henry whispering together. Slowly, every member of the family became aware of Cave's absence, and, from time to time, a head turned in expectation. By the end of the service, he was still nowhere to be seen.

The service ended with the traditional candle-lighting, and everyone filed out of the church singing "Silent Night." Outside, the somber air was broken by tolling church bells that signified the midnight hour—and the beginning of Christmas Day. Wild whoops from tired, but excited, children filled the air, and adults hugged and kissed one another.

Caught in the midst of several of her mother's friends, who were exclaiming over her dress, Sarah searched the crowd for Henry. Finally, catching his eye, she excused herself and made her way to him.

"We can't seem to find Cave, Sarah," Henry began in a perplexed voice, his eyes continuing to scan the congregation as they exited the small church. "I did want him here when I make my announcement. Did you see him? He came to church with us, but he never entered the church," Henry added.

"I believe he may have returned home. I spoke to him before the service, and I saw him return to the carriage." Sarah hesitated and took a deep breath. She wasn't sure what to tell Henry. "He knows our news already," she continued at last. "I'm sorry it couldn't be your surprise. He—saw my ring."

"Well, then, if he knows the news already, I don't have to wait for him to tell the others," Henry smiled excitedly. "Come on. I want you with me when we tell them," he said, taking Sarah by the hand as he spoke. "We'll really have some celebrating to do when we get home. I'll bet old Cave already has the party ready. That's probably why he left church. I can't wait to see his reaction!"

"I hope you never learn of the reaction I got from Cave," Sarah said to herself, seeing Henry's happiness at sharing his news with his brother. She knew now Henry had no indication of Cave's feelings, and she would never be the one to tell him. She could only hope Cave would also keep silent. She never wanted to come between the brothers. It must remain their secret—hers and Cave's—whatever the cost.

CHAPTER FIVE
March 1845

SARAH, SUSAN, AND THEIR mother were busily engaged in sewing for Sarah's trousseau one squally afternoon in early March when Aaron came to the door of the sitting room to announce Henry's arrival. Laying aside the pillowcase she had been working on and straightening her hair as she walked, Sarah hurried to the vestibule to see him. It had been several days since he had visited, and she looked forward to spending some time with him on this bitter afternoon.

As she entered the room, however, it was clear Henry was not prepared to stay. Standing inside the double doors, he still wore his coat, which was dotted with raindrops and tiny beads of sleet, and he had not removed his overshoes, which were splattered with mud.

"I wasn't expecting you, Henry," Sarah began, then stopped as she noticed his ashen face. "You look worried. Is something wrong?"

"It's Tibitha," Henry answered, shaking his head.

"Is the baby coming, then?" Sarah smiled. "Give me a moment, and I'll get my cloak. I promised to help."

"No need," Henry answered, placing his hand on her arm and choosing his words carefully. "The baby's already here. It came during the night. The weather was so bad, though. I couldn't have come for you. Mary was with Tibitha. Doctor Strudwick managed to get there, too—despite the weather.

"The baby's fine," he added hastily as he noticed the worried look on Sarah's face. "It's a beautiful little girl with flaxen hair just like Tibitha's—although there isn't much of it," he added, smiling wanly. "Tibitha and John have named her 'Elizabeth' after our aunt, who cared for us when our mother died. She never had any children, and Tibitha thought she would be pleased."

"I'm sure she will!" Sarah added, noting the guarded look in Henry's eyes. "But there's something you're not telling me. I can read it in your face. How is Tibitha. When can I see her?"

"I'm afraid not for a while," Henry answered sadly, shaking his head. "The doctor has ordered complete bed rest and no visitors. It was a very difficult delivery—you know how frail Tibitha is. She's still quite ill, but the doctor thinks she'll live. It's doubtful, however, that she could ever survive another childbirth, and he told John that."

"How terrible for them. And both John and Tibitha were planning such a large family. . .," she continued. Tears filled her eyes as she remembered the glow in Tibitha's eyes when she had shown Sarah the nursery—with room enough for all the babies she and John had wanted.

"John is reconciled. I've been with him all evening," Henry answered, reaching up a gloved finger to brush away one of Sarah's tears. "He says he's just thankful the Lord spared Tibitha this time. And he's overjoyed to have a daughter. It really is a miracle, you know—seeing a new life begin. You should have seen John's face when Dr. Strudwick put little Elizabeth in his arms."

"I wish I could have been there. . .," Sarah added sadly. She'd promised Tibitha so many times that she would be there for her, and now. . .

"It was all for the best. Tibitha wouldn't have wanted you to risk coming such a long way with the weather such as it was. Rest assured, though, that I'll come for you the moment Dr. Strudwick allows her to receive company," Henry smiled again, taking Sarah's hands in his gloved ones.

"Now, I really must go. I need to take the news to my father and stepmother. They'll be anxious to hear. But I wanted to tell you first," he added, turning to the door.

"Oh, do be careful in this weather!" Sarah called, following him to the door, then backing away as a blast of sleet-laden wind swept into the vestibule.

"I promise to be very careful," Henry called back, pulling his greatcoat tightly about him. "After all, I have some important business to attend to come October," he yelled over the whistle of the wind as he climbed into his buggy and waved a farewell.

≈ ≈ ≈

AFTER THE LATE sleet storm, spring seemed to pounce on the countryside. Buds swelled and burst, robins picked at worms in the red Carolina mud, servants opened windows to admit the warm breeze laden with the smell of newly-mown grass and freshly-turned dirt, and the field hands, with Samuel's ever-present overseeing, laid the basis for the new year's crops. Samuel was optimistic about a bumper crop and spoke of good fortune smiling on the Holeman family in this year of 1845. Everyone seemed in good spirits as they planned for the upcoming wedding.

Jean Holeman and her older daughters spent their mornings putting the finishing touches on Sarah's trousseau or having fittings for the wedding dress and her attendants' dresses. Afternoons often found Henry visiting or, if the weather permitted, taking Sarah for a buggy ride.

Little by little, Tibitha did improve, and one day Henry surprised Sarah when he stopped at the Quackenbush home. "Is Tibitha up to visitors, then?" Sarah asked in delighted surprise. "Oh, I'm so anxious to see her—and Elizabeth."

"And they're both anxious to see you!" Henry smiled, helping Sarah from the buggy. "Tibitha made me promise to bring you today."

They found Tibitha in the darkened parlor, fully dressed and waiting for them. As she rose and approached them, Sarah was struck by her appearance and tried to disguise her alarm. Tibitha's once luxuriant hair was wound tightly in a bun at her neck, while thin wisps framed her drawn, pale face with its deep-sunken blue eyes. Always thin, Tibitha now appeared almost wraith-like, and her clothes hung on her tiny frame. But her smile was genuine as she extended her hands to her friend.

"I'm so glad Dr. Strudwick has finally allowed me to have visitors. You were the first I asked for!" Tibitha exclaimed, embracing Sarah. "I know you've come to see Elizabeth, but I've just gotten her to sleep. So, if you have the time, perhaps we can visit some before she wakes. It won't be long," she smiled. "That child is too afraid of missing something to sleep more than a few minutes at a time!"

"Of course I want to see my future niece," Sarah said, pulling back at last from the embrace. "But it's really you I came to see. I've been so worried about you, Tibitha! I was afraid for a while that we would have to have the wedding in your bedroom to have you present."

"You know I wouldn't miss it," Tibitha smiled faintly. "I'm determined to be totally up and about by then. Your wedding will be the social event of the year, and nobody deserves happiness more than you and Henry," she added, taking Henry's hand as he led her back to her chair.

Before either Sarah or Henry could reply, a loud "Harrumph" erupted from the far corner of the room near the fireplace. Glancing in that direction, Sarah saw with dismay the figure of Cave Stroud lounging in a chair before the fire, hidden in shadow. "You put too much stock on the importance of our families, my dear, to think the rest of Hillsborough will care about a simple little wedding," he sneered, directing his comments to Tibitha alone.

"Cave," Tibitha admonished, a crimson blush covering her pale face. "Of course people will care. Whatever has come over you?"

"He's probably right," Henry called jovially. "But it's the most important event of our lives, and that's all that counts," he added, slipping his hand around Sarah's waist.

"Well, it's clear my presence is no longer needed here," Cave announced, getting to his feet. "And I really must be going anyway. I promised John I would stay until he got back, but now that you have such sterling company, I don't think I'll be missed.

"Why not fix yourself something to drink, Henry?" he offered. "Celebrate the upcoming big event and all. The maid left lemonade and glasses in the dining room."

"Splendid idea. It's a warm day, and I'm sure we could all do with a glass," Henry replied, extending his hand to Cave before exiting into the dining room.

"Sarah, would you see Cave to the door?" Tibitha asked. "His coat's in the hall. I hate not being able to play hostess, but just getting downstairs tires me so much still."

"Of course," Sarah answered, hurrying to the hall—eager to see Cave off. As she reached for his coat on the rack, however, she saw Cave at her elbow. "So, Miss Holeman," he began with a sneer, "still planning the big day, I see."

"It's in October," Sarah nodded. "But I'm sure Henry has told you. With my mother planning it, it's sure to be quite an affair. We hope to see you there."

"I think you've made it quite clear which of us you want to see that day," Cave countered, angrily reaching up to grab his coat from her hand. "So don't waste your time looking for a matched set by your mantle."

"Cave, I'm so sorry. I. . .," Sarah began, backing away.

"Save the apology, Sarah. Insincerity doesn't become you," Cave interrupted her, throwing his coat over his arm and stomping noisily down the steps—without looking back.

≈ ≈ ≈

One summer afternoon as Sarah, dressed in her riding attire, approached the barn for a long run, she heard footsteps hurriedly approaching around the side of the barn and saw Henry running breathlessly up behind her. "I came to take you riding," he announced with a grin. "But Aaron told me you'd beaten me to the idea. I have something exciting to show you. Will you come with me? My horse is at your door. I'll just go and get him."

They rode in silence for a while, enjoying the beauty of the countryside.   The towering pines provided a canopy to shield them from the August sun, and their needles made a lush carpet on the path. Finally, Henry turned his horse into a newly-cut path through the trees—slowing as he did so, for Sarah to catch up. Then, with a sweeping motion, he gestured toward the banks of the swiftly-flowing, muddy Eno River, now visible through a jumble of blackberry bushes at the end of the road. "Isn't it perfect?" Henry asked. "What a view! I had to show it to you."

"Oh, Henry! It's the property for the school! Have you found a buyer at last?" Sarah asked, knowing how much the project had weighed on Henry's mind. "Of course I want to see it. May we?"

"Right this way, Milady," Henry gestured gallantly, leading the way up the path. "Just imagine," he said with a faraway look in his eyes, "a whole campus laid out before us. It will be set on a large, common square with buildings on three sides, facing the river.

"Up there on the hillside is the perfect spot for the headmaster's home, where he can oversee the whole campus and watch the river change with the seasons. The new railroad station will be just over that rise, so the students can come and go quite easily. Who knows, maybe someday we'll attend a convocation here as parents," he continued, smiling down at her with an attempted leer. Sarah colored at his statement and averted her eyes. In her excitement over the wedding, she had not yet begun to think of the children that would come. It was a sobering thought after the toll she had seen Elizabeth's birth take on Tibitha. But, after all, the future—and children— were still a long way away.

Caught up in his vision and oblivious to Sarah's discomforting thoughts, Henry walked his horse to the shade of a tree, dismounted, and reached up to help her dismount as well. Then, quickly securing both horses, he took her hand and led her to the end of the clearing. "Look," he said, gesturing into the distance. "Over there, imagine a whole garden of red and yellow roses. I know how much you love those at the Caldwell Academy, and I'll bet other ladies might be more willing to leave their sons here where they would be surrounded by such beauty. You do agree, don't you?" he asked, watching her eyes for her reaction.

"That would be perfect," Sarah nodded, sensing his excitement. "In fact, the whole area is perfect. I love it. I don't understand why several buyers haven't been vying for this land from the first."

"Now," Henry continued, leading her into the shade beneath a large oak, "Since I've shown you my future business plans, I'd like to talk about our personal plans. You know, you haven't even asked once where we are to live after our wedding," he smiled, taking her hand.

"Since you haven't said anything, I just assumed we'd live at your father's," Sarah answered quietly, turning to him. In truth, the subject was one Sarah had been dreading. It would be hard for her to adjust to the lifestyle of the large and boisterous Stroud family. And she knew she could not bear to be in Cave's company on a daily basis. Besides, she really did want a home of her own.

"I hadn't spoken of it until now because I've been doing a lot of thinking—about my life and about our marriage," Henry began. "You know how I've agonized over the plans for this property and how many hours I've put into them. There hasn't been a night since we purchased this land that I have gone to bed peacefully. I don't want to enter our married life with the same worries, Sarah. It's not fair to you—or me. I'm not like my brothers, and I really need to face that fact.

"Despite being a partner in our business, Alfred had really been quite removed from our speculative plans, preferring to handle other more stable real estate problems in town. And that's fine. He's better at keeping the books and performing checks and balances for the company.

"Cave seems to thrive on all sorts of schemes for making money and is the entrepreneur. He hatches the ideas and has a grand way of making even the most remote idea seem plausible. Why, he could sell the bed of the Eno River for a new town site, and it would probably succeed.

"I can't be like either of them. I don't like figures and bookkeeping, and I can't stand the pressure and uncertainty of land development deals. I want to work with people and make them happy. I want to be my own boss. I want a business where I can lock the door at lunch and come home to see you and our children with no worries and no one waiting for me."

"Are you saying you're leaving the company?" Sarah asked, confused. "I thought the three of you were in it together. . ."

"Of course. And I couldn't, in good conscience, leave Alfred and Cave to handle all the projects alone. But there's another option—one that I want to talk to you about," he continued. "We need to make this decision together."

"Certainly. Go on," Sarah smiled nervously.

"Well, it seems our company has a chance to purchase a mercantile business in Wake Forest," Henry continued excitedly. "It's a small dry-goods store on the main street with a home adjoining it. It just came to our attention yesterday, so I rode over to see it. The store is nicely kept with a real oak counter and oak floors. The home is two stories with dormer windows. It's not very big, but the furnishings are beautiful, and they go with it. There's a huge magnolia tree shading the dining room and a rose garden on the far side, near the shop.

"You'd love it. I know it. I could just picture us there— doing what we want to do with no pressures. What do you say? Do you want to try it, or would you rather stay in Hillsborough? Wake Forest isn't that far. We could come home often," he concluded, searching Sarah's eyes for her response.

A chance to start their own lives—away from the Stroud plantation and all the pressures of Henry's work—was more than Sarah had ever dreamed of. Throwing her arms around Henry's neck, she cried, "What a wonderful idea! I love it, Henry. I'm so happy. . .with everything!"

≈ ≈ ≈

THE LONG-AWAITED opening of the new Orange County Courthouse took place in September. The red brick building fronted by tall, Doric columns had been designed by a local architect, John Berry. It stood at King and Churton Streets—in the center of town—and was already being touted as the most beautiful building in Hillsborough.

The opening took place on the courthouse's front lawn, where chairs had been set out in rows facing the building. Sarah sat with Tibitha, John, and Mary in the front row. Henry, Alfred, and Cave, whose company had been instrumental in the construction, were seated on the stage as honored guests.

As the ceremony began, an honor guard bearing United States and North Carolina flags marched sharply down the lawn while a band played. Being a hot day, the speeches were short—for which everyone seemed grateful.

The ceremony ended with a sumptuous feast set out on tables beneath the spreading oaks. Pleading Tibitha's still-delicate health, John and she took their leave immediately, and Mary strolled off across the lawn in the direction of some friends. Sarah, however, was not alone long, as Alfred Stroud sought her out in the crowd. "Henry's been delayed by a short business meeting," he explained. "He asked me to see to your comfort in his absence. At any rate, I was looking for an excuse to talk to you, and this seems to be the best time."

Turning to the tall figure beside her, Sarah thought again how good looking all the Stroud men were. Alfred was two years older and was taller and slimmer than Henry and Cave. His honey-colored hair was darker than the twins' flaxen locks and perfectly matched his hazel eyes, which glowed almost golden in the afternoon sun. "What is it, Alfred?" Sarah asked. She regretted that she had not taken time to get to know this quiet brother better.

"Come with me to get some punch, and we'll talk on the way," Alfred suggested. "I'm very thirsty from so much talking. I really don't have the knack for small talk that Henry does and find it all rather tiring. I'll be glad when this day is over," he sighed, taking a glass of punch for himself and pressing one into Sarah's hands.

"Now," he continued, "Henry's so excited about the move to Wake Forest. I think it's a wise one for him, but I want to know your feelings. Was I wrong to present the idea to him? I'm sure it will be hard for you to leave your family and friends. Are you unhappy at the prospect?"

"Not at all. I'm as excited about the move as Henry. It will be wonderful having him next door all day instead of miles away in town," Sarah answered.

"It's just that, well, you see. . .," Alfred continued, hesitantly. "I've been worrying about Henry for some time. Cave is all business, as you know, and he seems to be forever taking on new projects. Recently, he's placed all the burdens for our proposed academy on Henry's shoulders. Goodness knows Henry has done his best. I've seen the hours he puts in. Over the last few months, however, Cave has seemed to find more and more fault with him and has been quite short with him on several occasions. Henry's said nothing, of course. But he didn't need to. Any fool can see the pressure he's been under.

"At any rate, your marriage deserves the best possible start. I felt that might be found away from Hillsborough. Henry is a people person, and the mercantile seemed a perfect place for him right now. Please don't tell me I was wrong, for I never wanted to hurt you," Alfred ended with a blush.

"So it was totally your idea! I didn't know. How can I ever thank you?" Sarah asked, rising on tiptoe to place a kiss on Alfred's cheek.

"What's this? I ask my brother to keep my fiance out of trouble for a few minutes and then come back to find him allowing her to throw herself all over him instead. For shame, Alfred Stroud. When did I ever treat you so?" Henry teased, coming up behind Sarah and placing his arm possessively about her waist.

"Henry!" Sarah gasped, turning around. "I didn't know you'd returned."

"Obviously!" Henry noted, then hastened to add, "But now if I didn't trust both of you, I would be a fool, wouldn't I? So I assume there was a just cause for the kiss I just witnessed."

"Alfred was asking if I was happy with our move to Wake Forest, and I was thanking him for his concern," Sarah answered. "I'm sorry, Henry. Are you thirsty? Let's walk to the tables and get you something to drink."

"I can take a hint," Henry answered with a wink at his brother. "We'll speak no more of it. But I can see I'll have to spend more time with you myself to keep you from looking at other men."

CHAPTER SIX
October 1845

SEPTEMBER'S BEAUTIFUL WEATHER DETERIORATED toward the end of the month. Lingering, gray clouds brought days of drizzle and nights of whipping gales, which drove the rains sideways against the house. Mornings dawned pale and wan with only a hint of sun, and the whole horizon was obscured by fog, which rose from the warm earth.

"Now, don't go frettin' and messin' up that pretty forehead of yours with wrinkles," Nana told Sarah one morning in early October as she entered her room to find her staring out the window and sighing. "You know the weather changes at the drop of a hat this time of year. Besides, there ain't a thing you can do about it."

"I know you're right, Nana," Sarah answered, turning away from the window. "But we've planned a garden reception, and I do so want everything to be perfect."

"As long as you folks has been plannin' this occasion, you know it's gotta be perfect—whatever the weather," Nana answered from the armoire.

Less than a week later and true to Nana's prediction, the weather did change dramatically on October 8, Sarah's wedding day. Sarah awoke to find sunlight streaming into her room and a sea of faces peering eagerly at her. With a groan, she tried to pull the covers over her head, but the gathering of six little faces refused to leave.

Finally, Sarah sat up and motioned for them to climb on her bed. With shouts of glee and much bouncing and shifting of gowns and nightcaps, they finally settled down and looked expectantly at Jane, who was holding one hand behind her back. "Go on," Susan said. "It was all your idea."

"All right," Jane answered, taking a breath. "We've been working on a gift for you. We hope you like it," she finished quickly, pulling a package from behind her back and depositing it in Sarah's lap.

"Hurry up, open it!" Martha cried, her blue eyes wide under her pale lashes.

Tearing off the paper, Sarah found six white hand-towels with the initials "S H H" embroidered in gold. "Girls, they're beautiful!" Sarah exclaimed, hugging each one. "How did you do them without my knowledge?"

"Jane helped us," Julia said. "Do you really like them? I had some trouble with the 'S.' I had to rip it out three times."

"Jane had to hold my hand," Harriett confessed. "But I threaded the needle myself."

"They're truly the most beautiful gifts I've received, and I'm sure Henry will think so, too," Sarah answered truthfully, touched by the love in all of her sisters' eyes. "We'll put them out only for special company—especially you six when you come for a visit. And you are going to come often, aren't you?"

"Well, I declare, what's all this goin' on so early in the mornin'?" Nana asked, shuffling into the room. Looking at the little girls with mock disapproval, she added, "Since you've woke up Miss Sarah—her needin' her sleep an' all—maybe I'd better just bring her breakfast in here so she can at least get some food in her for her big day."

With this, Nana vanished and returned carrying a silver tray piled high with bacon, eggs, fluffy white biscuits, and steaming grits. Shooing the little girls off the bed, she announced, "Now, clear a place 'fore this gets cold. Mind you, Miss Sarah, don't go givin' any to these hungry mouths. Their day will come."

~ ~ ~

AT FOUR O' CLOCK, buggy wheels ground to a halt on the drive, and footsteps echoed on the front steps. Before the knocker sounded, Jean Holeman and Susan each took an elbow and whisked Sarah from the parlor, where she had been looking over the wedding flowers, up the stairs to her bedroom.

As they closed her door, Sarah recognized Henry's laugh from downstairs. He'd promised to come early with Cave and dress in Samuel's study. "At least he's here," she breathed with a sigh. "But now, what will I do for the next two hours?"

The next two hours passed rather quickly, however, as Nana came to dress Sarah for the wedding and fix her hair. Her dress was made entirely of white lace, with a fitted bodice and a full, hooped skirt. In her ears, she wore her mother's diamond earrings, loaned to her for the occasion. Her lace handkerchief had been carried by her grandmother on her wedding day, and sufficed for "something old." At her neck, a gold locket studded with a single diamond provided the "something new," as it was a wedding gift from Henry. "I'm sure we've forgotten something," Sarah thought as a knock sounded on the door.

At her invitation, Tibitha entered the room, followed closely by her sister Mary. "We've brought you a gift,"

Tibitha said proudly, producing a tiny bit of blue satin trimmed in lace.

"Of course," Sarah sighed. "Something blue!"

"It's a garter, Sarah, which has been worn by all the Stroud women since my grandmother's wedding fifty years ago. I'm afraid it's only on loan, however, for it must go to Alfred or Cave's bride in turn," Mary explained. "Here, let's see how it looks."

As the strains of the wedding march drifted upstairs from the parlor harpsichord, Sarah turned to the large, oval mirror in the corner of her room to put on her veil. Behind her reflection, she could see her father watching her from the doorway. As she turned, Samuel smiled and offered his arm to his daughter, patting her hand as he had when she was a small child.

"It's going to be lonely around here," he told her with tears in his eyes. "You were our first, and you'll always be very special to us. But your mother and I know how much you love Henry and can only hope there'll be a place for us in your new life."

"We won't be that far away, and it won't be forever. Henry wants to try the mercantile business for a while, but Hillsborough will always be our home," Sarah replied, kissing her father's cheek.

As they approached the top of the curved staircase, Sarah saw for the first time the large assemblage gathered, and for the first time she became nervous. Looking around frantically for Henry, she saw him at the parlor entrance. He smiled a welcome as he caught her eye, but her eyes flew instead to the figure by his side. Where she had expected to see Cave as his best man, Alfred stood instead, smiling confidently. Sarah turned a worried look toward Henry, who shrugged his shoulders nonchalantly to let her know it was not illness or an accident that had kept Cave away.

"So, he couldn't face the ceremony after all," Sarah thought. As relieved as she was that she would not have to share her wedding day with Cave, she was afraid his absence meant he had not yet gotten over her rejection, She knew he was only putting off the inevitable. "But today is my wedding day, and I refuse to let Cave Stroud spoil it by his presence or his absence," she vowed, holding her head high and beginning her descent.

≈ ≈ ≈

THE WEDDING WENT off without a flaw—a tribute to good planning, Jean said later, and perhaps it was. When the ceremony ended, the guests enjoyed a buffet dinner in the large family dining room. Most then began drifting outside to enjoy the early autumn evening. An orange harvest moon rose majestically through the distant pines, bathing the whole garden with its luminescence—making evening walks and chats possible without artificial light.

Sarah and Henry, arm in arm, strolled from the house toward the rose garden, alone for the first minute since they had said their vows. "What happened to Cave?" Sarah whispered, not wishing to alert any of the guests gathered nearby that anything had been amiss.

"I honestly don't know," Henry answered, shaking his head. "Sometimes, I'm at a loss to explain my brother. While being so identical outside, we certainly do view life differently. For him, business always comes first. He came to me this morning and told me that he had heard of a man in Charleston who was interested in building a military academy somewhere in the South. Of course he decided to go to see him immediately.

"I would have thought our wedding would be cause enough for him to delay the trip. But you know Cave," Henry added.

"Luckily, I had Alfred to fill in. I wanted to tell you, but your mother put such a guard on you there was no way to let you know. You didn't mind, did you?"

"No, really, I love Alfred, and he did splendidly. I don't mind at all. I was just afraid something had happened to Cave," Sarah whispered back as a group of former school friends approached them.

Two hours later, with the festivities still going strong, Henry managed to slip to Sarah's side just as a group was leaving. "Do you think you could manage to drag yourself away to change now before anyone else finds you? It's getting rather late, and I'm quite anxious to get my bride alone," he said, a combination of love and pleading in his eyes. "I've asked Alfred to see to our buggy and have it waiting in front. Please hurry, won't you?"

"Of course. I didn't realize how the time had flown," Sarah answered, smiling and giving him a peck on the cheek. "Cover for me, and I'll be back as quickly as I can. I don't want to keep my new husband waiting," she replied, raising an eyebrow and offering a seductive smile, which set Henry laughing.

"Just make it quick, or I may have to come up after you and really set tongues wagging," he called after her.

Entering the house, Sarah was stopped for a moment by an elderly friend of her mother's, who was seated alone in the parlor—considering herself too frail for the night air. Sarah went to her side for a moment to accept her best wishes. Then, making her apologies as quickly as possible, she made her way to the stairs.

"I hope Henry isn't too impatient," she mused, glancing at the grandfather clock as she passed. "Poor thing, to have to tear himself away from all that female attention."

Sarah was still chuckling to herself at the picture of Henry surrounded by a bevy of ladies and trying to tear himself away to get to the buggy as she reached the second-floor. The din of the wedding guests filtered through the windows. But upstairs there was not a soul in sight. The gas lamps had been lit in each room, but the wicks were low to lend a romantic atmosphere to any who came upstairs.

Sarah paused at the landing to look down the dimly-lit hall and take in the familiar surroundings one last time. At the end of the hall, she glanced through her open door at the large, canopied bed with its white, crocheted spread. Remembering her sisters' happy chatter as they had gathered excitedly on it that morning with the hand towels they had so lovingly made for her, she brushed away a tear. She would miss them all so much. But she had made her choice. She loved Henry, and it was time for them to make a home for themselves. And he was waiting for her.

She'd need to find Nana quickly if she was ever to get out of this dress, she decided. Perhaps she was in the sitting room. Mother had ordered punch and cookies placed here for any guests who needed a rest and had asked Nana to look after the room—while also watching over Sarah's younger sisters, who had already been sent to bed.

Walking across the hall to the sitting room door, Sarah gasped to see a familiar figure standing by the window—his back to the room. "Goodness!" she laughed. "You really gave me a start. I thought you were teasing about coming after me. You shouldn't be up here, you know." Glancing about to be sure no one else was nearby, Sarah, with a gleam in her eye, swung the door closed and threw her arms about her husband.

As he turned from the window, Sarah felt strong arms pull her to a muscular chest so tightly that she could feel his heart pulsating against her breast. Getting more than she had bargained for and fearful of being discovered, Sarah regretted her impulsive action and looked up to plead with Henry to save their reputations. As she caught the eyes above hers, however, she pulled quickly away when she found herself gazing into the eyes of not Henry—but Cave Stroud!

Grasping her by both shoulders, Cave held her at arm's length so that he could see her face. "That's quite a different reception than I had hoped to get," he smiled wickedly. "And you a married woman and all. Have you changed your mind as to which Stroud you prefer?"

"Cave? How did you get in here?" Sarah demanded, pulling away.

"I'm an invited guest, am I not?" Cave asked, coolly. "And, my dear, you are forgetting the resemblance I bear to the groom. I had only to nod to the few servants I saw to receive a most-solicitous smile. Why, Nana's even gone to bring me a cup of coffee. . ."

"But. . . Henry said you had gone to Charleston," Sarah stammered. "I don't understand."

"I do plan to go to Charleston—tonight," Cave nodded. "I delayed only long enough to offer my best wishes to my favorite sister-in-law. Although, if I had known the reception I would get, I might have attended the wedding as well," he grinned, noticing Sarah's obvious discomfort.

"If you were still in town, why didn't you attend the wedding?" Sarah countered. "Henry was quite disappointed, you know."

"But I'm sure the same sentiment never crossed the bride's mind," Cave answered. "You'll remember, I told you some time ago not to look for a matched set on your wedding day. You will also remember, my dear, I take a back seat to no one. This was Henry's day. I told my family goodbye this morning. As I was leaving town, however, I realized I had not done the same for my new sister-in-law. And since she so kindly reminded me a few months ago that we are all 'family' now, I decided to afford her the same courtesy."

"Cave, I appreciate your coming, but Henry. . .," Sarah said, frantically glancing toward the closed door. She knew there was no way she could ever explain this scene to her husband—or to her parents or Nana if one of them should enter the room.

"Will be quite content to wait for you outside," Cave interrupted her. "My brother would never risk your mother's wrath by following you upstairs. So, you see, your fears are groundless," he added—as the door swung open and hit the wall with a bang. Startled, both Cave and Sarah turned to stare at a sleepy little girl in a long gown and nightcap clutching a china doll and rubbing her eyes.

"Oh, Sarah, I'm so glad I can see you and Henry before you leave. I waited up even though Nana said I should go to sleep. When I heard voices in here, I wanted to come and say goodbye," little Harriett burst out. "You won't tell Mommy or Nana, will you?"

Relieved at the interruption, Sarah bent down before the tiny child and gathered her into her arms. "Why, I think that's the nicest compliment we could have received to have you wait up just to see us. Don't you, 'Henry'?" she asked, turning to Cave, who could only nod in agreement. "Of course we won't tell. But we wouldn't want either of them to come up here and find you awake, now would we? So before you are found out, I'll take you back to bed myself and tuck you in. Tell Henry 'goodnight.'"

With only a brief backward glance at the bewildered figure in the shadows, Sarah gathered the little girl and her doll into her arms and quickly departed the room. Depositing

Harriett in bed with a big kiss and pulling the covers up to her chin, Sarah called, "I love you, Harriett," and ran to the stairs.

≈ ≈ ≈

CLOSING THE FRONT door behind her, Sarah took in a large breath of fresh night air to quiet her racing nerves. The nagging thought that Cave might be seen leaving the house caused her to search the darkness frantically for Henry and the buggy. Suddenly, from the side of the house, she heard a low murmur, which grew louder and louder. Looking in the direction of the noise, she saw a long line of guests, led by her parents, approaching from the rose garden.

"Trying to sneak out on us, were you?" Samuel bellowed to a chorus of laughter behind him. "After all your mother and I have done for you, you planned to ride off without so much as a goodbye. Come here, young lady, and give your old daddy a big kiss. That is, if that new husband of yours doesn't mind!" he added, looking around for Henry, who approached with the horse and buggy from the opposite side of the house.

"Caught in the act!" Henry laughed. "Can you blame me for wanting to get my bride alone?" he joked. A burst of male laughter was echoed by a tittering of female voices as everyone rushed forward to add their best wishes.

Approaching Sarah's side, Jean appeared to be the only one who noticed that she was still in her wedding dress. "Sarah," she whispered, bending to kiss her daughter, "why haven't you changed?"

"It was so difficult getting away from the guests, and Henry wanted to leave, so I decided to leave the garden as I was. I hope you don't mind—about the dress. It's lovely. I'm sure I'll have many other occasions to wear it," she added.

"I'm sure I don't mind, Dear, but how will you feel arriving at the Tavern House in your wedding dress?" Jean teased, ruing her daughter's lack of etiquette.

The chorus of voices died away in the distance as Henry and Sarah drove down the moonlit drive. Henry, responding to the good-natured jeers following them, turned and waved several times before placing his free arm around Sarah's shoulders. Never once did Sarah look back, however. She wanted no reminders of the scene she had just left. Fighting back the anger welling inside her, she prayed that Cave had now managed to slip out the back way and was finally on his way to Charleston. Even then, however, she knew she would never be free of him.

But this was her wedding night, and Henry was beside her. She had all she had ever wanted. She had to remember that. Finally, snuggling against her husband's side in the chill night air, she turned to gaze at the brilliant moon, which was lighting the way to their future.

THE WHITE TAVERN House glowed in the soft moonlight as Henry turned the buggy onto King Street in downtown Hillsborough. Gas lamps flickered at every window, and dinner guests waiting their turn at the fully-laden tables or walking off the crisp, fried chicken or country ham dinners strolled outside or into Mrs. Nash's walk next door.

"I had no idea there would still be so many people around," Sarah remarked, lifting her head from Henry's shoulder as he turned the corner. Her mother had been right. There was no way she would be able to avoid the eyes of half the town as she entered in her wedding dress—thanks to Cave.

"All the better to show off my bride," Henry smiled down at her. "Since we could only invite half the town to the ceremony, I wanted to make sure the other half shared my good fortune as well. And I'm not disappointed," he added, pulling the buggy to the curb in front of the inn and dismounting.

Helping Sarah from the buggy and ushering her inside, Henry glowed as the eyes of every bystander—and those of all the patrons in the dining room—followed the young couple.

While Henry registered at the desk, Sarah stood by the stairs—her wide hoop filling the entire foyer. She was mortified as she noticed the whispers sweeping the room and knew herself to be the object of each conversation. "Curse Cave Stroud," she mumbled under her breath. Oh, why didn't Henry hurry?

In moments, however, Henry turned from the desk, flourishing a key and waving it toward Sarah. He was clearly enjoying the raised eyebrows and jovial comments of the men in the smoking area beside the desk, most of whom Sarah recognized from town.

The kindly, silver-haired proprietor, Mr. Nichols, smiled at Sarah and motioned to a young boy in uniform as he entered from the back door with Henry and Sarah's valises. Slipping past Sarah, the boy made his way upstairs. Taking Sarah's arm, with a smile at his audience, Henry ascended the stairs—failing to notice the crimson stain that had crept over Sarah's face.

Handing the young boy a coin, Henry watched him run merrily back down the stairs. Then, looking to make sure no other guests were about in the wide upstairs hall, he turned to Sarah, smiling. "Well, Mrs. Stroud, this is it! Want to change your mind yet?"

"Before I get a chance to see our new home?" Sarah joked.

"Actually, I think it's fitting that we spend our first night together here—at the Tavern House. Since the two of us may be running this establishment some day. . ., well, it seems only right that I carry you over this threshold first," Henry added, turning the key in the lock and swinging the door open—while bending to pick Sarah up in his arms.

As he entered the room, Sarah's wide hoop caught in the doorway, stopping Henry's progress. Watching him struggle a moment to free the dress, Sarah laughingly reached out at last to fold in the sides of the hoop, which caused the whole skirt to swing up over Henry's head.

"Sarah, I can't see a thing," Henry laughed back as he staggered into the room, tripped over the footboard of the large, four-poster bed, and landed the two of them in its center. "Actually, this was all a diabolical plan to get you where I want you!" he added, raising himself on his elbows and leering down at her as Sarah giggled.

"Now, seriously, tell me what you think. I did so want everything to be perfect. But I don't seem to have done a very good job of it so far," he added, standing up, pulling Sarah to her feet, and making a sweeping gesture around the room. "Mr. Nichols has been kind enough to give us his best room for tonight."

"It's a charming room. I've never been upstairs before," Sarah answered, looking around at the high, feather bed with its green, flowered coverlet, the tall, mahogany highboy and matching armoire, and the dainty, roll-top desk set between the dormer windows. Catching sight of the desk, Sarah let out a sigh and hurried over to it—burying her nose into a bouquet of one dozen, long-stemmed, red roses.

"They're beautiful!" she cried, returning to Henry to throw her arms around his neck. "You knew how much I'd love them. Wherever did you find roses in October?"

"While I'd like to take the credit," Henry answered, grasping her by the shoulders and looking into her eyes, "I didn't order them. Perhaps it's a gift from Mr. Nichols. There seems to be a card. . .," he added, pulling her by the hand back to the desk and handing her the small, folded note.

Eagerly opening the card, Sarah scanned the writing. As she did so, her face fell, and she quickly thrust the card into Henry's hands. Surprised, he, too, opened the card and read: "Remembered how you loved these. Sorry I could not have been at your side. Cave."

"How thoughtful!" Henry exclaimed, handing back the card. "Cave didn't forget us after all. He must have arranged to have these delivered before he left town. All day—I'll admit—I've been rather angry that he didn't stay to stand up for me and share in our happiness. I guess this is his way of apologizing for not being there. And what a perfect gift. He certainly knew the way to your heart," Henry continued jovially—failing to notice the crumpled card now lying at Sarah's feet.

"And now," Henry smiled, taking Sarah's hands and pulling her to him in an embrace, "it's time to find out what married life is all about!"

As his lips met hers, Henry's fingers played with the long line of buttons down the back of Sarah's dress. When the last button was unfastened, he slid the shoulders of her dress slowly down her arms until the yards of fabric pooled at her feet.

Taking her hand and helping her step out of the countless layers of white lace, Henry held his bride at arms' length, his eyes taking in every inch of her before he pulled her to him once more. Their shadows played on the wall beside the bed and wavered in the lamplight as the cool, evening air parted the thin, chintz curtains.

Across the street, a large, Chestnut stallion snorted, his flanks wet and heaving. Behind him—in the shuttered offices of the Hillsborough Improvement Company—an errant moonbeam caught a lone figure bent over an empty desk.

CHAPTER SEVEN
June 1846

THE HOUSE IN WAKE Forest was so tiny it could have fit into one of the wings at the Holeman home. Since it fronted on the town's main street, it was also subject to all the traffic going into and out of town. After spending her whole life on the plantation, Sarah thought she would never get used to the horses' hooves and buggy and carriage wheels clattering down the street at all hours of the day.

It was her own home, though. And Henry was next door at the store all day, where he could pop in for lunch or tea, so that made it perfect. The first few months, she spent every spare moment polishing the lovely, mahogany furniture until it shone, even though Henry laughed at her for doing the work herself, since she had brought two of her parents' most trusted servants to Wake Forest.

Tom was Aaron's son, and every bit as fine a man as his father. It was his job to care for the two horses and see to the garden, which he seemed to love. In his spare time, he ambled next door to help Henry load supplies and keep the shelves neat.

Lucy was a quiet girl and the daughter of the Holemans' cook. Although only seventeen, she had already learned the fine art of Southern cooking from her mother and was able to place many delicious dishes on the Stroud table. Since the house was small, Lucy also doubled as the housekeeper.

Henry was more content than Sarah had ever seen him, and she was thrilled to see how much he liked his regular contact with the Wake Forest residents. It was not long before everyone in town had tried the new dry goods store and agreed it carried the best stock in town and had a fair and likeable proprietor. Sarah was spared any further contact with Cave, who—by all accounts—was, indeed, in Charleston. He had not been seen since the day of the wedding, and Alfred admitted he'd had little contact with him. If Alfred felt strapped with running the company alone, he never admitted it and seemed happy to see Henry so content.

Sarah was weeding beside a rose bush on a rather warm day in June when she heard the wheels of a carriage approach and stop in front of Henry's store. Looking up for a moment, but noting nothing out of the ordinary about the carriage, she went on with her weeding. Suddenly, a voice interrupted her reverie, "Pardon me, I'm looking for Henry Stroud's store. Can you tell me if this is it?"

Rising from her knees and brushing the red, caked clay from her dress, Sarah raised a dirty hand to tuck a stray hair into place and turned to face the stranger. As she did so, both she and her visitor gasped, for there on the walk—with only the fence to separate them—stood Cave Stroud. His look was one of disbelief and horror, and he stared at Sarah as if seeing an apparition.

"Sarah," he breathed at last, "I didn't recognize you. What in the world are you doing digging in the garden like a servant? The Sarah I knew would never have dirtied her hands. What can Henry be thinking of to allow you to make such a spectacle of yourself? I assure you, I would never have allowed you to grovel in the dirt for all the town to see!"

As Cave walked around the fence and opened the gate, he glimpsed Sarah for the first time in full view. Anger sparked in his narrowed eyes as he observed her well-advanced pregnancy. "I can see my brother lost no time making good his claim on you. Do you ever wonder, Sarah, how different things might have been?" he asked.

"I've made my own choices, Cave, and I've never been sorry," Sarah answered, brushing her hands off on her skirt. "The garden is my hobby, and Henry has encouraged it. And we are both thrilled to be expecting a baby," she offered as the back door of the shop opened and Henry appeared. Shading his eyes from the noonday sun and glancing toward the muffled voices, Henry broke into a grin and then into a fast trot as he covered the few feet to the fence where Cave stood, hand on gate.

"Cave, I had no idea you were in the area. Are you back for good, or are you returning to Charleston? I hope you at least have time to join us for dinner and see what you're missing by avoiding married life." Henry said, circling Sarah's thickened waist.

"I can vouch for it, Brother. There's nothing like coming home to this lady at the close of a busy day," he ran on, oblivious to the frowns appearing on both Cave's and Sarah's faces.

"Now, we won't take 'No' for an answer. Sarah, please ask Lucy to set another place on your way in to dress for dinner. I'd like to show Cave the store before we eat. After all, he does own a fair share of it," he continued, slapping his brother on the back. "Goodness, but it's good to see you again. It's been too long."

"Not long enough—from where I'm standing," Sarah fumed, kicking the bedroom door shut behind her a few minutes later, stubbing her toe and sending herself hopping in pain. Despite her protests, however, Sarah took an inordinate amount of time readying herself for the meal. She chose her newest gown of pale peach muslin, which had a bodice laced with black ribbon, to allow for her waist's rapid expansion. A pair of black pearl earrings, which Henry had given her for their six-months' anniversary, completed the costume.

"Now, let Cave Stroud tell me I look like a servant," Sarah huffed, closing the door more gently this time, and walking regally toward the stairs and the unpleasant meal she knew she must endure.

At dinner, Cave asked all the right questions about the store, and Henry delighted in sharing his venture with his brother. Feigning interest as Henry addressed a remark to her from time to time, Sarah was, nonetheless, grateful that the brothers' conversation left no need for her to respond.

As the clock in the vestibule struck one, Henry jumped to attention. "I had no idea it was so late!" he called. "I must have customers lined up on the walk fuming for me to reopen. Don't let me rush either of you, though. I'm afraid I've dominated the conversation all meal. I'm sorry, Sarah. I'm sure you'd like to talk to Cave alone and find out about society in Charleston and what the new fashions are. Why don't you two stay right here and have your dessert and visit?"

There was complete silence at the table after Henry left. Then Lucy brought in fresh strawberry pie. Rolling his eyes heavenward at the first bite, Cave turned to the girl with a roguish grin. "Lucy, after the meal you fixed, I'd carry you back to Charleston if I wouldn't feel so guilty at leaving Henry and Sarah here to starve."

"Mister Cave, you don't expect me to believe you ain't got finer cooks in Charleston, do you? But you sure know how to make a body feel appreciated, don't he, Miss Sarah?" Lucy answered, leaving the room with a self-satisfied smile.

"He certainly does," Sarah called after her. She could not help remembering the times Cave's eyes had raked her figure and registered his approval so completely. Subconsciously, she ran her hands over the breadth of her enlarged stomach and glanced down.

"Do I detect something other than bliss at the forthcoming, blessed event?" Cave began, following her hands with his eyes as she quickly folded them in her lap. "Ashamed at the loss of your charms, Mrs. Stroud?" he continued, reading her thoughts. "Nonsense, my dear. I'm sure Henry has told you countless times that you look radiant. But then what does he know about vanity? He never had any. Only you and I can understand that.

"But don't look so glum. My niece or nephew will get here soon enough, and then you can once again begin to charm the gentlemen of Wake Forest as you did those of Hillsborough. You miss those days, don't you, Sarah?"

Her eyes flashing angrily, Sarah responded, "The truth is, I have never been happier. And I'm proud to be carrying Henry's baby. Now it's time for you to go on with your life. Nothing would give Henry and me greater pleasure than to receive an invitation to your wedding and later buy baby gifts for our own little niece or nephew."

"Perhaps I will give marriage a try. It seems to agree so with Henry," Cave answered with a laugh. "But now," he continued, wiping his mouth and rising to leave, "duty calls. I must be off if I expect to survey Henry's needs in the store and get back to Charleston any time in the near future.

"No, don't bother to see me to the door," he said, waving Sarah away as she began to rise. "I might do something both of us would regret—despite your condition. Goodbye, Sarah."

≈ ≈ ≈

THE FEW SHORT weeks before the baby's birth passed quickly. By August, Henry was able to close the store for a few weeks and take Sarah back to her parents' home, where she would have the family doctor and Nana to care for her and the baby.

The day was unbearably warm, that September sixth of 1846, and not a leaf stirred on the plantation. "I'll never carry a baby through the summer again," Sarah vowed as she leaned on her old windowsill and gazed out across the fields, brown from the drought. She turned to smile as Nana entered the room with her breakfast tray, but grimaced and grabbed for the bedpost instead as the first contraction hit her.

Placing the tray on the dresser and helping Sarah back into bed, Nana grinned and replied, "I 'spect none o' us will get much rest this day!"

Henry arrived back at the Holeman home at noon carrying a large bouquet of late summer roses. Without a glance, he sped past the dining room, where the rest of the family was taking the midday meal, and took the stairs two at a time. Bounding down the hall, he stopped at the door. Remembering Tibitha's difficult time with Elizabeth, he was surprised to see Sarah sitting up in the bed reading.

"Mister Henry," Nana demanded from a chair near the bed, "it's about time you got here. Miss Sarah's been waitin' for you so she can go on with this birthin'. Now get in here!"

As Henry moved hesitantly toward the bed, Sarah put her book down and smiled at Henry and the roses. "How are you feeling?" Henry asked, handing the flowers to Nana and taking Sarah's hand. "I would have been here sooner, but Aaron and I had to find Dr. Strudwick first, and. . ."

"Henry Stroud, you look like you need the doctor more than I," Sarah laughed, noticing the flush in Henry's cheeks after his run up the stairs. "Nana has everything under control," she added, squeezing his hand. Then, as another contraction took hold of her, she began to squeeze harder. Her face contorted with pain, and she gasped for breath.

"Nana!" Henry called frantically to the old woman, who stood by the dresser arranging the roses.

"I expect I know why the Lord decided women should bear his babies," Nana sighed, laying the flowers on the dresser and shuffling to the bed to wipe Sarah's forehead with a cloth. "Not much here you can do after all," she scolded. "Now shoo, and let us women get on with this." .

Shortly after supper, Doctor Strudwick arrived smiling, his bag in hand. The slight, stooped man with the thin, white hair and moustache and kindly, pale blue eyes had attended almost every birth in Hillsborough for more than thirty years.

Running everyone from the room, the doctor examined Sarah and pronounced, as Nana had, that all was progressing well. Giving Nana the orders she knew by heart, the two went to work.

Within minutes, the family gathered downstairs in the parlor could hear the plaintive cries of a newborn. Henry was on his feet immediately. But Samuel took hold of his arm. "Give them a few minutes, Henry. Sarah will want to look presentable before she shows off her new creation. Nana will come for you when she's ready. Trust me. I've been in your place too many times," he smiled, his eyes sweeping lovingly over his family. "Do you suppose we've gotten our boy in the family yet, Mrs. Holeman?" he teased.

"I've told you all along Sarah was carrying a girl. But you must hope, I suppose," his wife answered. "That baby was much too low for a boy. I hope you won't mind having a girl first, Henry. I never thought to ask you."

"Somehow, I can't imagine having anything but girls. I've been surrounded by so many for so long. I hope she looks just like her mother," the new father smiled. Then, letting out a sigh, he added, "Oh, what's taking them so long?"

"Only a few more minutes, I'm sure," Samuel put in.

"Daddy, can we go in, too, when Nana comes, please?" Harriett begged. Being the only one in the family who had not been through a birth, she was anxious to see the new arrival.

"There'll be time for all of us to see the baby. And I expect we'll hear more of it than we want to every night for a while. Be patient. I promise you'll see your new niece or nephew before the night is over," her father answered, grinning at the little girl.

Suddenly, a heavy tread sounded on the stairs. Looking up, the family saw Nana on the landing, her face wreathed in smiles. Forgetting that it was not his wife this time, Samuel started to his feet. Then, remembering himself, he reached for the stunned Henry sitting immobile at his side. "Well, Son, what's keeping you?" he asked. "Your family is waiting!"

A bond was established at first meeting of father and daughter. As Dr. Strudwick placed the newborn child in Henry's arms, her crying ceased. Opening her deep-blue eyes, she gazed directly into Henry's eyes, for only a second. Then her eyes closed again, and she snuggled peacefully into his arms and slept. Nana motioned to a small bassinet in the corner, where Henry deposited his tiny bundle, too awed to speak.

Turning to Sarah, who lay propped against the pillows, pale but radiant, Henry breathed, "She's perfect and an exact copy of her beautiful mother."

"Oh, Henry, isn't she the most beautiful baby? And all that dark hair! Why, she can wear ribbons already. Do you think she'll keep her blue eyes?"

Folding linens in the corner, Nana could not resist breaking in. "It won't be long before they change to brown, like yours. They're too dark to stay blue. You'll see. What're you two goin' to name her?"

"Actually, we've had a name picked out for some time. We're going to call her 'Mary Frances' after Henry's mother and stepmother. It does seem to fit her, don't you think so, Henry?"

"It's perfect, like my two girls," Henry said softly.

∼ ∼ ∼

IT WAS LATE afternoon, and Henry was enjoying the last day with his family before returning to Wake Forest. Sarah was in the bed sewing some lace on a baby bonnet, while Mary Frances—in a rare moment—slept peacefully nearby. Suddenly, the door opened, and Harriett and Maria burst into the room carrying candy sticks in very sticky little hands. "Shh," Henry warned, putting a finger to his lips. "You'll wake Mary Frances. We just got her to sleep!"

"But, Henry," Maria put in, her blue eyes peering up at him beneath her tousled, brown curls, "Uncle Alfred and Uncle Cave are downstairs and want to see the baby."

"They brought us candy, too!" Harriett added, her little face red with excitement—and sticky peppermint.

"Maria, Alfred and Cave are not your uncles. They are Mary Frances's uncles," Sarah corrected them, wincing inwardly as she realized the role of uncle Cave would now play in her daughter's life.

"Do you feel up to visitors?" Henry asked, turning to his wife. "If it's too much for you, I can see them downstairs. They can see the baby another time."

Longing to have them do just that, Sarah would have pleaded fatigue. But knowing how proud Henry was of his daughter and how much he wanted to show her off, she answered, "I'm fine. And I surely wouldn't deny Mary Frances a chance to meet her uncles."

"Can we tell them to come in, then?" Maria asked, sucking the candy remnants off a finger.

"Of course. In fact, I'll go with you," Henry said, rising and tousling Harriett's dark ringlets as he ushered the girls from the room. "I didn't even know Cave was in town. What a great surprise."

"Yes, isn't it!" Sarah added to herself.

In seconds, Henry was back, flanked by the two smiling Stroud brothers. Without a glance at Sarah, Cave walked deliberately to the lace-covered bassinet and stood perusing the peacefully-slumbering child. Alfred, on the other hand, immediately approached the bed, took Sarah's hands in his and planted a kiss on her forehead. "Motherhood agrees with you, Sarah. You look lovely.

"Now, Old Man," he said, turning to Henry, "tell me what I hear is not true, and you're not going to leave these two beautiful ladies of yours alone while you return to Wake Forest tomorrow."

"I'm afraid I must go back, Alfred, much as I would like to stay. It was Cave who pointed out to me a few weeks ago that the business is too important to leave unattended. And I owe it to our company to see that it succeeds," Henry answered.

"Bother the business, Henry. It's not every day that your wife has a baby!" Alfred added.

Suddenly, Cave's voice filled the pause. "If it were up to you two, we would be penniless. That's why I came back from Charleston. I had to make sure there was still a business to come back to. We can't afford to lose the business while Henry plays nursemaid."

"It's all arranged," Henry answered calmly. "I'm sure I'm leaving Sarah in good hands until she and the baby can travel." Then, brightening, the new father moved toward the bassinet. "But come on. You two haven't told me yet how beautiful my daughter is! What do you think?"

"Why, Henry, she seems to have all her mother's good looks. Aren't we fortunate she doesn't favor you?" Alfred said jovially as he approached.

"Do you think she will be as hardhearted as her mother as well and break all the hearts in town, too?" Cave questioned, looking toward the bed for the first time to see Sarah's reaction.

"I'm sure she'll break at least a few," Henry answered proudly, failing to notice Cave's dig.

≈ ≈ ≈

WITH THE "DOG days" of summer bringing a virtual standstill in business each year, annual August visits to Hillsborough became the norm for the Strouds. Since Mary Frances was kept busy with aunts, grandparents, and Nana fussing over her, Sarah and Henry had a great deal of time to go riding and to picnic by Nunn Creek.

"I declare this has been the best vacation ever," Sarah admitted one afternoon as she sat leaning against Henry's shoulder by the creek, watching a tiny school of minnows swarm in the shallow pool at their feet.

"You really do love it here, don't you?" Henry asked, turning to her.

"It's where I grew up," Sarah answered.

"No, it's more than that. You belong here, Sarah. You come alive whenever we come back to your home. You never seem the same in Wake Forest."

"But I'm happy there," Sarah said. "I'd be happy anywhere if you were there."

"But you'd be happier here. And, frankly, so would I. I miss riding in the woods, and I want our daughter to grow to love the out of doors, too. I think it's time to consider moving back home," Henry said.

"Do you really mean it? But what about the store?" Sarah asked.

"How do you think I got it in the first place? Our company acquired it to sell. We can continue our original plans and find a buyer," Henry explained. "Besides, I'll be more valuable to the company here. Cave insists on staying in Charleston, and—while he never complains—Alfred has seemed overburdened every time I've popped in at the office. I'm sure he'd welcome having one of us back."

"It's a perfect plan. But where will we live?" Sarah cried, her eyes serious.

"What about right here on the banks of Nunn Creek? We could put our bed on that large limb hanging over the creek. I seem to remember you climb trees quite well. It should be perfect," he said, smiling. "Let me see. . . over there can be the dining room. . ."

"Oh, Henry, do be serious," Sarah pouted. "I thought you meant it. And here you had me all excited. . ."

"I do mean it. Won't it be exciting building our own home? I'd really like it to be right here where we've had such happy times. And when I carry you over the threshold," he continued, scooping Sarah up and carrying her to the creek, "I'll have to be sure I don't drop you in the creek on our way to the door."

≈ ≈ ≈

THE HOUSE, WHICH was to back on the creek, was to be an imposing, white wood structure with two full floors and a long attic playroom with windows on each end. Each of the main floors was to have a sheltered porch overlooking the surrounding woods.

Samuel was overjoyed at the idea of having his eldest daughter and her family nearby and was only too willing to sell Henry acreage. As the papers were signed, Samuel grabbed Henry's arm. "You don't know how happy you have made Jean and me. It will be such a joy to have Sarah nearby again and to watch your family grow. And I'll be content knowing Sarah will always have a roof over her head."

"You need never fear for her well-being, Sir. If something happens to me, my brother Cave will see to it that she and our children are cared for. As my twin, I trust him to take care of my family as if they were his own," Henry replied.

"Do you think that's wise, Son?" Samuel asked, a frown drawing his bushy eyebrows together. "I must admit I have reservations about your brother, fond as I am of you. What provisions have you made for them?"

"All my property will revert to Sarah at my death. Cave will see to that. She'll never have to worry. Besides," he grinned, "I don't plan on leaving this Earth any time soon. We have a house to build!"

BEADS OF PERSPIRATION clung to Sarah's forehead, and her dress felt like a damp rag after the long journey from Wake Forest. Funny, it never seemed long when they came for Sunday dinner or for vacation. "Mommy, I'm hot!" Mary Frances—her flushed face framed by dark, wet curls—complained beside her.

"I know, Precious! I'm sorry. But soon you'll be at 'Gamfa's,' cooling your feet in the creek," she reassured the little girl.

"How much further?" Mary Frances whined.

"Not much longer. Why, your daddy and I used to ride in those woods off to your left," Sarah said, pointing toward the path beside the river, where a midmorning haze still hung between the tree branches.

"I'm hungry!" Mary Frances began again.

"Oh, Mary Frances, how can you think of food when it's so hot?" Sarah asked, hearing Tom's chuckle from the wagon in front of them.

"Be patient, Honey," Lucy answered, turning around in the seat beside Tom to look at the adored child. "My mamma taught me to cook. She makes the world's best chicken and biscuits, and she knows you're comin'."

"Actually, the thought of food in this heat makes me nauseous," Sarah continued to no one in particular, as she felt the bile rise in her throat. Choking it down, she reached for the water bottle. "It must be the heat," she told herself.

Within a few minutes, the well-worn drive to the Holeman home came into view. Before the horses reached the door, Samuel was on the veranda. Alive with excitement, Mary Frances stood up and reached out to her grandfather, who gathered the tiny, damp bundle into his arms for a bear-hug.

"I've missed you, Gamfa," she said, pulling back to look into his face.

"Are there any kisses there for me?" Jean smiled as she approached.

"Lots of kisses for later. But I'm too hungry right now," Mary Frances announced. "Mommy said you'd have chicken and biscuits, and I'm so-o-o hungry," she mimed, holding her stomach and sending her family into peals of laughter.

"That little girl is the best thing that has happened to this family in a long time," Samuel smiled. "But don't wait too long before giving her a playmate. I'm not getting any younger. And you've a big house to fill now."

CHAPTER EIGHT
June 1849

THE FIRST VISITOR TO the new home was Alfred, who came for dinner and to fill Henry in on the business he was to resume. "I can't tell you how glad I am to have you both back," Alfred admitted. "I didn't want to complain. But the company has been taking up all my time. I'll be glad to turn over half of it again. Not that I'm too upset at avoiding the plantation work," he smiled. "But I've literally had no time to pay court to any of the young ladies of Hillsborough. After all, you and Sarah make marriage seem so desirable. . . Since you don't seem to be helping the population of the town enough, however, I feel the burden may fall on me before too long, and I'll need to have some prospects."

"What do you hear from Cave?" Henry asked, changing the subject as he noticed Sarah's blush. Their lack of other children had been a disappointment, and he didn't want to spoil their first night in the new home.

"He's still in Charleston. Says he's working on lots of deals to bring manufacturing to Hillsborough. He's still determined that's the only hope for the South. I believe he has extended a business trip into permanent residency, though. In fact, speaking of lovely ladies, you don't suppose that's the reason he hasn't returned to town?" Alfred asked innocently. "You're closer to Cave than I am, Henry. Has he ever mentioned any ladies—or a special one?"

"Actually, Cave never mentions much other than business in his letters," Henry answered, cutting the conversation short.

"You were rather quiet tonight, Sarah," Henry said to her later, taking the brush from her hand as she sat at her dressing table and running it through her thick hair. "Did Alfred's joke about children upset you?" he asked, catching her eye in the mirror. "It shouldn't, you know. Mary Frances is the most perfect child in the world, and I'm the most fortunate husband and father. I couldn't wish for anything more."

"You wanted a large family, though, didn't you?" Sarah asked. "That's what you said when she was born."

"Of course I did. But we have so much. It seems selfish to wish for more."

"But you would like more children, wouldn't you?" she persisted, turning from the mirror to look at him.

"Why, Mrs. Stroud, are you proposing we start right now to fill up the new nursery? I'm willing if you are!" he added, putting the brush down on the dressing table and lifting Sarah into his arms.

Sarah said nothing for a minute. Finally, looking at him demurely, she replied, "It's impossible to start something that has already begun."

Henry held Sarah at arms' length to look at her. "Just what are you saying, Sarah? Was that a message?"

"I've suspected for several days. But I was waiting for the right time to tell you," Sarah answered. "When Alfred brought up children tonight, I couldn't wait to let you know."

Henry's yell shook the house. Putting her hand over his mouth, Sarah stifled an explosive giggle. "Try to control yourself," she laughed.

"It's impossible to control myself when you're around," Henry said with a wicked grin. "Why not try for twins this time?" he added, pulling her to the bed.

≈ ≈ ≈

YOU'RE HOME EARLY," Sarah called to her husband from the veranda where she and Mary Frances were reading a book. "I didn't expect you until supper."

"Catch me, Daddy," Mary Frances squealed, sliding from Sarah's lap and running as fast as her long skirts and short legs would allow. Perching at the top of the steps, she spread her arms and waited for Henry to get into position beneath her.

"You two are incorrigible," Sarah laughed. "Mary Frances, be careful! Someday, Daddy may not be there to catch you, and you might break your pretty little neck."

The admonishment went unheeded by the little girl as she flung herself forward into her father's arms and wrapped her tiny arms around his neck. "Daddy won't ever leave me, will you, Daddy?" Mary Frances questioned, looking into his eyes.

"I'm afraid you're both stuck with me forever," Henry grinned, taking the seat beside Sarah with Mary Frances on his lap. "But don't you two want to see what I've brought from town?" he asked, reaching into his pocket and pulling out a large envelope. "It's a letter from Cave. It's short, but that's Cave's way. I thought you might be interested," he added, turning to Sarah.

"What does he say?" Sarah asked.

"Well, in essence, he says he's returning to Hillsborough—for good. He really doesn't give a reason. Here—I'll read you that part," he said, removing the single sheet of paper and beginning to read. "'I've made some good contacts in Charleston, and I think the time is ripe to try to convince some of them that a textile manufacturing plant near Hillsborough might be a good investment. After all, the raw products are much closer than they are in the North, and the natural power supplied by the Eno River ought to convince any doubters.

"'The new railroad will be a great selling point, as well. At any rate, I will, more than likely, turn up on your doorstep within the month. And I might have a surprise or two for you as well.'

"There, what do you think about that news?" Henry smiled, leaning toward Sarah. "I knew you'd be excited. It'll be like old times having him at the office and nearby again. We'll have to plan a party!"

≈　≈　≈

IT WAS A cold Sunday for early October. A fire was burning brightly in the sitting room fireplace. Mary Frances, for once, was playing quietly on the hearth rug with a new doll she had received on her third birthday. She had named it "Baby Stroud" and was very proud to have her very own baby before her mother had hers.

Henry was reading the paper when buggy wheels sounded on the gravel outside. "Who would come calling without notice, and on a Sunday, too?" Henry questioned.

"I'm sure I don't know," Sarah answered, putting down her book with a sigh and following Henry to the door. Mary Frances, hearing the commotion, dropped her doll and rushed to the door as well. Determined to be the first to arrive, she almost knocked over Sarah, who was not too steady on her feet.

"It's another daddy!" the little girl squealed, opening the door.

Henry let out a whoop and ran across the veranda, scooping Mary Frances up in his arms as he ran and leaving Sarah gaping from the doorway. Mary Frances had been right. It was—at least to her young mind—another daddy, for Cave Stroud stood at their own front steps.

"Mary Frances, this is Uncle Cave," Henry explained. "And you're right, he is another daddy—as alike as you'll ever see. Daddy and Uncle Cave are twins. Give him a kiss, won't you?" he asked, turning the child around in his arms to face Cave.

"Cave, this is Mary Frances. She's the spitting image of her beautiful mother, isn't she? How are you, Old Man? Why didn't you tell us when you were coming?" Henry smiled, clapping his brother on the back.

"I didn't tell you because we weren't sure ourselves when we could actually leave Charleston. Besides, we wanted to surprise you," Cave smiled.

Walking back to the buggy as he spoke, he reached his hand up to a diminutive young woman wrapped in a lap robe. As he helped her to the ground, Cave made the introductions: "Cornelia, this—if you haven't guessed—is my brother Henry. Henry, this is Cornelia Lloyd-Stroud, my bride. What do you think? Did I produce the surprise I promised?"

"More than I could imagine! You've rendered me speechless! But what am I thinking of letting you stand out here in the cold? Cornelia, welcome to the family," Henry said, extending his hand with a smile to the lady with the enormous blue eyes and light brown hair, who smiled shyly back at him as she took his hand. "Come meet Sarah," Henry continued. "I know she's dying to see you, too, Cave. We've been wondering when you would return. What a treat!"

Sarah watched from the door, unable to force her legs to carry her outside. To see Cave again after all this time, without warning, and in the same misshapen condition she'd been in before, to endure his piercing stare as he came up the walk, and to meet his new bride, whom she had not even known was in the picture, were all too much. Not knowing how to react, she was glad to have Mary Frances take the problem out of her hands by grabbing her dress and relaying all the information in a breathless three-year-old manner.

"Yes, Precious, Mommy knows Uncle Cave," she said to Mary Frances, while avoiding Cave's eyes, which she knew instinctively were on her at that moment. "But I haven't met his wife. Let me introduce myself," she said hastily, approaching Cornelia. "I'm Sarah. Forgive me for not coming outside. The air is rather chilly, and I don't want to take any chances," she said, laying a hand on her extended midsection.

She knew it was a lie. Henry would know it, too, since they had argued yesterday when she had been out in the garden for several hours and he had scolded her for risking a chill. But she counted on his excitement over Cave's arrival not to notice.

Cornelia put her hand in Sarah's. "I've heard so much about you," Cornelia smiled warmly. "I hope we can grow to be good friends. I'm going to need lots of advice if I am to set up housekeeping here."

So Cave was home—with a new bride, Sarah mused, watching the couple take the chairs Henry had pulled to the fire for them. And Cornelia was lovely. He seemed to have chosen well. Perhaps, now, she and Cave could forget the past. . . She was so lost in thought that she didn't hear Henry ask her to find refreshment for the weary travelers and was embarrassed when he called her name a second time.

"You can hardly blame Sarah for being preoccupied, Brother, when you keep her in a perpetual state of motherhood," Cave responded, turning and looking her up and down. "It agrees with you, Sarah," he added with a grin. It was clear. Nothing had changed between them.

~ ~ ~

THE NEW BABY arrived on January 3, and both households had been in an uproar since. Jean had assigned Nana to help with

Sarah and the new baby for as long as needed, since Harriett was able to care for herself and Lucy had her hands full with taking care of Henry and Mary Frances and the household duties.

The birth, once it began in earnest, was an easy one. And soon Nana proudly called Henry to meet yet another Stroud girl. "If you're disappointed it's not a boy, Mister Henry, don't you go upsetting Miss Sarah by saying so," the old nurse admonished as she preceded him up the stairs. "She done her best, and that's the truth."

"Why, I'm delighted with another girl. And I will be next time, too, if Sarah's willing," Henry chuckled. "You know how she hates to give up her riding and gardening."

"Not to mention her tree climbing, right, Mister Henry?" the old woman added wickedly.

"That must be our secret!" Henry grinned, placing his finger over his lips as they approached the door.

"Oh, Henry, it's another girl, and she looks so much like Mary Frances. Isn't she adorable? Look at her tiny hands and feet," Sarah said as Henry approached the bed to kiss his wife.

"What shall we name her?" Henry asked.

"I'd like to name her for Jane. It would thrill her no end," Sarah announced. "What do you think?"

Pausing a moment, Henry responded at last, "I think another sister might be rather put out."

"But we can't give her six names. That would be absurd. Besides, we'll have others," Sarah answered.

"I'm not speaking of the younger girls," Henry went on. "They'll love her whatever her name is. I'm thinking of Susan. She is next in line."

"Then, why not name her for both of them?" Sarah smiled. "Susan Jane is a lovely name. And then two aunts will adore her."

"Susan Jane, it is then," Henry announced. "Now, Nana, may I hold my new daughter?"

Placing the baby back in the cradle, Henry turned to Sarah. "Do you feel up to another visitor?" he asked. "After all, she's going to have a big stake in raising her baby sister."

"Mary Frances! Of course. Do bring her in."

Henry found Mary Frances with Lucy in the attic playroom. "Is the baby here yet?" she asked. "Look, Daddy, I've fixed up my doll house so we can play with it together. When can she come to play?"

"I don't think Susan Jane is able to play just yet," Henry chuckled. "But I can take you to see her—if you'd like."

"Is that her name, Daddy?" Mary Frances asked. "Just like Aunt Suthan and Aunt Jane?"

"Do you like it?" Henry wanted to know, picking his daughter up and looking into her eyes.

"It's a nice name, I guess. But I'll just call her 'Sudie,'" Mary Frances announced, wriggling from his grasp and bounding down the stairs.

"I suppose we don't have a say in the matter!" Henry shrugged to Lucy as he followed his happy toddler from the room.

CHAPTER NINE
March 1853

MARY FRANCES WAS READY to enter school, and Sudie was a dimpled three-year-old when the next little Stroud put in an appearance one blustery day in early March 1853. Once again, Henry expressed his delight at the birth of yet another girl. Claudia was so different from the other two that—although third—she quickly found a place in everyone's heart.

Her hair was white-blond and as soft as corn-silk. Her large, gray eyes dominated her face. "There's no denying it. She's a Stroud!" Henry said proudly, touching the almost transparent skin with a forefinger as she lay in the cradle. "I was beginning to think I had nothing to do with the children, since the other two look so much like you and your family."

"Why, Henry," Sarah said, sitting up in bed to look at him earnestly. "I didn't know it mattered."

"Of course, it doesn't," Henry joked. "It's just that she reminds me so much of Tibitha and Mary when they were babies. She's so tiny. She looks as if she might break!"

"She'd better not, because I know two rambunctious little

girls who'll make her fight for anything she wants. She'll toughen soon enough," Sarah predicted.

∼ ∼ ∼

SARAH, YOU AMAZE me," Jane said one afternoon as she watched her sister bathing Claudia. "You handle her so well. She's so tiny. I'd be afraid to touch her."

"Nonsense," Sarah answered. "She only looks breakable. Here, have a hand," she continued, reaching the soapy infant over to Jane, who shrank back as if she had been stung. Sarah laughed. "If the company you're keeping with Willie Roberts means anything, you might have one of these yourself before too long."

"We're just friends," Jane protested. "Willie and I both like to paint, so we like to spend time together when he isn't needed on his father's farm. It isn't serious—not like Susan and Francis," she added, referring to Susan's fiance, Francis Jordan. Susan had met Francis on a visit to Wake Forest, and it had been love at first sight for both of them. Francis was tall and thin with thick, sandy hair, which always seemed to stand on end where he had run his fingers through it, and penetrating hazel eyes, which held his audience spellbound. Although he was a serious divinity student, he was also a wonderful storyteller and had quickly become a favorite in the Holeman home when he spent his summers as an intern at the Mars Hill Church.

"Susan and Francis," mimicked a voice from the hallway as Julia walked into the room. At eighteen, she was the idol of every young man in Hillsborough. Her bouncy, blond curls, blue eyes, and rosy skin, coupled with a vibrant personality, kept every gentleman in town waiting for just one glance.

"Honestly, I can't imagine waiting for one man for all the years Susan has been waiting for Francis. She's wasted five years of her life!" Julia continued, untying her bonnet as she walked into the room. Spying a mirror above the dresser, she touched a curl into place. Sarah and Jane exchanged looks. "You won't find me waiting until I'm twenty-two."

"Francis had to finish Divinity School first. Besides, did you ever stop to think Susan might be in love with Francis and might not mind the wait?" Sarah put in, lifting the baby from the sudsy water and laying her on a towel as the little legs kicked back, spraying water.

"Oh, pooh. I've been in love with lots of men, but none I'd wait five years for," Julia said with a toss of her head, sitting on the bed and handing Sarah a diaper from a stack beside her.

"Speaking of Susan and Francis," Julia continued, "Mother asked me to remind you that you need to see Mrs. Hicks as soon as possible to be fitted for your gown for Susan's wedding."

"I haven't forgotten," Sarah sighed. "I was just hoping to get more of my figure back before I get measured," she added, smoothing her skirt over her stomach.

"That's why I've decided never to have any children," Julia announced, shaking her curls. "I couldn't bear to look like a cow!"

WHILE NOT THE grand affair Sarah's wedding had been, the wedding of Susan and Francis was a ceremony in keeping with their more simple preferences. It, too, took place in the Holeman home. Susan's long, brown hair was swept back into a low bun, which was sprigged with baby's breath and covered with a transparent veil. She had chosen a simple dress of white lawn with tiny pleats from the high neck to the narrow waist, where they spilled over a large hoop. The long sleeves were gathered at each wrist and fastened with a buttoned cuff. A simple cameo Francis had given her at their engagement was her only jewelry.

Her only attendant was Jane, who looked lovely in a dress of peach lawn in a style similar to Susan's. Francis's brother John stood up for him. The remainder of the family was seated in the front parlor—along with their guests—to await Susan and Samuel's arrival.

"The house looks lovely," Sarah confided to her mother. "The lilies are really all the room needed."

"It was Susan's wish to keep the affair simple," Jean whispered, "although no wedding is ever simple."

Squeezing her hand, Henry called Sarah's attention to him. "I can't believe it's been eight years, Sarah," he whispered as their eyes met. "It seems only yesterday I was at the bottom of those stairs waiting for you to walk into my life. When you came down those stairs, you were the most beautiful vision I had ever seen. And, Sarah, you are more beautiful today that you were then."

"Can it really have been that long ago?" Sarah asked, smiling at the compliment. "Do you remember how taken Susan was with you then? She adored you so, you know. Do you miss that now that she's all grown up with a man of her own?" Sarah teased.

"Certainly not. In fact, it's a relief to no longer have to live up to her expectations," Henry smiled. "I hope Francis can!"

The wedding feast was set up in the gardens where the roses were still in full bloom—the first frost having held off as of yet. Carrying her plate of food to the bench under the magnolia, Sarah sat down to watch the children playing nearby. It seemed only yesterday she had been one of them, she mused. Lost in thought, she suddenly sensed someone behind her. Turning, she jumped visibly when she saw Cave looking down at her. "Henry's gone to help decorate the buggy," Sarah said, hoping that was what he wanted.

"I know that," Cave added coldly, draining his punch cup—his eyes never leaving hers.

"Where's Cornelia? I didn't see her in the house," Sarah remarked, looking around.

"At home, where a good wife should be. She doesn't parade her condition for all to see," Cave added, circling the bench to sit beside Sarah.

Catching up yards of light blue fabric, Sarah moved to give him space as Cave chuckled wickedly. "I remember another day in this house when you couldn't wait to throw yourself at me. Do you remember that, Sarah?"

"That's unfair, Cave. I mistook you for Henry. I didn't even know you were still in town," Sarah added.

"Still, with a display like that, you're lucky that I didn't throw you over my shoulder on the spot and whisk you off to Charleston with me—married or not," Cave laughed.

"You had no business being in the house that day. I don't know what possessed you. We were just lucky that neither Henry nor any of the guests saw us," Sarah whispered, looking around to be sure no one was within earshot.

"I suppose you'd prefer that no one see us together now, as well," Cave answered, noting her glance. "Very well, dear sister, I can take a hint. I only came to offer Cornelia's greetings and her apology for not attending. Now, with your permission, I'll return to fill her in on the festivities," he added, rising.

"Please give her my best," Sarah added weakly, watching him stalk away.

"There you are!" Henry called, rounding the corner of the house in a rush. "I've been looking all over for you. I knew you wouldn't want to miss the 'getaway.' Susan has gone to change. Come on. We can catch them if we hurry," he cried, pulling her to her feet. Then, following her gaze, he noticed

Cave's back as he crossed the rose garden. "Was that Cave with you?" he asked. "I barely got a chance to say hello. I'd hoped to catch him later."

"He's going home," Sarah answered, smoothing her skirt as she rose. "He didn't want to leave Cornelia alone for too long."

"I thought perhaps he couldn't stand the competition when he saw me coming," Henry laughed. Then, turning to look seriously at his wife, he added, "You know, Sarah, your love was the only thing in my life Cave couldn't win away from me. Heaven knows, he tried. I think it was all a game with him, but—I admit—it made me angry when he used to pop up every time I had you to myself for a little while.

"I even wondered for a time if you were the reason he left for Charleston. If I'd lost you, that's what I might have done. Then I realized Cave isn't me. Business is his life. That's why he left. But I was secretly glad to have you to myself all those years while he was gone."

～ ～ ～

SARAH," HENRY QUESTIONED the day after the wedding while he and his wife sat on the veranda watching Claudia sleep in her pram and the two older children playing in the leaves beside the drive. "I have something important to ask you. But don't give me an answer too hastily. Take time to hear me out first."

"All right. I know you wouldn't ask it if it weren't important to you," Sarah answered, turning to him.

"Do you remember right before we were married when the new courthouse was dedicated?" Henry asked.

"Of course. Everyone in town was there. It's still the most beautiful building in town," Sarah answered. "And I remember that you and Alfred and Cave got to sit on the podium because you'd sold the old courthouse to that young man from

Virginia for a new church. It was one of your first transactions, wasn't it? I remember watching the men move the building to the corner of Queen Street. I was in town with my mother and Susan that day. I felt so proud knowing you'd had a hand in the whole transaction. The old courthouse is still in use, isn't it?"

"Yes, and that's what I want to talk to you about," Henry nodded. "You see, it was Cave's fast talk that convinced Reverend Dodson to move here from Virginia. I've felt terrible that Cave and I were responsible for bringing him to town. And then neither of us joined his church. Alfred has been attending, but, as a bachelor, he hasn't added much. The congregation is still quite small. What the church needs is more young families.

"How would you feel about becoming charter members of the new Baptist church? Reverend Dodson approached me in town just the other day. It seems that they're seeking a charter on November 19. I know it will mean leaving our home church. Since my business is in town, though, it makes sense to mingle with the people with whom I work each day.

"Alfred has already asked for a letter of dismissal from Mars Hill, as have Tibitha and John. Even Susan Graham, Governor Graham's wife, who went to school with you and Tibitha, has asked to join. We'll form a new group of friends. What do you think?" Henry asked.

"I had no idea. I mean. . . This is just so sudden," Sarah answered, her eyes searching Henry's. "And it's hard to conceive of ever leaving Mars Hill. Every important occasion of my life has been involved with that church. Mother and Father will be hurt, too. It would mean they wouldn't be seeing us or the children on Sundays as well," she mused.

"I'm not sure I can give you an answer so quickly. But perhaps you're right. Maybe it's time we did get more involved in town. I'll think about it. I promise," Sarah smiled. "But I didn't say 'Yes' yet."

"I'm glad you want us to become more involved," Henry added sheepishly, "because I have something else to tell you. I'm sorry to spring everything on you at once. But—with my work and the girls—it's so hard to find time to talk these days. Well, it seems I've just been asked to join the Masons. You know, they meet at the old Opera House near my office—right across from the Tavern House."

"I know where it is," Sarah nodded. "Susan and I used to love to swing around the columns out in front."

"My father's been a member for years, you know. And Alfred joined when we were in Wake Forest. Now, Cave and I have been asked to join. It's a great honor, and it would be a real asset in our business. But there are several problems, as I see it. First, it would take time away from you and the girls. Second, it's a secret organization for men only. There'd be things that I would be sworn to keep secret from you," Henry concluded.

"What sort of things?" Sarah asked.

"If I knew, they wouldn't be secret!" Henry laughed. "There's nothing subversive about it, if that's what you mean. They're mostly involved in philanthropic activities through-out the county—from what I've heard from Father and Alfred."

"As long as it's not another woman," Sarah smiled, "I sup-pose I could accept it—especially if it will help the company. Why don't you find out more about it? I guess I have been rather selfish wanting to bury you out here in the country with me and the girls."

≈ ≈ ≈

IT WAS A bleak, overcast Sunday in November 1853 when Sarah stood inside the old courthouse—now modeled into a passable church—to hear her letter of dismissal from Mars Hill accepted and to pledge her support for the new church. Henry and their two little girls stood with her—Claudia having been left in Lucy's care.

As they left the church after the service, Henry took her hand. "I know how hard this was on you, Sarah. I hope, however, you will look back with pride in years to come at our position as charter members. Now, business concluded, why not treat ourselves to dinner at the Tavern House before we return home?" he smiled. "It's a miserable day, and a hot meal will cheer all of us."

"Oh, Father, could we really? I love the Tavern House. If we promise to be good, could we play in the courtyard after dinner?" Mary Frances asked, jumping up and down with excitement as Sudie—watching her sister—began to do the same. Sarah burst out laughing and had to turn away. Henry was always hooked.

The family ate in the east dining room with its low windows overlooking King Street. The fireplace sizzled as a new, wet log was hauled in, and the smell of country ham and biscuits permeated the air. Sarah felt her apprehensions fall away as she shed her cloak and looked around the small, cozy dining room. Smoothing her skirt and taking the chair Henry pulled out for her, she turned toward her offspring.

Mary Frances had climbed into one of the high-backed, wooden chairs and now sat as tall as she could—trying to reach the table without assistance. Watching her sister, little Sudie had tried to do the same and now hung over the rush seat of the chair—her legs dangling a few inches from the floor.

Before either Sarah or Henry could react to Sudie's plight, Rich Nichols, the tavern owner, appeared at her side. Reaching onto a shelf above her head, the short, stocky man with the silver hair and twinkling blue eyes lifted down a large book, caught the toddler around the waist, and placed both book and child on the narrow, rush seat. Sudie giggled as he bowed low.

Mary Frances, denied the center of attention for a moment, frowned at Mr. Nichols until he turned and noticed her. Pulling a weak, late fall rose out of a vase on the mantle, he bowed low before her as well and dropped the rose into her lap.

Henry laughed, "No wonder this establishment is so popular if you treat all the ladies that way!"

"Ladies are a welcome diversion around here," Rich Nichols answered, "especially when they are as pretty as yours. I declare, Henry, you do have more than your share," he added, smiling at Sarah.

"I understand, Mrs. Stroud, that Henry will join us in the lodge next month. May I say that I feel his election into membership is one of the best things to happen to our organization," he continued.

"Are you a Mason, also, Mr. Nichols?" Sarah asked, trying to ascertain the type of men Henry would be associating with.

"For more years than I care to count," he added, running his fingers through his silvered hair, his blue eyes twinkling with merriment as he understood Sarah's question. "They're dedicated men, Mrs. Stroud. I assure you. You'll be proud of Henry's association, I dare say.

"Now what can I get for you? The country ham is especially good, and the beans are still fresh, although with today's weather, they may be our last for a while."

"Whatever you suggest," Henry answered. "We're famished!"

"What a delightful meal, and how solicitous Mr. Nichols is," Sarah remarked as she and Henry lingered over tea while the girls ran off to the courtyard. "I declare, Henry, this is a lovely establishment. You haven't spoken of it in a while," Sarah said, searching his face. "But do you still harbor a dream of owning this place someday?"

"I can't think of anything I want more, Sarah. Just look at this place. It's the loveliest inn anyone could imagine. I'm just waiting for the right time. There's so much going on at the company right now. . . I can't, in good conscience, leave Alfred and Cave with all the work. But I'm willing to bide my time. And when Rich Nichols gets ready to sell, I intend to make an offer," Henry added, stretching his legs out to enjoy the fire.

"Did I hear an offer to buy my Tavern House? I didn't realize I had offered to sell. I declare, Mrs. Stroud," Rich Nichols said, turning to her to avoid embarrassing Henry, who was glowing red at having been overheard, "those Stroud men can't wait for a body to ask before they begin to improve this town right under his nose. Why, I'll bet you already have a buyer. Am I right?

"I'll tell you what," he added after a pause. "If and when the missus and I decide to throw in the dishtowel—and I don't feel ready yet, mind you—I'll let you be the first to know. But I don't want this place turned into a rambling hotel for rich guests from up North. So don't let your brother go selling it to some big businessman to try to improve upon!"

"I assure you, Mr. Nichols," Henry answered, finally finding his tongue, "I wouldn't change one board. I love this old place—always have, since my father brought me in here when I was about Mary Frances's age. It's more than a building. It's a part of history. I pledge to you, I'll protect your interests. Only, let me know when to find that buyer," he said, avoiding looking at Sarah, for he knew only too well her right eyebrow would now be lifted in displeasure at the small omission of the buyer's name.

CHAPTER TEN
November 1855

THE NEWS HENRY HAD been waiting for came even earlier than he had expected. Taking the stairs two at a time, he found Sarah in their bedroom preparing for bed. She looked up inquiringly when he burst into the room, pausing with her brush in hand.

"What's the matter?" Sarah asked, alarmed at his breathless state. "I was worried when you didn't come home from the lodge meeting on time."

Grasping her by the elbows, Henry lifted her from the stool and hugged her to him. While she pulled back to read his face, he smiled, "No, no, it's not bad news. It's the best news of our lives. You'll never guess. . .," he paused, still out of breath.

"I suppose not, and it doesn't look as though you're in any shape to tell me. Come over to the bed, catch your breath, and begin again," Sarah teased, pulling him to the bed and sitting down beside him. "Now, what has you so excited?"

"After the lodge meeting, Rich Nichols asked me to join him at the Tavern House. I expected it to be some lodge business he wanted to discuss, so I went—rather reluctantly—and. . . Oh, you'll never guess!"

"Of course I won't—if you keep refusing to tell me!" Sarah giggled.

"It's just this," he continued, taking both her hands and looking directly into her eyes. "He's ready to sell the Tavern House and wants me to find a buyer! Can you believe it? After all these years, he's ready to sell. He said he and Mrs. Nichols would like to move to the country to 'take life easier,' as he put it. Isn't that the most amazing news you ever heard?"

"But do we have the capital to invest at this time? I thought owning the Tavern House was years down the road. With the cost of Mary Frances's and Sudie's schooling, with Claudia, and with the new baby coming," she continued, looking down at her advanced state of pregnancy, "how can we afford to buy it?"

"You're right. We certainly can't afford to buy the inn right now, but our improvement company can. Why, Alfred was saying just yesterday that it's time for us to invest more in area businesses. And what more lucrative business do you know of in town? There's not a person in the whole of Orange County who hasn't frequented the Tavern House. And with the depot now so close, the inn is drawing lots of travelers, too," he added.

"At any rate, I intend to talk to Alfred as soon as I've gotten all the facts. Then, if he's with me, we can approach Cave with the idea. Of course I don't plan to tell them I intend to run it until after they agree to the purchase! So don't let on," Henry smiled.

"Oh, Sarah, say you'll go into town with me tomorrow and look at the Tavern House. We need to look carefully—at what it has, at what it needs, at what we could do with it. You have such wonderful ideas. In fact, let's bring the girls and make it a family outing," Henry gestured with a large sweep of his arm.

"They love that old place, too. Besides, they'll need to pick out their bedrooms when the time comes."

"To what?" Sarah asked, turning to stare at Henry with her mouth open. "I think I heard you wrong."

"Didn't you realize running the Tavern House will mean we'll have to move there? Being an innkeeper is a twenty-four-hour a day job. I thought you knew that. I never even dreamed. . . I was just so happy that you and the girls could be with me all the time. I'm sorry, Sarah. I never would have sprung this on you if I'd realized. If you don't want to move, I'll understand," Henry went on, gathering Sarah—mouth still agape—into his arms.

"I need time to think," she said at last. "I know it's your dream, but. . . it will change all of our lives. Is there room, do you think, for all of us? Four children will need lots of growing space. And there may be more. And what do we do with this house?"

"We keep it, Sarah, for the time being. Your father sold us the land, so it wouldn't be fair to sell to a stranger. And there may come a time when we'll want to move back. But there's plenty of room in the inn's west wing, where Rich's family lives. And if we move into town, the girls would be close enough to run home from school for lunch. With the large courtyard to play in and Mrs. Nash's garden for walks, the girls will have all the play room they need. Please tell me you'll go with me tomorrow and keep an open mind."

As THE LITTLE family alighted in front of the Tavern House, Rich Nichols spotted them from the desk and hurried to hold the front door. "Why, Henry, what a surprise. I had no idea this business deal involved the whole family. Getting the young ones started early in the business, are you?" he added with a wink.

"Come in, all of you. Let me help you with your coats. Sarah, wouldn't you like a chair and some tea? Take a seat by the fire, and I'll get Martha. I'm sure she'd like a chance to visit with you and the girls while Henry and I talk business. It's seldom we have a chance to have young people in the place."

The short, rotund lady with white curls appeared from the dining area, untying her apron, and bending down to the little girls all assembled before the fire. "What good fortune has smiled upon us today!" Martha Nichols said. "Cook was just asking me what to do with the new batch of gingerbread. She needed someone to taste it for her, and I couldn't think of a soul until you three appeared. Could you do it if I took you off to the kitchen?"

"Could we, Mommy, please?" Sudie asked. "Mary Frances and I will take care of Claudia. We promise."

"Don't eat too much. We may decide to stay for luncheon," Henry warned, looking toward Sarah, who nodded her approval as the girls dashed off with Mrs. Nichols.

"If you'll excuse us, Sarah," Mr. Nichols said with a mock bow, "I believe your husband and I have business to attend to. The girls will be well cared for. Cook has had lots of experience. Martha will be right back, and perhaps she'll give you a tour."

Left alone, Sarah took time to gaze about her. She remembered Henry had told her a fire had destroyed the old, Colonial tavern that had stood on the spot, and the Tavern Room downstairs still bore the charred logs to prove it. The present inn had been built on its foundation in 1768. But the inn was in beautiful shape, and the furnishings were exquisite—many more than a century old.

Sarah remembered with fondness her own wedding night at the inn while Henry filled her head at dinner with all the facts she now remembered. Even then, he had exacted a promise from her to help him run it someday—when the time was right.

"I suppose that time is now," Sarah sighed. "And I did promise. But with the girls and the new baby on the way. . . I did so hope for a little more time. And I never imagined moving to the inn. However would we manage it all?"

AFTER TEA, SARAH took the promised tour of the inn, beginning with the upstairs guest rooms and the spacious front porch filled with wicker rockers. "From this porch, I keep informed of all that's happening in town," Martha Nichols smiled. "When I hang the flag out each morning, I can see who's going to the courthouse for business and can even see that handsome husband of yours and his brothers come to work across the street.

"And it's such fun watching the men at the lodge meetings. Their meeting room is just opposite," she added, pointing across the street to the large, red brick building with its Grecian columns. "They never realize they're being spied upon when I sit up here with my needlework. After all, I have to be sure Rich is where he says he is when he goes to those meetings," she continued, placing her hands on her ample hips and laughing at her own joke.

When Henry found his family an hour later, the girls rushed to tell him of their morning's adventure—especially the gingerbread. "Well, it sounds as though you've had a wonderful time," Henry added at last. "But what about Mommy? What did you think?"

"It's all lovely. And the Nicholses have done so much with the inn. I had no idea the family quarters were so spacious," Sarah answered truthfully. "Have you men concluded your business?" she asked then, in an effort to change the subject before Henry could pin her to any further revelations.

≈ ≈ ≈

I AM A bit concerned," Alfred was saying to his father as Henry joined the two in the study. "What do you think of the likelihood of Franklin Pierce running for a second term, Henry? I must admit, the problems in Kansas and the violence over the slavery question have me very worried about the future of the Union and his ability to direct it," he concluded, leaning forward to tap his pipe into the nearby ashtray.

"It's his lackluster approach to the problems that worries me most," Henry added, pulling a chair beside his father's and reclining with his feet stretched toward the fire. "The sectionalism is becoming more pronounced—and will turn more violent—and I question Pierce's ability to hold the country together for five more years."

"You aren't afraid of a war, as Cave is, are you, Henry?" Hawkins Stroud spoke slowly, smoke curling around his sandy head as he puffed on his pipe.

"I'm not sure, Father. But our country can't continue to endure the bitterness that exists now. I'm afraid of a showdown of some sort, sooner rather than later. I pray it doesn't end in war," Henry replied.

Father and sons sat in companionable silence a few moments—each lost in thought and watching the fire. A log dropped in the fireplace, breaking the silence. As if stirred to activity by the noise, Hawkins Stroud leaned forward to direct a piercing gaze at Henry from under bushy brows—a look that had once sent chills up Henry's spine. "Henry, what's this about you discussing the sale of the Tavern House with Rich Nichols? He says you're looking for a buyer."

"I wasn't aware he even wanted to sell, Henry. When did he contact you?" Alfred asked, sitting upright to look at his brother.

"After the last lodge meeting, he asked if I would look over the property and tell him what I thought. He and Martha are planning to move to the country in April, and he wants our company to handle the sale," Henry answered truthfully, running his fingers through his hair as the only sign of his nervousness.

"Do you really think it's a wise undertaking?" Alfred asked. "That building is almost a hundred years old. What shape is it in? I know it was burned at one time, and I would question the stability of the foundation. Perhaps it would be better to tear it down and offer the property for sale."

Starting up in alarm, Henry answered quickly, "Alfred, the Tavern House is beautiful. It was totally renovated just before Rich bought it fourteen years ago. It would be a crime to lose the inn. It's too valuable a piece of history. It should be preserved at all costs—as it is—for future generations to enjoy. Besides, I promised Rich I would find a buyer who loves the inn as much as he and Martha and would continue to run it just as he has."

"You seem to have a lot of confidence in finding such a buyer," Alfred said. "Do you have one in mind?"

As Henry hesitated, his father put down his pipe, leaned forward, and fixed Henry with his eyes. "Son, you aren't thinking of trying to run the inn yourself, are you? I know how you've always loved that old place."

"Well, actually," Henry began. "Well. . ., yes, as a matter of fact, that's just what I'd like to do. I'm sorry, Alfred, I was going to talk to you about it as soon as I got all my facts in line. I don't have enough capital personally to meet the purchase price—although it is very fair. If the Improvement Company were to purchase the inn, Sarah and I could move in and run it. I feel certain we could turn a profit."

"You've had this in mind for years, haven't you, Son?" Hawkins asked shrewdly. "I remember your eyes the first time I took you and Cave in there for dinner. I remember how you questioned Mr. Lockhart and made him take you on a tour. I guess I saw it coming. Although, since you haven't said anything in so long, I thought maybe you'd forgotten your obsession with it."

"Henry, if it means so much to you. . . I had no idea. . .," Alfred answered thoughtfully. "Of course, I'll go over the books with you and consider it as an investment. And I'll help you with Cave if I'm in favor of the deal," he continued, smiling knowingly.

"But what about Sarah? How does she feel? I imagine it's not a good time to present this to her, with the baby so close. . ."

"She's known my feeling since we were courting," Henry smiled. "But neither of us suspected Rich would be ready to sell this soon. She was in favor of the idea until she realized running the inn would mean moving there. You know how she loves our home. It will be a hard decision."

"Let's set aside some time tomorrow at work to go over all your paperwork, and I'll give you my opinion as soon as I can," Alfred promised. "Then, we'll work on Cave—together."

∽ ∽ ∽

WHAT KIND OF a fool idea is this to purchase the Tavern House?" Cave asked the following afternoon after Henry and Alfred had approached him with the idea. "I can't see why anyone would want to run an inn. I can't believe we're even related, let alone twins. And Sarah. . . How can you possibly ask her to give up all she has and take her there to wait on people and clean their dirty linens? Well, she can't say she wasn't warned about you, and she did have other chances. Perhaps it's no more than she deserves for choosing such a dreamer."

"Cave, that isn't fair!" Alfred bellowed, rising from his chair and leaning across his desk toward his brother. "Henry says he's been honest with Sarah from the first. She knew about his desire to run the inn and even planned it with him."

"Ah, but that was when it was in the dreaming stage. Now that it's about to become a reality, will she leave that big house she loves so much and move into the cramped quarters at the Tavern House? What guarantee do we have that if we acquire the property she'll agree to go and we won't be stuck with an inn and no innkeeper?" Cave inquired, glaring at Henry.

"He always cuts to the core," Henry mused to himself uneasily, trying to return Cave's stare. "Sarah loves the inn as well," he answered. "And the girls do, too. Once we move in, the girls can attend school in town and be close all day. They can come home for lunch. . ."

"And serve tables in the meantime," Cave put in, settling back in his chair once more and placing his fingers together before him with a concentrated effort, designed to show his disdain of the whole plan. "I can see it all now."

"We can't even discuss this if you show no more consideration of Henry's feelings," Alfred told Cave angrily.

"It's all right," Henry replied, cutting his brother off. "Cave's questions aren't any more than I've been asking myself. All I'm asking is that you both look over the portfolio I've comprised and let me know your thoughts. The Nicholses do not plan to move until April. At the moment, all I have promised to do is try to find a buyer."

"I'm certainly willing to look it over. How about you, Cave?" Alfred asked, turning to his brother.

"Never hurts to look over a business deal," Cave mumbled under his breath. "I'll agree to that much. But as to you running the inn, Henry, that's a sight I'd like to see. And I can't wait to see Jean Holeman's expression when she tries to explain her daughter's new profession to her lady friends!"

~ ~ ~

DESPITE THE HARD time Cave had insisted on giving him, Henry left the office elated. It was a crisp day. The cedars in Mrs. Nash's garden were outlined clearly against a sharp, blue sky, and the smoke curling up from the Tavern House fireplaces gave the whole scene a welcoming atmosphere, which drove Henry across the street and into the door.

"Henry?" Rich Nichols called, coming around the desk with an inquiring look on his pleasant face.

"Relax, Rich. I've just presented your papers to my brothers, and they've agreed to look them over. Everything seems to be in fine shape. Actually, I just came in for some of your famous hot cider as a talisman against the cold on my ride home," Henry smiled.

"By all means," the proprietor smiled back, ushering Henry down the stairs to the Tavern Room.

It was there Tom found him fifteen minutes later. "Mister Henry," he began when Rich had heard Tom's plea and escorted Henry to the back door of the Tavern Room, where Tom stood waiting with cap in hand. "Lucy done asked me to come fetch you. It's Miss Sarah, Mister Henry. She's ready to have this new young 'un."

~ ~ ~

WHO DOES SHE look like?" fifteen-year-old Harriett asked, looking from the cradle at her feet to her own reflection in the mirror. Blue eyes peered back at her, framed by dark lashes and equally dark ringlets. "Is there red hair in Henry's family?"

"Henry says his grandmother—whom I never met—had red hair. He thinks Maria's a throwback. She is rather unique, isn't she? I declare, I can't seem to do the same job twice. Each of the girls is so different," Sarah answered from the bed.

"Was Henry disappointed that it was another girl?" Harriett asked, sitting on the foot of the bed.

"He was delighted. It's amazing how much he loves each girl. I'm sure Maria will be no exception. She's a good baby— and very healthy. It's a good thing, since she'll have to undergo many changes her first year. I'm afraid I won't have as much time for her as I had for the other girls if I have to arrange the move in the next five months and help Henry set up the inn."

"Sarah, why did you agree to move to the inn? No man could drag me away from my house and move me into an old inn in town. I wouldn't stand for it," Harriett snapped, eyes flashing.

"You would if you loved him," Sarah answered in a low voice. "This has been Henry's dream since long before I met him. I could never deny him that dream. You should have seen his face the day Maria was born, when I told him I would agree to move. He was so excited. You should have heard him scream!"

"You should have heard Mother's scream when Daddy told her your plans!" Harriett countered. "She said she would be mortified when all her friends saw you working in the Tavern House and would never be able to lift her head up in church again. Martha and I were in the next room, and we almost died laughing."

Sarah sighed. "Oh, dear, I was afraid she would take it like that. Heaven forbid that one of her carefully-trained ladies should dirty her hands at manual labor. I wish she could understand—in fact, I wish I could, too. Well, I've given my word, and there's no going back. Who knows, maybe someday I'll love that old inn as much as Henry."

Chapter Eleven
April 1856

The wagon wheels rumbled down the gravel drive—the unbalanced load shifting as Henry rounded the curve and took the rutted road to the Holeman house a mile away. Sarah, waiting by the front door in the buggy, gasped until the contents righted themselves and the wagon disappeared through the trees. Their belongings were all loaded, the windows shuttered, and the door locked. There was no reason to delay further.

"Mommy, you need to hurry to catch up with Daddy and Sudie," Mary Frances said impatiently from the seat beside her, where she sat cradling the sleeping Maria in her lap. Nodding absently, Sarah lifted the reins and signaled the horse to move. As they reached the Holeman road, she turned her head one last time to watch the budding dogwood and redbud trees disappear around the bend.

In moments, the house and its expanse of gardens were gone, and the hard-baked, red clay road stretched ahead of her—past her parents' home and on into the pristine little town of Hillsborough. "Even the road seems to be drawing me back," Sarah mused, watching it disappear under the horse's hooves.

Suddenly, the road and all the surrounding woodland blurred into one swirl of brown and green, as Sarah's eyes filled to the brim and tears rolled down her cheeks. "How silly of me to have become so attached to a house," Sarah thought. "And it's still our house to come back to some day. I have four adorable little girls," she continued to herself, glancing briefly at the chubby little Maria snuggled in her sister's arms, "and a loving husband, and a new venture to share with my family. I should be thanking God for my good fortune."

Yet, it didn't matter what she told herself. She knew it did matter. Three of her girls had been born in that house; the garden she and Mary Frances had started was left behind; and all the fields and woodlands, which had called to her from her childhood, would now be miles away.

Life in the city would be completely different with only the small courtyard of the inn or Mrs. Nash's garden for walks. And they would be so tied to the inn. They would never be able to leave it behind. She dare not even try to imagine the work it would entail to run such an establishment and care for four little girls as well. It was a lot to sacrifice for someone else's dream.

Oh, the Nicholses had done a beautiful job with the inn, and the furniture and atmosphere were charming—for an evening. To live there permanently, however, was something else again. What was it Henry saw in that century-old building with its peeling, white columns and sagging porches? Where was the magic for him? Listening to his glowing descriptions over the years, she had tried to see the building through his eyes. Nevertheless, she had never figured it out. Now, here she was, ready to give up the life she had always known to live his dream with him—and she was not even sure she could.

Aware of eyes upon her, Sarah raised her head to see Henry just ahead—smiling back at her from the front seat of the wagon, where he, Sudie, and Claudia were companionably seated to guide the horses to their new home. Attempting to smile back, she waved, as did Mary Frances. "It won't be long now! A penny for the first one to spot the turn," Henry called back. "Who's excited?" A chorus of delighted squeals answered him.

The magic was there. She could see it in his face and hear it in his voice. The girls had felt it, too. Henry's excitement reached out to her, and suddenly the doubt was gone. She knew at that moment she could make his dream her own—whatever it took!

∼ ∼ ∼

HENRY DIRECTED THE wagon past the inn and turned into the drive, motioning Sarah to do the same. As they neared the stables, the three little girls jumped from the wagon and buggy and ran to the kitchen door. Sure enough, Cook was there, arms akimbo, her apron straining over her ample frame and her dark hair hidden beneath a kerchief. She smiled as the trio raced past her legs to find the treats she always kept waiting.

Sarah wearily made her way through the courtyard and up the back steps of the inn with the sleeping Maria in her arms. Wanting to find the cradle and deposit her quickly so that she could get to the business at hand, Sarah walked past the front parlor without looking around.

"When a body comes all the way to town for a housewarming, he expects to be noticed," Samuel's loud voice bellowed from the room beyond. Turning, Sarah spied her father standing beside the fireplace—flanked by Julia, Martha, Maria, and Harriett, who were all smiling broadly. Julia quietly took little Maria from Sarah and disappeared into the family wing with her.

Before Julia could return, Alfred appeared through the back door carrying a trunk. Tom and Henry followed, each similarly burdened, as Martha, Maria, and Harriett hurried after them to help unpack each of the little girls' trunks. Since all the furnishings for the inn had been left, it did not take long to place the family's own personal belongings in the various rooms of the west wing. It seemed only minutes before everything was properly placed and Lucy was bringing in a big tray of Cook's famous gingerbread and lemonade.

"Looks pretty settled to me already!" Alfred laughed, looking at the dirty, perspiring group in front of him. "But, Henry, you still have one task."

Seeing Henry's quizzical look, Alfred continued, "I thought you might want this before you open for business." As he spoke, he walked to the door and carried in a large parcel. Handing it to Henry, he smiled, "Well, don't just stand there. Open it."

"Hurry up, Daddy!" Sudie cried, jumping up and down, as all three girls gathered around excitedly to watch.

"I'm hurrying," Henry called back with a grin, tearing at the paper like a small boy on Christmas Eve. "Why, Alfred, wherever did you get this?" Henry cried, tearing off the last of the paper and proudly displaying a large wooden signboard that read, "The Orange Hotel / Henry Calvin Stroud, Proprietor."

"Well, I didn't think you'd want to stand outside and tell every guest the new name of your inn. So I ordered a sign big enough for every traveler passing through town to read. Do you like it?" Alfred asked, waiting for his brother's reply.

"It's perfect," Henry answered, holding the sign at arms' length to visualize the effect. "Come on, everybody, and help me hang it," he called over his shoulder, vanishing out the door with Alfred and the girls behind.

Waiting until the others had left, Samuel walked to his eldest daughter and put his arm around her shoulders. "I always said you were something special," he smiled, placing his free hand under her chin and lifting her face to look into her eyes. "And nobody can tell me differently. What you are doing is the most unselfish thing I can imagine. Only you and I know how much you are giving up and how much you're suffering right now.

"And you're right, Sarah. It will be hard. Don't think it won't. There may be many nights when you'll cry yourself to sleep. But remember what Ecclesiastes says: 'There is a time for every purpose under heaven.' This is the time to live Henry's dream. The Lord will see you through. Trust in him, Sweetheart.

"In time, though, I predict that you will come to love this old inn as much as Henry because it will contain your sweat and tears as much as his. And within a few years, you, too, will be willing to give your life to protect it from harm.

"Although your mother wouldn't come with us today, she, too, will come around in time. Whatever you may think, her main concern has been for you. She knows what it takes to run a large establishment. But I don't believe she knows Sarah Stroud as well as I. I know that you, if anyone, can do it—alone, if necessary—, although I hope you never have to prove it."

At her father's words, Sarah's eyes filled with tears. "Oh, Daddy, I didn't know anyone else knew. Henry is so happy. . . And I thought I had hidden my feelings so well. . ."

"You can never hide them from me, Sarah, so don't ever try. When life deals you more than you can bear, I'll be there. Remember, too, whenever the urge to roam the countryside comes over you, we're only a few miles away.

"Now, how about some of Cook's gingerbread? The work's over, and it's time to celebrate. Let's find the girls," Samuel added, giving his daughter a squeeze and propelling her back into the family quarters.

≈ ≈ ≈

RUNNING THE INN was more work than Sarah—or even Henry, for that matter—had ever imagined. Although Rich Nichols had left the business in pretty good shape, the physical structure still needed a good bit of work. "Better to get it in shape now—before we reopen," Henry had said as he and Tom set about repairing loose boards on the front porch and scraping the columns for painting.

With the help of her sisters and Tibitha, who now lived just down the street, Sarah undertook the recovering of the parlor furniture and overseeing the cleaning of the floors and woodwork. She and Henry were so exhausted each evening that they fell into bed as soon as the last little girl was tucked in. "It will get better," Henry assured her one evening. "As soon as we get all this work done, we can just sit back and enjoy our guests."

By the time the inn was ready to reopen, however, Sarah could have served Henry his words on a platter. "Enjoying" their guests meant being ever ready to answer any questions, listen to all complaints, and correct any problems from a missing bar of soap to a fire in the kitchen.

Then, there were the books. Sarah felt this was one place she could contribute the most—being confined to the family quarters for a good part of each day with little Maria. She tried her best to keep up with the ordering of food, supplies, and replacement linens—using the excellent notes Rich Nichols had left. Try as she might, however, Cook, Lucy, or Tom were always on hand to report shortages of flour, spices, soap, napkins, hay, or spirits.

"I declare," Sarah remarked to Henry one rare evening as they reclined in the courtyard after the dinner crowd had left and watched the children play, "I never dreamed one establishment could need so much. It seems we never have an even balance of anything. Do you suppose it will get easier as we become more accomplished?"

"My dear Mrs. Stroud," Henry answered, affecting an awkward bow from the wicker chair in which he was seated, "of course it will get easier. Do you think the Nicholses would have stayed so long or been so reluctant to leave if it had been so difficult for them? It always takes a while to learn a new venture. But it will pay off. You'll see. By next summer, we'll be old hands at all this and will feel as though we've always run this inn.

"In the meantime, let's take the day off tomorrow. It's Fair Day, so everyone in town will be attending. We can close the dining room for the day—since there will be more than enough food at the various booths. I'll ask Cook to prepare picnic baskets for all our inn guests. Then we six can be free to enjoy this fine weather and the fair. You'd like that, wouldn't you?"

"More than anything. But are you sure?" Sarah asked.

"Very sure, Sarah. I didn't buy this place to wear us out, but rather for us to enjoy. And enjoy it we shall. Let's start tomorrow. I'll tell the girls."

≈ ≈ ≈

It was a happy party that set off down King Street the next morning. Sudie skipped ahead, determined to be the first to see the new ponies. Mary Frances followed with Claudia in tow, the little girl's eyes as big as saucers at seeing all the people and tables full of wares—for, at three, she could not remember the previous fair, which had been held two years ago. Henry carried Maria in his left arm and tucked the right one lovingly around Sarah's shoulders. "Such a perfect day!" Sarah remarked. "I really needed this. We all did."

"And the best thing is that we can walk to and from the fair this year without traffic. Living in town does have its advantages," Henry smiled.

As they neared the exhibits, Henry cried out, "Look who's here!" as Tibitha, John, and Elizabeth approached. "Come to enjoy Fair Day as well, I see."

"Oh, may I hold Maria, Uncle Henry?" eleven-year-old Elizabeth begged, her blue eyes eager. "I do so love to play with her. Would you mind if I took her to show some of my classmates? I'll bring her back for lunch. I promise."

"Of course, Elizabeth. That would be a great help and give us some time to enjoy the fair," Henry answered, handing the chubby baby over to her cousin. Holding Maria's hand, Elizabeth helped her wave before skipping off with blond braids flying and the baby on her hip.

"Elizabeth loves babies so," Tibitha sighed, watching her daughter until she had vanished in the crowd. "What a pity she can't have a brother or sister of her own."

"She's never suffered," John said lovingly, putting his arm around Tibitha's shoulders. "She's spoiled rotten by both of us. Besides, she has more than enough cousins to go around."

"That's true," Henry laughed. "She can borrow one any time she wishes. And. . .," he added conspiratorially, "there are more where they came from."

"Henry," Sarah admonished him, blushing and playfully punching her husband in the arm, "we weren't going to tell yet. Now you've spoiled the surprise."

"Oh, Sarah, are you expecting again so soon?" Tibitha asked. "What wonderful news, but are you sure it's advisable? After all, Maria's only—eight months old," she added, mentally counting the months since the baby's birth.

Taking the cue that "girl talk" was to ensue, John led Henry to a display of pipes and tobacco as the ladies continued to talk. "However will you manage?" Tibitha asked, her eyes alert and interested—despite the hurt the talk of babies always brought to her. "With four little girls to run after, an inn to run, and this new pregnancy, I really fear for your health."

"Doctor Strudwick's worried, also, Tibitha, to tell you the truth. He's ordered me to take it easy," Sarah confided. "I don't want to burden Henry with more worries, however, so I haven't told him that. He's so excited and is already planning to annex another part of the inn to provide enough space."

"Let me help you," Tibitha offered. "Elizabeth loves the girls so much. We could take the little ones several mornings a week this summer and give you a little time to rest."

"What a wonderful idea. I really could use a break, I admit. I'm feeling rather run down. In fact, I feel rather faint right now in this heat," Sarah answered, putting her hand to her head.

"Here, Sarah," Tibitha said, taking her sister-in-law's hand. "Sit here on this bench for a few minutes, and I'll bring you a lemonade. Would you like me to fetch Henry for you?"

"Oh, no. Please don't tell him. It will pass. He's been under such a strain, and he doesn't need me to add more worry. But a lemonade would be wonderful. Thank you," Sarah added, sitting down slowly. Breathing deeply, she removed her gloves and laid them beside her before dropping her head back and closing her eyes.

"Well, if I didn't know better, I'd say this was Sarah Holeman, the former belle of Hillsborough, who gave every young man in this town a reason to live—if only for her smile. But no, the Sarah I knew would never have allowed her hands to look this way," Cave offered, taking a seat beside her and lifting one of her hands. "What a waste of a beautiful woman," he continued, shaking his head. "What is that brother of mine thinking of to allow you to work like a servant?"

"Things will get better, Cave," Sarah sighed, sitting upright and looking into her brother-in-law's eyes. "A new venture is always a chore. I don't think Henry had any idea of the work when he purchased the inn."

"Correction, Sarah. When he talked Alfred and me into purchasing the inn with him. He promised it would turn a fair profit. But we have yet to see it."

"It's only been three months. A new business takes time," Sarah continued wearily. "Really, Cave, I came out today to get away from business for a short spell, if you don't mind. If you care to talk, could we discuss something besides profit margin and supply?"

"Funny, I remember a girl standing right here about thirteen years ago who wanted to know all there was to know about the Hillsborough Improvement Company and the future of Hillsborough. Do you mean you're no longer interested in the price of tobacco and cotton or in how the new nominee for president, James Buchanan, will run—or fail to run—the country?"

"Cave, please, I. . .," Sarah began. Feeling her head become light, she paused and held her temples. "Please, Cave, could you help me out of the sun?" she pleaded before collapsing against his shoulder.

Surprised, Cave turned to look at the inert form beside him. Supporting her weight with his left arm, he turned to brush the damp hair from her forehead and gaze at her for a moment. "You're still the most beautiful woman I've ever seen, Sarah Stroud," he said in a low voice.

His thoughts were interrupted by the returning Tibitha, who ran in alarm as she saw Sarah faint, spilling the lemonade she had been carrying and dropping the glass beside the bench. "Cave, help her to the shade immediately. We must find Henry and get her home to bed as soon as possible. She's not well."

"Go find Henry, Tibitha. We mustn't delay," Cave said, suddenly aware of the gravity of the situation. "Tell him to meet us at the inn. I'll carry her home myself. I wasn't aware that she was ill; although she did look rather pale."

"She's expecting again, and it's really too soon. Dr. Strudwick is very concerned, but Sarah has begged me not to tell Henry how serious it is. You won't tell him, will you?" Tibitha responded, holding her brother's arm to exact his promise.

"Of course not," Cave answered, gathering the unconscious Sarah into his arms and heading back through the crowds, smiling and nodding to each passerby who turned to look and then gape in surprise. "It will remain our secret, Sarah," he added, lowering his chin to rub it across the top of Sarah's head.

Then, looking at the pale body in his arms, he threw his head back and hissed under his breath, "Curse you, Henry Stroud, for causing her so much pain."

∾ ∾ ∾

WHAT HAPPENED?" SARAH asked, attempting to sit up in bed. As she lifted her head, however, a rush of dizziness overtook her and forced her head back to the pillow.

"You fainted at the fair. But you're home now. The doctor's on the way," Cave added gently beside her, reaching out to take her hand.

Suddenly recognizing Cave, Sarah quickly withdrew her hand. "What are you doing here? Where's Henry?" she demanded without thinking.

The smile on Cave's face vanished immediately, and he retreated several steps from the bed. "Tibitha has gone for him, Sarah. Never fear, your knight in shining armor will soon be here," he replied sarcastically.

"But why. . .?" Sarah began.

She stopped in mid-sentence as Henry and Tibitha rushed breathlessly through the door. As Henry bent over Sarah and took her in his arms, Cave—unnoticed by the two—backed toward the door.

"Cave, thank goodness you were near to bring Sarah back," Tibitha said, catching Cave as he moved past her and squeezing his arm. "I don't know what we would have done otherwise."

"Yes, Old Man, thank you ever so much," Henry added, turning to his brother. "John and I had only gone a short distance, assuming the ladies wanted to talk. I had no idea. . ."

"Cave brought me back?" Sarah asked, looking from her husband to her sister-in-law, and then focusing on Cave.

"You were talking to him when you fainted," Tibitha answered when neither Cave nor Henry offered an explanation. "Don't you remember? He carried you back here while I went for Henry. We came right back. But it was difficult getting through the crowds. Don't worry. John and Elizabeth are with the girls and will keep them so you can rest here until the doctor comes."

"You. . . carried me back?" Sarah stuttered—gazing in disbelief at Cave, who stood coolly returning her gaze.

"You're not heavy," Cave answered, by way of explanation. "And if you're worried about your reputation, remember the resemblance I bear to your dear husband. I nodded to each passerby as if I were Henry carrying you back to the inn in a swoon for a secret tryst. So your reputation is perfectly safe—and enhanced if anything—judging by the looks we got."

"Thank you," Sarah offered, blushing with embarrassment. "I'm so sorry. I—I don't know what happened. I don't even remember you being there," she stammered.

"That's the story of my life," Cave muttered under his breath. Aloud, he answered, "Think nothing of it, Sarah. I was just doing my brotherly duty. We can't have you disgracing the family name by lying like a vagrant on a park bench. Now, if you are in no further need of me, Fair Day or not—someone has to look after the affairs of the company," he added, leaving the room.

"Poor Cave," Tibitha sighed after he left the room. "All he ever thinks about is business. I fear he even has little time for Cornelia these days."

CHAPTER TWELVE
February 1857

ON A COLD, SNOWY night in late February, Sarah felt the first pangs of labor from her fifth pregnancy. Dr. Strudwick, roused from a warm bed, dutifully made his way to the inn for the delivery. Henry also managed to bring Tibitha and John from their home down King Street, but it was too late and the weather too bad for him to go for any of Sarah's family.

In the family sitting room, trying to keep warm in front of the fire, Henry waited, worried as he had never been before. "Why not go to bed, Henry?" John asked, sensing his worry. "You have several hotel guests and will have to be up to see to them in the morning. Dr. Strudwick and Tibitha have things in hand, and Lucy's with them, too. We'll let you know as soon as the baby comes."

"Thank you, John, but I couldn't sleep. I can't help worrying about both Sarah and the baby. She's never had a pregnancy like this one. She isn't well, and I'm afraid the birth will be a difficult one. I'm not sure she has the strength to go through it," Henry answered, running his fingers through his thick hair.

"Sarah's a fighter, Henry," John assured him. "She'll come through this all right. We just have to have faith. I remember how distraught I was when Elizabeth was born. I was so worried for her and for Tibitha. Tibitha was so ill afterwards. I vowed never to put her through that again."

"Then you know how difficult it is," Henry said, at last, standing and walking toward the fire. He stared for a moment into the flames, seeking answers that would not come. Then, turning, he continued, "Perhaps I've been selfish wanting a large family. Sarah has suffered so. It must have been hard on you and Tibitha all these years, too. I never realized. . . And here I've been bragging so about each new arrival. Can you and Tibitha ever forgive me?"

"We're family, Henry," John offered, shaking his head. "We've rejoiced and suffered with both you and Sarah over each of your children—as you did with Elizabeth. It's the Lord who gives to us—and takes away. We all must leave things in His hands. And right now the best thing either of us can do is to pray that he spares Sarah and that tiny child she is about to bring into the world."

The two sat in companionable silence for the next several minutes, each lost in thought. A log fell into the glowing fireplace, and Henry stirred as if from a dream. He glanced expectantly toward the door, but, seeing no one, turned back to the fire, catching John's eyes upon him. Having nothing more to say, however, John, too, turned back to the fire, as if watching it wane was the most important task either had to do.

The pale pink rays of a very wan dawn were just peeping through the shutters of the sitting room when a footfall in the hall stirred both men awake in their chairs. "Is it time to open the hotel?" Henry asked, supposing it to be Lucy or Tom coming for orders to begin the long day.

Then, coming more fully awake, he started to see a very tired and disheveled Tibitha standing in the doorway. "Is it Sarah? Is the baby here yet? I didn't hear a cry. . .," he began, rising, straightening his rumpled clothing, and walking toward her. He wanted to run, but something in his sister's demeanor made him turn away and walk slowly, instead, afraid to meet her eyes.

John, too, had risen and was looking at his wife quizzically, fearing the worst. "What is it, Sweetheart?" he began, watching as she struggled with her emotions—unable to speak.

Henry longed to push her to find the words she could not say. But he also did not want to hear whatever it was. Hers was not the happy face of one announcing a new birth to the new father. "You must tell us, Tibitha," he said at last. "Can I see Sarah?"

Finding her voice with a question she could answer truthfully, Tibitha nodded. Then, putting her arm out to catch her brother, she held him back a minute. "There's something you should know," she said. "The baby is here. It's another girl. Sarah says you wanted to name her Rebecca. . ."

"That's wonderful news, Old Man. Congratulations!" John called out, breaking the stillness of the room.

"But," Tibitha added, "she's very tiny—very much under the ideal birth weight. She's alive. But you didn't hear crying because her first cry was so faint. She's sleeping now.

"Dr. Strudwick asked me to bring you in. You and Sarah have some decisions to make. He's also asked John and me to find a minister. Should we get Reverend Dodson, or would you prefer Francis?"

"Sarah would prefer Francis," Henry added, his head in a daze. "But the roads are still so icy. . . I hate to send anyone."

"I'll go," John said. "We'll be back as quickly as possible. Tibitha, take Henry in to Sarah. She must be devastated."

Sarah lay in the big bed, her long, shiny, dark hair forming a halo around her head as it spread out on the pillow beside her. Her hands were folded on her newly-flattened stomach as if feeling the emptiness left inside. She lay gazing only at the ceiling and did not even seem to hear Henry as he entered the room and approached the bed. As Henry reached out to untwist her fingers and take her left hand in his, she turned her face at last to him, and he saw the tears that lay upon her cheeks. "It's all right, Sarah," he began. "She's alive. She'll make it. We'll will her to. With all the love in this family. . ."

"She's too tiny," Sarah cut him short by lifting her fingers to place them over his mouth. "Oh, Henry, it's all my fault," she sobbed, tears wrenching out of her body as if they would tear her apart.

"Sh-h-h, Sarah. It's nobody's fault. Dr. Strudwick will do all he can," Henry began again. "And if he can't. . . Then, it's the Lord's way, and we have no right to question. You must still yourself. It isn't good for you after the birth and all," he added as more sobs shook his wife's frail body. Then, gathering her in his arms, he felt the tears start down his own cheeks.

"May I see her?" he asked, turning to the doctor, who stood by the tiny cradle under the window—almost lost to sight in the gloom of the darkened room.

"Of course," Dr. Strudwick answered, turning to acknowledge Henry's presence and stepping aside.

The tiny form that lay in the bed was so small and lifeless Henry wondered for a moment if one of the girls had placed a doll there instead—as a joke. She was perfect. Henry could see that. But her skin was almost transparent, and he could trace the tiny veins across her face. Her head was turned toward him in sleep, and her only sign of life was the dilation and contraction of her tiny nostrils as she labored to breathe.

"How long before Francis can get here?" the doctor whispered.

"How long can she last?" Henry countered.

"I'm not sure," the doctor answered slowly, pausing to study the tiny form. "Not long, I'm afraid. Do you want to bring in the other children—or would you prefer not to? And I'm afraid you and Sarah must decide if you want to name her or not," he added.

"Not name her? Not give her an identity?" Henry hissed incredulously, all the pent up anxiety and heartbreak unleashing itself on the doctor. "She's a person. She's our flesh and blood—our daughter. For however long the Lord has given her to us, we will cherish her and give her all the rights of humanity.

"She'll be baptized as soon as Francis gets here. And her sisters and the rest of the family will be present. They're all a part of her birth and her life, and they have a right to love her as well."

"Very well," Dr. Strudwick said slowly, ignoring Henry's outburst. "Tibitha, I think it's time you and Lucy woke and dressed the children."

~ ~ ~

FRANCIS ARRIVED BEFORE noon, as did all of Sarah's family, Alfred, Cave, and Cornelia. Alfred and Henry carried Sarah to the little family sitting room, where the baby's cradle had been placed. With the children and the rest of the family looking on, Francis blessed the child and gave her the name Rebecca Thomas Stroud. After everyone had a chance to see the new arrival for a brief moment, both she and Sarah were whisked back upstairs, where Dr. Strudwick stood watch for the rest of the day.

Sarah remembered later that Henry never left the little cradle, delegating all hotel responsibilities to Tom and closing the dining rooms indefinitely. He seemed unable to look at Sarah in the bed behind him and only stared at the tiny, unmoving form in the cradle, bending over occasionally to grasp a tiny set of fingers.

Sarah felt numb. The pain of childbirth was nothing compared to the emptiness she felt inside. Even though the baby still lived, Sarah was realistic enough to realize they would not have her for long. She was too small. Try as they might, no one could keep that fact from her.

There was no hearty bawling from the cradle, and no one had tried to give her the baby to nurse. She could feel the milk building inside her, which only served to make the mental anguish more unbearable. She was thankful that Henry did not speak, for to say anything would have brought back the tears, which had already left her head pounding and her eyes raw. Finally, her body devastated by the birth and her subsequent grief, Sarah fell into a sleep of complete exhaustion.

It was with total disorientation that she awoke sometime in the early morning hours to see a small lantern burning on the table beside the cradle. Henry and Dr. Strudwick stood head to head looking down. Pushing herself onto her elbows, Sarah saw the doctor lift one tiny arm and shake his head sadly. Henry turned quickly, and she could see the light sparkle on the tears that streamed down his face.

As the truth dawned, Sarah convulsed in tears. Seeming to notice his wife for the first time, Henry turned to her, took her in his arms, and the two of them sat locked in an embrace, while neither tried to check the tears that commingled down their faces and necks.

Standing by helplessly, Dr. Strudwick covered the tiny form with the blanket and walked to the door. In moments, Tibitha and John tiptoed into the room, and John and Dr. Strudwick lifted the tiny cradle and carried it from the room. Tibitha stayed only a moment longer to gather up all blankets, diapers, and baby clothes so lovingly laid out less than twenty-four hours earlier. Then she, too, silently left the room, leaving the grieving parents in the semi-darkness, lost in their own private grief.

≈ ≈ ≈

DR. STRUDWICK HAD been firm in his insistence that Sarah was not to leave the hotel for the funeral. She had been too sick and was much too weak to walk to the church or cemetery or to be out in the late February cold. But they could not keep her from watching from her own veranda. It hurt more than Sarah could have admitted that she, the mother, could not even attend her own daughter's funeral.

Sarah stood on the upstairs veranda, supporting her weight on the railing as she watched the little procession make its way from the church on the next block down King Street to Churton Street and into the small cemetery, which was only a block away. As they passed the hotel, Mary Frances and Sudie, flanked by their grandmother and Aunt Susan, waved forlornly at their mother, who raised her hand in acknowledgment.

Henry, head bowed, walked with Francis in front of the tiny casket, borne by Alfred, Cave, John, and Samuel. He did not look up as he passed, and Sarah doubted he even knew where he was. He had barely spoken in the last three days. But Sarah understood. There were no words to express their grief.

She knew where the Stroud family plot was located, so she allowed herself to visualize the little party ascending the wide, stone steps and stopping beneath the magnolia tree. She knew she would never ask for a description of the graveside ceremony.

Turning from the railing, she pulled the heavy robe closer about her, for it was bitter cold, befitting her own mood.

Tibitha stood by her side and, pulling Sarah's arm around her own slight shoulders, allowed her sister-in-law to lean on her for support.

The unbearable silence of the empty hotel surrounded them until—in the distance—Sarah heard the laughter of the youngest children playing with Lucy in the courtyard, oblivious to the pain inside.

CHAPTER THIRTEEN
April 1857

BRIGHT SUNLIGHT PLAYED ON the ceiling—the magnolia tree beside the window making a pattern of dark and light that wavered around the room. A gentle breeze wafted through the filmy curtains, bringing with it a heady perfume of lilac. Sarah stirred and, eyes still closed, pulled the white, lacy coverlet over her head, almost obliterating the dark hair spread on the pillow.

She sensed—rather than saw—that Henry had risen and left quietly for his morning duties in the hotel—as he had every day since the week after the baby's death. He had not wanted to disturb Sarah in her illness and grief. She was glad, for she had preferred to sleep as much as possible for the past six weeks rather than face her loss. Now Sarah knew it was time to resume her duties. She had imposed on everyone too long. But she just needed a little longer. . .

She had almost succeeded in returning to sleep when she heard footsteps in the hall. As the door opened slowly, Sarah did not stir, hoping whoever it was would leave her alone again.

"Sarah," said a familiar voice by her ear. "I'm not going to go away. I know you're awake, and you're going to hear me out before I leave."

Sarah pulled the coverlet higher over her head and turned her face to the wall, not wanting to hear whatever her mother was going to say. She could not think yet, could not make any decisions. And her mother's tone told her she would have to.

"You once told me something I've never forgotten," her mother went on. "You were sitting by the big window in the parlor watching the rain fall in sheets. When I remarked how dreary April always was, you looked at me in total disbelief. 'How can you think that?' you asked. 'April is the most beautiful month because it brings an end to the cruelties of winter and gives everyone and everything a fresh start.' It's April, Sarah!

"The cruelties and heartbreak of the past winter are behind you, and you have a chance for a fresh start. You've lost one child. But you have four others who need you. Not a day goes by that they don't ask for you and beg to see you. Lucy has done a remarkable job of keeping the household running. But now it's time for you to resume your place.

"Henry, too, needs a wife. He's suffered his own private grief—over Rebecca and you as well. Nobody knows why things happen as they do. They're all a part of God's plan. He alone decides the time for us to be born and the time to die. It's no one's fault. You must understand that. Don't allow your family to continue to feel the guilt they do over Rebecca's death. Life is for the living. We can mourn the dead—there is a time for that—but then we must put mourning aside and continue to live for those around us and for ourselves as well. It's time for you to come back to us, Sarah.

"Now let's get you up and dressed. I'll call Lucy," her mother continued in the no-nonsense voice Sarah remembered so well from her childhood. "The girls and I will wait for you in the courtyard. They've asked Cook to prepare a party."

"I don't suppose I have a choice," Sarah answered petu-
lantly, raising herself on her elbows and swinging her legs over
the edge of the bed.

"No, you don't," Jean said firmly, walking toward the door.
It was not until she was safely out of sight in the hallway that
she lowered her shoulders and leaned against the wall with an
audible sigh. Getting Sarah through this had been one of the
hardest things she had ever had to do. Having lost a child
before Sarah was born, she knew only too well the depression
Sarah was feeling.

SARAH'S REINTRODUCTION TO the world was abrupt. And she realized she could never recapture the lost weeks of her confine-
ment. The girls had changed so much. Mary Frances, at ten,
was turning into a little lady—and a very attractive and headstrong one at that. With her dark hair and intelligent eyes, she
gave every indication of becoming a carbon copy of her mother.
She was thriving at school and seemed to be involved in almost
every activity.

Sudie was a total tomboy. Horses filled her seven-year-old
world, and she could usually be found in the stable with Tom.
Whenever possible, she would disappear with Grandpa
Holeman to ride in the woods for the day. With her flying,
brown braids that never stayed still and four missing teeth in her
wide grin, she looked like an elf from one of her picture books.

Wisps of flaxen hair surrounded Claudia's pixie face and
highlighted her enormous blue eyes. She had so far proved
the most precocious of the children and, at four, was already
trying to read from Sudie's picture books.

Maria, at sixteen months, was a darling. Her unruly, red
curls framed a round face that was always smiling, and her
ungainly waddle as she tried to keep up with her sisters brought
smiles to all who saw her. Sarah was sorry she had missed so

much of her early development and was only thankful her mother had arrived in time to snatch her out of her self-pity.

If Sarah thought she had missed a lot with her family, it was not to be compared with what she had missed in the world around her. The Orange Hotel was always abuzz with the latest news, and many political questions were argued and even solved—to their owner's satisfaction—over a glass of ale in the Tavern Room.

As the proprietor, there was no news in the county—or even the state, for that matter—of which Henry was not aware. He longed to discuss many ideas with Sarah, as he had in the past. However, finding her so weak before the baby's birth and so depressed after it, he had stopped sharing any ideas other than ones essential to the family's well-being for almost a year. He found, instead, a ready forum each evening in the Tavern Room, where many businessmen in town often gathered before going home.

It was there Sarah found him one Friday evening after the children were in bed. She needed a bill clarified, and, being impatient, decided to seek Henry out before closing hours.

She made her way cautiously down the stairs to the basement, where the Tavern Room lay stretched out before a large fireplace. Dark, wooden tables covered the stone floor, most of them filled with men in various states of dress. The smoke from many cigars lay heavy on the air, and Sarah had trouble at first spotting Henry at one of the rear tables with Alfred and Cave.

Seeing him in conversation, Sarah thought better of her impulsiveness and turned to head back upstairs. She had been spotted, however, and Alfred motioned her over with a big smile.

By the time Sarah arrived at the table, all three men had risen and Alfred had pulled out a chair for her. Embarrassed, since all talk in the room had ceased and all eyes were following her, Sarah took the offered seat as quickly as possible to avoid further disruption. "Henry," she began, after briefly acknowledging Alfred and Cave, "I'm sorry to bother you. I wouldn't have come unless it was for a good reason. But I need some help understanding a bill so I can put the books in order."

"I'm glad you came, Sarah. It's time you got out more," Henry stated. "First, let me see that bill and clear your mind. Then why not stay for a while and hear our discussion? You've been rather out of touch lately."

After having the billing matter from the new supplier explained to her satisfaction, Sarah was ready to leave. But all three Stroud men were too persuasive, and she admitted to herself that she really was starved for meaningful conversation.

"We were discussing the slavery question when you came in," Henry explained.

"As businessmen. . .," Cave began.

"And women. . .," Henry added, looking up from the ledger book with a smile at Sarah.

"And women," Cave conceded, "the slavery issue really does not control our way of life, as it does for both of our planter-fathers. However, it does affect every one of us as citizens of North Carolina and of the South. This sectionalism cannot continue indefinitely before it blows into too heated a controversy to keep the country together. I, for one, fear it can only result in war—a war that will be the destruction of more than our way of life.

"If it happens, it will be a war such as none of us has ever dreamed of—with a loss of more lives than we care to imagine. It will be a war neither side will win—despite the outcome. And the repercussions will extend far beyond our own lifetimes and even those of our children and grandchildren."

"I'm afraid you're only too right, Cave," Henry added with a sigh. "I had hopes we could all learn to live peacefully and respect one another's economic needs and customs. But more and more that seems to be an unreachable dream. You always were the realist. . ."

"Actually, my time in Charleston and my ties with Cornelia's family have given me more insight into the problem. South Carolina has been threatening secession since the Compromise of 1850, when California was admitted as a free state. There are some avid and outspoken politicians in Charleston," Cave put in.

"Does any state have the right to secede?" Sarah asked.

"I'm afraid that question is one the Constitution didn't actively address. And it's open to many interpretations," Alfred answered, shaking his head.

"But would you favor secession if the other states called on us to join them?" Sarah asked, looking from one brother to another.

Cave and Alfred turned to Henry to allow him to answer first. "I'm a North Carolinian first and foremost. I don't favor slavery as an institution. I never have. You know that, Sarah. But I do see it as an economic necessity for the South. I also do not favor secession. However, if slavery were abolished and our citizens stood to lose their livelihood for lack of labor, I would favor some action. If our leaders chose to secede from the Union and form a new Confederacy to foster the economic needs of our Southern states, I would support my state without hesitation," Henry concluded.

"I agree with you completely," Alfred nodded in approval.

"If we cannot—as a Union—keep the needs of every state and every citizen uppermost," Cave added, "then it would be time to dissolve that Union. I do not, however, feel that time is yet at hand when we have just won three concessions in the Dred Scott decision. I pray it never does come to that. But I fear it may. Unfortunately, the time may not be far off."

≈ ≈ ≈

EVENING SHADOWS PLAYED on the shiny, white railings of the upstairs veranda while the late summer cicadas called raucously from the oak tree across from the hotel. Sarah rocked contentedly in the white, wooden rocker, her mending in her lap, as she watched the four little girls play up and down the veranda. Mary Frances and Sudie were lost in a game of jackstraws, while Claudia attempted to instruct Maria in the proper etiquette for a tea party.

Henry was attending a lodge meeting across the street, and Sarah, remembering Martha Nichols's comments about watching the lodge proceedings from the veranda, had chosen her spot judiciously. Something big was happening tonight. But she had no idea what it was.

Just before they had left for the meeting, old Hawkins Stroud had approached Sarah on the sly to ask her to have a few bottles of spirits and some good cigars ready in the Tavern Room for after the meeting. And judging by the number of buggies that had pulled into the dirt road beside the old, red brick building—and the equal number of members who were arriving on foot—it must be a monumental occasion.

The lodge building blended into the shadows. But light blazed from the three upstairs windows where the louvered, green shutters had been thrown open to catch what little breeze wafted down King Street on the hot, still summer night. Sarah could see several men already seated around the large oak table, which stood in front of the windows. Others milled around talking. She wished she could hear what they were saying. But the sound of the cicadas and the children's chatter prevented that.

"Mother," Mary Frances called, her soft voice carrying the length of the veranda. "Is it time to take in the flag? It's almost dusk. And it's my turn tonight."

"It's my turn," Sudie put in, dropping her jacks and coming to stand beside her mother. "Mary Frances got to do it last night."

"That was because you and Grandfather didn't get back from riding in time, and I had to do it for you," Mary Frances retorted with her hands on her hips—ready to do battle if necessary. "You should thank me—not try to take my turn away!"

"When will I be big enough to take in the flag?" Claudia wanted to know, joining in the controversy.

"When you can reach across the railing to the flagpole, Silly," Sudie answered. "But you're too puny yet. So it will be a l-o-n-g time. Now, Mother, really, isn't it my turn?"

"Girls, girls. Your bickering is very unladylike. And I'm really tired of settling disputes. It's Mary Frances's turn. She did do it for you last night, Sudie, when you forgot. Still, it seems she could be a good sister and allow you to do it tonight instead," Sarah said, her eyes pleading with Mary Frances to agree.

"All right. If she wants to be such a baby about it. I hope she falls off the balcony trying to reach it!" Mary Frances retorted as a parting shot, picking up the jacks once more.

"I am not a baby!" Sudie stormed, stamping her foot. "I'm seven years old, and I'm in the second grade. And I can even beat you at jack straws—sometimes. Does that make me a baby?"

"That settles it," Sarah sighed, putting her mending basket aside. "I'll do it myself. Why, everyone along King Street can hear you arguing. Aren't you ashamed?"

"Well she started it," Mary Frances replied.

As Sarah carefully unhooked the flag from its position on the pole above the inn's front door, she looked at it as if seeing it for the first time. How many people in Hillsborough even remembered that a British flag had hung over the inn door when Cornwallis had stayed in this very building? How many remembered how hard their forefathers had fought to end British rule and to bring the thirteen sparsely-settled colonies into a viable union? So much sectionalism had now developed that people had forgotten the reason they had come together in the first place. Was it too late to save the Union, as Cave thought?

"Mother," Mary Frances questioned, looking at Sarah quizzically as she stood holding the flag against her heart. "Is something wrong?"

Sarah smiled, returning to the present. "I was just recalling a conversation with your father and uncles," she explained, shaking the flag and beginning to fold it.

"I wish Father were here," Sudie commented. "Why does he have to go to those old lodge meetings anyway?"

"I'm sure I don't know, Honey," Sarah sighed, sitting back down and picking up her mending basket, for she, too, wondered the same thing. "I guess that's something only the men can answer. They like to have their little secrets."

"But don't you ever wonder what those secrets are?" Mary Frances asked, puzzled. "I do. In fact, I tried to look in Father's secret drawer once."

"Mary Frances, you didn't!" Sarah snapped, coming to attention at her daughter's confession.

"I didn't see anything!" Mary Frances pouted. "The drawer was locked. It's just full of some old papers. I could see them stuck out of the drawer."

"Want to know something else?" Sudie asked, waiting until she had everyone's attention. "That piece of marble on the top of Father's desk is loose. I saw him pull it up and put some papers under it. We could go look while he's out."

"We will do no such thing!" Sarah admonished them. "I cannot believe either of you would think of snooping in your father's desk."

"It was just an idea," Sudie added in defense, shrugging her shoulders before turning back to her game.

A cheer from the windows across the street interrupted the discussion. All five pairs of eyes focused on the three open windows, as even Claudia and Maria gave up their play and ran to peer through the balustrades.

"What's happening?" Claudia asked, climbing onto the lower railing to peer across the street. "I see Grandpa Stroud and Uncle Alfred and Uncle Cave. But I can't see Father."

"What are they doing?" Mary Frances questioned, coming to stand beside Claudia and bending down to peer under the branches of the old oak tree in front of the lodge.

"I don't know," Claudia answered. "But they're real happy."

"Look," Sudie added from her position farther down the veranda, "there's Father. He's standing at the front of the big table with a hammer in his hand. What do you think he's doing? Come see, Mother!"

"I think he's asking the men to be quiet by beating on the table," Sarah smiled, straining to see where Sudie was pointing.

"Why can't he just ask them to be quiet?" Claudia asked.

"Maybe they don't listen any more than you four do," Sarah smiled. "Now it's late. Don't you ladies think it's bedtime?"

"Oh, not yet, Mother. Not when it's just getting interesting," Mary Frances begged. "Please?"

"Not another minute," Sarah said firmly, picking up the squirming Maria, who made every attempt to get down and rejoin her sisters at the railing. "Besides, it looks as though the meeting is breaking up. I'll be needed downstairs. Here, Mary Frances," she continued, handing her the squirming toddler, "take your sisters inside and ask Lucy to get the little ones in bed. I must go to the Tavern Room for a moment. I'll come back to tuck you in as soon as I can," she added, herding the four little girls through the door into the upstairs hall.

CHAPTER FOURTEEN
August 1857

SARAH NODDED TO SEVERAL guests as she crossed the lobby, arriving in front of the big front desk just in time to welcome the first Masons into the hotel. "Mrs. Stroud," one called, "congratulations are in order."

"You should be very proud of your husband," added another.

Sarah acknowledged them all with a smile and waited for Henry and his father and brothers to enter. Finally, she was rewarded when the door swung back, bumping the wall, and Hawkins Stroud strode through. Seeing his daughter-in-law so close at hand, Hawkins grabbed her around the waist and swung her into the air. "Say hello to the new grand master of Eagle Lodge #19, Henry Calvin Stroud," Hawkins called, placing Sarah back on the ground and gesturing toward the door where Alfred and Cave appeared, carrying Henry on their shoulders.

"Sarah," Henry called as he entered the room, "I guess my father has told the whole town the news by now. What do you think?" he asked as his brothers deposited him beside her. "Does this call for a celebration?"

"Your father ordered one earlier tonight," Sarah answered through clenched teeth as she held her comb between them and attempted to replace the bun her father-in-law's hug had displaced. "The Tavern Room is ready, although I never realized you were up for grand master. What exactly does that entail, Henry? Will it take a lot of time?" she continued to question as she watched the happy party head downstairs.

"I'm not sure yet what any of it entails," Henry admitted, turning back on the stairs to look at her. "But I'm willing to do whatever is necessary. We needed someone who could keep an eye on the lodge. And who better than me, since we live across the street? The meeting room is also very small. So I'll be keeping a lot of the papers and books over here where they'll be easily accessible."

"Well, are we celebrating or not?" Cave inquired, herding the remaining Masons toward the stairs to the Tavern Room.

"Come join us, Sarah," Henry called over his shoulder as he was swept up once again by the crowd.

"Another time," Sarah answered, shaking her head. "It doesn't look like you need me. And I promised to look in on the girls."

≈ ≈ ≈

THE JOB OF grand master took a lot more time than Henry had realized. And before long, the desk and the study floor surrounding it were filled with papers and books. For weeks, Sarah stepped dutifully around the pile—which seemed to grow larger daily. Finally, she asked Henry to sort through the pile and file whatever he could. "Of course, when I have time," he smiled.

As the weeks wore on, however, the pile only grew larger. Finally, one bleak, rainy day in October, when the older girls were in school and the little ones napping, Sarah decided to take matters into her own hands. "After all," she mused, "it is a fire hazard. Someone must take control. I won't look—just straighten."

For almost an hour, Sarah was true to her word. She straightened papers and replaced them in overturned boxes, stacking the boxes against the wall. When the boxes were straightened, she began on the desk. Knocking the pile of papers into a neat stack, Sarah decided to place them inside the desk drawer.

Try as she might, however, she could not open the drawer. Finally, she gave up and stood with the papers in her arms, blowing a wisp of hair out of her eyes, tapping her foot, and trying to decide what to do.

Suddenly, she remembered that Sudie had told her the top of the desk above the drawer was loose. Placing the papers on the chair seat, she lifted the marble slab and found that the drawer she had been trying so hard to unfasten lay open beneath her gaze.

Placing the slab carefully against the wall, Sarah bent to examine the drawer's contents. It contained several interesting objects, including a lapel pin, a tassel for a hat, several small books with what seemed to be coded writing, and a small, leather apron folded up in the back.

One by one, Sarah removed the objects to examine them near the window, where there was more light. As she was unfolding the apron, the door slammed and Henry's footsteps approached her.

"What do you think you're doing?" Henry bellowed, as she had never heard him do before. "Everything in that drawer and those boxes is secret," he called out, coming to stand beside her and wrenching the apron from her hands. "It's against the rules for anyone other than a Mason to see any of these. I thought you knew that!"

"Why, Henry, I don't see why you're so upset. I was only straightening your desk, which you never seem to have time to do. There's only a pin. . .," Sarah began, picking up the membership pin in her fingers.

"Put that down!" Henry snapped as Sarah quickly dropped the pin back into the drawer as if it were on fire. "No one who is not a Mason may touch that. Just leave the room, Sarah, please, before I say or do something I shouldn't. I need time to think. This is an infraction. As the grand master, I must report it. But I have to decide how I can do that. And I have to put all of this back before someone else sees it."

"Here, let me help," Sarah added, picking up the apron from the chair where he had dropped it and stifling a giggle as she thought how seriously Henry was taking her innocent cleaning job.

"You think this is all some type of joke, don't you? Well let me tell you how much of a joke it is. That apron you are holding is an international distress signal. When displayed, that apron is a symbol to all Masons everywhere that the person displaying it needs the help and protection of any Mason who is nearby. This is a very serious matter and not to be taken lightly. I can't believe you've been into all of this. How can I ever explain it?" Henry cried in exasperation, sitting down wearily and placing his head in his hands.

"Oh, Henry, you're making such a big thing out of this. If it will help, I'll go with you to the next lodge meeting myself and explain that I saw some of your things while I was cleaning up. I'll be a dutiful wife and confess my infraction and beg the men's forgiveness. Will that do?" Sarah offered, still amused with the gravity Henry seemed to be placing on the situation.

"I suppose it's all we can do," Henry added glumly. "We'll have to throw ourselves on the mercy of the whole membership. They may remove me as grand master, however. Oh, how Cave will gloat. He told me when we brought these things in here that you'd be into this stuff in no time. But I never believed him."

"If you men had put it all away, I wouldn't have had to touch it," Sarah said angrily, fuming at Cave's unfair criticism. "I've asked you for weeks to pick these things up. The children could just as well have picked up some of them. Both Mary Frances and Sudie knew of the drawer and swore that the top was loose. . ."

"They haven't. . ., " Henry cried, jumping up to stare at Sarah in alarm.

"Henry, will you relax?" Sarah continued. "They haven't touched a thing. But that doesn't mean they wouldn't have if it had been left here much longer."

"Well talking won't make it any better," Henry answered sadly. "Why don't you go see to the girls, and I promise I'll put all this away."

≈ ≈ ≈

AS SHE ENTERED the front door with Henry and climbed the wide stairs to the room she had so often viewed from across the street, Sarah determined she would not allow these men to bully her. They had used a part of her home to store their precious papers. Yet not one of them had taken the time to secure whatever they deemed so private. Therefore, they were as guilty as she was.

"You all know my wife, Sarah," Henry began as the assembled men, including Henry's father and brothers, nodded. "She's come with me to the meeting tonight because she has something she must tell you," Henry offered, indicating for Sarah to take the floor as he gratefully took his seat at the head of the table.

Sarah stood before the men, tall and unbowed. She paused before beginning to speak, looking from one face to the other with her right eyebrow raised ever so slightly, like a school-teacher. Having watched her give this look to the children countless times, Henry grinned in spite of himself. He had been so worried about putting her through this. But now he could feel the uncomfortable shifting. It was the men who were ill at ease—not Sarah!

"My husband has brought me before you to tell you that I have committed the unspeakable sin of seeing some of your secret papers and ceremonial equipment. The boxes you brought to our hotel were left lying on our study's floor for weeks. Nobody, including my husband," she said with a withering glance at Henry, "thought fit to secure them against prying eyes. As you know, we have guests in the hotel every hour of every day. Any one of a number of people could have seen the papers as easily as I.

"When two months had passed and still nothing had been done with the papers, I took it upon myself last week to straighten them and move them out of the floor space. Henry came into the room as I was attempting to put them into the desk drawer. I had removed a pin, some small, black books, and a small leather apron. I had no idea what they were. But Henry was extremely upset and said that I must 'confess' this deed to you, which I have done," Sarah concluded, looking around the room at the serious faces.

It was not until she glanced at Cave that she noticed any change in the uniform expression all the men wore. He was sitting with eyes glued to Sarah's face. His elbows were on the table, hands joined palm to palm. He did not blink as Sarah locked eyes with him. But a small smile played around his lips. Finally, rising, he took Sarah's elbow and propelled her toward the stairs. "Thank you, Mrs. Stroud," he said formally. "You've told us what we needed to know. Now, if you will be so good as to excuse us while we discuss this, you may wait downstairs until we need you again."

"How dare he? How dare they all put me through this as if it were some inquisition," Sarah thought to herself, pulling her arm from Cave and turning to find her own way down the stairs. Her blood was seething. But she held her tongue, for Henry's sake alone. The lodge meant so much to him.

It was over a half hour later that Sarah, cooling her heels in the dusty room with the wood floor and hard, high-backed chairs, finally heard a step behind her. She turned to find Henry beckoning. "They're ready," he announced. As she rose, he came to take her elbow. But she brushed past him and ascended the steps unaided. She needed no help from any of these men. At this point, Henry was one of them.

"Mrs. Stroud," Cave began as she entered, "do you understand the importance of what you have seen?"

"I'm afraid not, Mr. Stroud," Sarah responded. "I have no idea what any of the books said. And I didn't look at the papers at all—only straightened them. The only things I saw were a pin, a tassel, and an apron—hardly anything to cause this uproar."

"Raise your right hand, Mrs. Stroud," Cave continued in the same formal tone. Seeing no harm in this, Sarah did as he asked. "Now, Mrs. Stroud, do you swear you will never divulge the contents in the drawer of your husband's desk to anyone?" Cave asked.

"I will swear to that," Sarah added. "After all, there is little enough I could tell about anyway."

"Does that satisfy each of you?" Cave asked, turning to the assemblage, who all nodded in unison. "Then, Mrs. Stroud, thank you for being honest with us. Our business with you is concluded. Your husband may escort you home," he added, suppressing a smile.

"I think Cave was laughing at me," Sarah said earnestly to Henry as they exited the building a few moments later.

"Never," Henry smiled at her. "We both were only admiring your spirit. Why I'll lay odds, after that performance, you could stare down an army and win!"

CHAPTER FIFTEEN
November 1857

Why, Jane, you look positively gorgeous!" Sarah announced, bursting into her sister's room. "Your hair is perfect for your dress and your veil. Did you do it, Julia?" she asked, turning to the young woman who was busily replacing combs and pins in a small case.

"It sure weren't me!" Nana spluttered, shuffling into the room. "That Miss Jane never has let me do her hair in no fittin' manner, an' I wasn't about to start now an' hear her fussin' on her weddin' day."

"Oh, come on, Nana," Jane coaxed. "Julia lets you spend enough time on her hair for both of us. I've just been freeing you up for her."

Laughing, Sarah sat on the bed. It was good to be home again where she could forget all the cares of motherhood and running the inn. Here, in the house where she had spent her childhood, time always seemed to stand still and she could join her sisters in their carefree world of hairdos, fashions, and beaus.

Looking up, she caught Jane's eye in the mirror. The bond between them was still there after all these years. "Actually, I came by early to tell you the honeymoon suite at the hotel is ready for you. Henry is downstairs with the buggy. We thought we'd take your valise back and set everything up for you before the ceremony."

"We don't need the honeymoon suite!" Jane cried, whirling around to face her sister. "I. . . I don't think I would know what to do in a honeymoon suite."

"You ain't 'spected to, Honey," Nana erupted with a throaty laugh from the side of the bed where she was folding clothing. "But, I 'spect Mister Willie's goin' to know quite well. He'll give you all the help you need!" she concluded, doubling over with laughter.

Sarah and Julia suppressed giggles and exchanged a glance. "I expect you have a lot to learn, big sister," Julia laughed.

"And just what do you know about it, Julia?" Jane asked indignantly, flushed with embarrassment. "I'm sure Mother would like to know where you've gotten your information."

"Come on, you two," Sarah said, trying to end the joke. "I feel as if I'm back with Mary Frances and Sudie. Let Julia finish your hair, Jane. Nana will help me with your things. They'll be at the hotel when you arrive. We'll be back for the festivities. And don't change your hair. It's positively breathtaking."

The early morning frost gave way to crisp, cool air and a bright blue sky. "A perfect day for a wedding," Henry smiled, guiding the carriage across the damp pine needle carpet to the Holeman property. "Even the dogwoods have kept on their fall finery for the occasion," he added, pointing to the crimson-berried trees that outlined the drive.

In the back of the carriage, the three younger girls squirmed and bounced trying to get a glimpse of Grandpa and Grandma's house to see who had already arrived for Aunt Jane's wedding. "Will you three p-l-e-a-s-e sit down," Mary Frances ordered in her most grown-up voice. "You're mussing my dress. Mother," she called, "please make them sit down."

"We're almost there," Sarah offered in exasperation. "Can't you children sit still for a few more moments?"

"But we need to hurry," Sudie called, leaning over from the back seat. "Claudia and I need to know how to spread the rose petals before the ceremony begins. Please hurry and stop, Father."

"All right," Henry called good-naturedly, reining in the horses beside the front door. "You girls go ahead and get out. I'll take the carriage around back."

"If Father hadn't spent so long with Uncle Cave this morning, we wouldn't have been late," Mary Frances pouted to her mother, alighting and attempting to smooth her wrinkled skirt. "Uncle Cave always seems to come around at the worst times."

"Hush, Dear. It was business. Your father and Uncle Cave have a very important meeting coming up. You mustn't question his judgment. We're here now. Let's try to have a good time," Sarah added with an exasperated sigh as she lifted Maria into her arms and watched Sudie and Claudia disappear through the front doors.

≈ ≈ ≈

Sudie and Claudia preceded the bridal party down the stairs, spreading their petals as they came. Julia, the maid of honor, was next, drawing oohs and aahs from the guests as she lifted the hoop of her deep-green velvet dress and made her way slowly toward the crowd.

Her entrance was cut short, however, as Jane and her father paused on the landing and all eyes turned to stare. Willie Roberts, looking uncomfortable in his formal tails, advanced to the base of the stairs, shook his sandy hair from his eyes, and beamed at his bride—his hazel eyes never leaving her face until she was by his side. His grin was unmistakable, and the crowd settled down to really enjoy this wedding.

"She looks positively glowing," Susan whispered to Sarah over her son Sam's head as she and Sarah each sat holding their youngest in the front pew.

"Doesn't she ever," Sarah smiled. "She deserves every happiness. And I intend to see that she gets it."

∾ ∾ ∾

MOST OF THE guests had departed, including the bride and groom, and Henry was heading to the carriage house when Cave cornered him beside the magnolia. "I've been trying to talk to you throughout the wedding," he said, exasperated. "That family of Sarah's certainly does monopolize you. I couldn't catch you alone for a moment."

"Well, I have time now," Henry answered, sitting on the bench beneath the tree and motioning Cave over. "What is it?"

"Colonel Charles Tew, the man from Charleston whom I talked to you about this morning, is already in town! He came into the office after you and Sarah had left for the wedding. He wants to see the academy property this very afternoon—as soon as we can take him there.

"Of course, he'll be staying in the hotel. I assured him we'll give him the best room for as long as he decides to stay," Cave concluded.

"That's really short notice," Henry responded. "I had no idea his arrival was so imminent. After I drop off Sarah and the girls at the hotel, however, I suppose I could spare the time to go with you to the property. He seems like the hottest prospect for our academy we've had yet. But as to giving him the best room, I'm afraid we can't do that—yet."

"Why not?" Cave gasped, staring at his brother as if he had gone mad. "What guest could be more important?"

"Jane and her new husband," Henry answered calmly. "Sarah, Susan, and the girls have been decorating the room for days. The bridal couple should be there already. They're staying the weekend."

"You don't mean to tell me that Colonel Tew will have to use one of the regular guest rooms, do you? Think about how important this man is. He's from one of the oldest families of Charleston, an honor graduate of The Citadel, and a colonel in the United States Army. He's used to only the best.

"I must remind you that Alfred and I own a third each of the Orange Hotel as well. And I believe it's time for us to vote our majority. You'll have to move Jane and her new husband elsewhere. Besides, they'll be content with any room you give them—and I assume you are 'giving' them the room since Willie really hasn't much money," Cave continued.

"That isn't the point, Cave. Sarah and I have given that room to Jane and Willie. And we intend to give them the most enjoyable honeymoon two people could have. After all, they'll have to work hard enough once they move to the farm. We wouldn't think of disappointing them on their wedding day," Henry added.

"Then I've said all I came to say. We'll talk more about this in town—after I've seen Alfred," Cave answered angrily as he rose. Brushing off his trousers, he turned. "We'll see who has the most pull—your brothers or that wife of yours and her precious family!"

∾ ∾ ∾

DROPPING HIS FAMILY off on King Street, Henry drove the horses behind the hotel, jumped from the carriage, and handed the reins to Tom. "Got to go to the office," he said. "Thanks, Tom." As he started to leave, a shiny buggy beside the building caught his eye. "Whose is that?" he asked, turning back to Tom.

"Mister Cave brought some big-city man in here earlier," Tom said. "He came all the way from Charleston, I hear. All I know is that's some rig, and he's some rich fella—judgin' by his clothes. Mister Cave told me to watch that rig with my life—an' I will, Mister Henry, I sure will!"

"Thanks, Tom. I know we can count on you. If Mrs. Stroud asks about me, tell her I'll be back soon. She'll probably be so busy with Jane and Willie, she won't even notice I'm gone, though," Henry added with a grin.

"Yes, Sir, Mister Henry," Tom answered, smiling as he watched Henry disappear around the front of the inn.

I REFUSE TO discuss this further," Alfred was saying as Henry walked into the Hillsborough Improvement Company's ante room. "Colonel Tew is a reasonable man. He has just shown up unannounced on our doorstep to see the academy prop- erty, and—money or no money—he can't expect to just waltz in here and take the best room in town. If he's that unreason- able, I—for one—do not want to do business with him."

"Do you hear what you're saying?" Cave shouted. "How many years have we waited to find a buyer for this property? Then, with the help of Cornelia's father—I might add with no help from you and Henry—we find Colonel Charles Tew of Charleston ready to invest his fortune somewhere in North Carolina to build the premier military academy of the South. And you expect to tell him he can't have the best room in the hotel because the little sister of the manager's wife is there with her farm-boy husband?"

"Yes, I do," Alfred announced calmly. "And I'll not dis- cuss it further." Leaning back in his chair and sliding both hands in his pockets, he leveled his hazel eyes on his younger brother, who sat with mouth agape.

Sensing that Alfred had the situation in hand, Henry remained outside the door and smiled to himself. Catching Alfred's eye, while still out of Cave's line of vision, he winked and walked out the door.

Entering his own establishment a few moments later, he found Sarah deep in conversation with a very well-dressed elder gentleman whose back was to the door. "Henry," Sarah said, spotting her husband. "I'm so glad you've returned. We've been waiting for you. This is Colonel Tew from Charleston. And this, Colonel Tew, is my husband, Henry."

"I'm so glad to meet you at last," Colonel Tew said, rising and extending his hand to Henry. He was indeed as impeccably dressed and as distinguished as Tom had led Henry to believe. He was quite tall and rather thin with chiseled features and deep-set brown eyes under bushy white brows. His deep tan accentuated his pure-white hair and curving mustache. His military training had given him a regal bearing, with a straight back and squared shoulders, so that he seemed to be at constant attention.

"Fine establishment," he added, his booming voice filling the room. "I've taken time to look around town this afternoon, and I like what I've seen. I hear there was a big family wedding this morning and that's why you were out when I met your brothers."

"Henry, Colonel Tew has done the nicest thing," Sarah said smiling. "When I explained that we would have to put him in one of the regular guest rooms because the largest room was taken by my sister and her new husband, he said he didn't mind at all. And he even sent them a large bouquet of roses as a wedding gift."

"I have a soft spot when it comes to newlyweds. I've been one myself a few times," Colonel Tew said, laughing at his own joke. "Besides, one never knows. I may be investing in the parents of a future student. Never hurts to keep up the public relations."

"Colonel Tew tells me he's interested in looking at the property by the Eno River as a possible site for the military academy he wants to build," Sarah said, turning to her husband. "You didn't tell me."

"I didn't know until after the wedding when Cave cornered me to tell me Colonel Tew was in town. And who could tell you anything in the carriage with four little girls all talking at once!" he grinned.

"Were those your little whirlwinds who went by me before you came in?" Colonel Tew asked, surprised.

"All four of them," Henry answered with pride.

"Good lookers, all," Colonel Tew said. "But not a single son to enroll in my academy. What a pity. But if given a choice, I'm rather partial to the fair sex, myself. And it looks like you've cornered the market, Mr. Stroud, on all counts," he added, looking at Sarah from under his heavy brows.

"Getting back to business. . ., that property of yours sounds like just what I'm looking for, Mr. Stroud. And you say it's right at the station of the North Carolina Railroad?"

"That's right," Henry nodded. "My brothers and I bought the land just after the railroad was planned—thinking it would be perfect for an academy."

"This little lady of yours has been filling my head with all the virtues of the property. She's even got the academy designed for me with the commandant's house—complete with a rose garden—on the hill overlooking the river. I must admit, I like the idea. If she isn't on your payroll yet, you'd better hire her. She's the best sales person you fellows have—not to mention the prettiest," Colonel Tew concluded.

"Actually, the design I told you about was Henry's idea," Sarah said, coloring under the compliment. "He told me about it many years ago when he first took me out to the site. I just thought it was so perfect."

"Well, my curiosity about this place is piqued enough. Now I'd like to see it for myself. Do you suppose there's time to go this afternoon?" Colonel Tew asked, pulling on his gloves and retrieving his walking stick from beside the sofa. "I'm not a man who likes to waste time if there's business that can be done."

"I don't see why not. We still have time before dark. And Sarah can see to the dinner crowd, can't you?" Henry asked, turning to his wife.

"Of course," Sarah answered. "But I'll be jealous I can't come along. That property is one of my favorite places."

"Tell you what, Mrs. Stroud. If I like the property as much as you do, I'll take you with me to buy the roses for that garden. And you and your husband shall be my first guests in the house on the hill," Colonel Tew responded with a bow, kissing Sarah's hand and following Henry out the door.

≈ ≈ ≈

HE LOVES IT!" Henry cried, banging the door as he entered the hotel later that evening. "Sarah, you did a wonderful job convincing him by telling him all the plans beforehand. Why, he just got out of the buggy and stood there looking around. Then he asked where the commandant's house was to be placed and walked up to take a look at the view. When he whistled, I knew we had it made!" he concluded, walking around the desk, picking up Sarah, and swinging her around in a bear-hug. "And I owe it all to you."

"Henry, we're in the middle of the lobby!" Sarah reminded him as he kissed her.

"The dining room's empty. And I don't see anyone about," Henry called, raising his head and looking around. "But if you'd prefer we carry on this celebration elsewhere," he grinned, raising his eyebrows, "I'm willing to accommodate you." Scooping his wife up as if she were no bigger than Claudia, he whisked her across the hall to the family quarters and kicked the door shut behind them.

~ ~ ~

SARAH AWOKE SEVERAL hours later. The room was dark, and the only noise she could hear was Henry's soft breathing as he lay with his arms still wrapped around her. Shifting her position, Sarah tried to go back to sleep when she heard the noise that had initially waked her. It was a soft tapping at the back door. As it continued, it grew louder. "Henry," she whispered, "wake up. There's someone at the back door."

"Well, they can just go away. We don't accept guests in the middle of the night," Henry answered sleepily, reaching for Sarah and turning back over.

"If you don't go, I shall," Sarah said firmly. "Besides, it will wake the children."

"Very well," Henry answered with a resigned sigh. "I'll go. But I'm not pleased. And I'm afraid I may be downright rude," he added, pulling on his trousers.

Pulling her feet up under her gown and wrapping her arms around her legs, Sarah waited in bed for Henry to return. She could not shake the internal dread that something was wrong—very wrong.

Finally, the door to the bedroom opened. "Sarah," Henry whispered, "we need to wake Jane and Willie. It's your father. We must go to him, now. Tom is seeing to the carriage. Aaron rode all the way into town to find the two of you. He's already summoned Susan and Francis."

"What's the matter?" Sarah cried, her voice rising in alarm. "He was fine this morning at the wedding," she continued, winding her hair around her fist to secure it on the back of her neck and reaching for the dress she had so casually discarded earlier.

"It seems he had some kind of attack shortly after the guests left. He thought he had only eaten too much. But when your mother checked on him after she had seen to the clean-up, she was alarmed at his color. He was also complaining of a severe chest pain. She sent Aaron for Dr. Strudwick, and he has sent for all of you.

"It sounds serious. I'll go with you. But I don't think we should wake the girls. I've alerted Lucy, and she'll see to them in the morning if we're not back," Henry added.

"Oh, poor Father. I can't imagine him in pain. He's always been so healthy. I'll go for Jane and Willie while you get the carriage. How dreadful for them—on their wedding night, of all times. I did so want to make it special for them," Sarah said, shaking her head and trying to block out the horrible thoughts that swam through her mind.

As Henry entered the hotel's darkened lobby on his way to the front door, he noticed a solitary figure standing near the fireplace—illuminated by the scant moonlight coming through the long window. "Colonel Tew!" Henry gasped in surprise, recognizing the stately figure in the velvet dressing gown. "Is something wrong?"

"Yes, something's very wrong, and you know that. But not with me. I've only just come to this establishment, but I feel sure you do not usually have visitors in the wee hours of the morning, nor do you and your wife take carriage rides at that time, either. I've come to see what I can do to help," Colonel Tew answered, turning an earnest face to Henry.

"It's Sarah's father, Colonel Tew. He's gravely ill. Sarah is waking her sister and brother-in-law so that we can go to him. I don't know when we'll return. I'm afraid I may miss our meeting with Alfred and Cave in the morning. Will you forgive me and make my excuses? I'm terribly sorry," Henry added.

"Go with your wife, Son. She's a strong lady. But she can't

go through this alone. Nobody can. . ." He paused as his voice seemed to break. Recovering, he continued, "Your brothers can handle the meeting. You've already given me your thoughts on the property."

∼ ∼ ∼

THE HOLEMAN DRIVEWAY was shrouded in fog and only faintly visible in the filtered moonlight. The dogwoods hung like withered ghosts, their crimson leaves folded under the weight of the moisture dripping from their ends. Rising like an apparition from the fog, the house glowed in the distance. The carriage lights had been lit, and a light burned in the foyer and the master bedroom. But the remainder of the house was lost in darkness in a world where time stood still.

Beside her, Sarah felt Jane shiver, and she pulled the warm lap-robe more closely about the three of them seated in the back of the carriage. No one spoke. Looking forward, she caught Henry looking at her from the driver's seat. He felt it, too—the sense of dread that had filled them all since Aaron's fateful knock.

Entering the front door, which was unlocked, the foursome hurried up the dimly-lit staircase. Jane paused briefly to touch the white satin ribbon still intertwined on the balustrades, as Willie bent to pick up a mashed carnation on the landing. The door to their parents' bedroom stood open at the end of the hall. A bedside lamp illuminated Dr. Strudwick, and family members surrounded the bed.

As they entered, all heads turned. But again, no one spoke. There were no words. Sarah and Jane approached the bed while Henry and Willie hung back, each holding his wife's waist for support. Francis, in the corner, raised his head in a solemn greeting.

Samuel lay on the bed, his head propped up by pillows. It was he alone who broke the silence. "I'm so sorry to have caused you all to come out at such an untimely hour," he began, his voice weak and raspy. "And on your wedding night, as well, Jane," he added, taking both his daughters' hands. "I tried to tell Mrs. Holeman it was only a case of too much merriment this morning," he continued, with an attempt at mirth. "But Dr. Strudwick thinks otherwise. I had hoped to give several more brides away in my lifetime."

"Oh, Father," Sarah protested, "please don't talk this way. You'll get better. You'll see. . .," she began. But as the tears started, she could not finish.

Stepping forward, Henry took the old man's hand from Sarah. "If it's any consolation to you, Sir," he began, "I'll always be here for your family—whatever they should need. . ." Then he, too, stopped, not knowing what else to say.

"I've been truly blessed," Samuel said slowly, looking around the room. "I've had the best wife a man could ask for," he added, looking at Jean, who stood immobile on the other side of the bed, "and seven beautiful and dutiful daughters. So far, they have brought me three wonderful sons-in-law, whom I love as if they were my own. I know I can leave my family in your hands. I'm not afraid of what lies ahead for them or for me. I'm only sad that I may not continue to be here to share the future with each of you. I shall miss you all," he concluded, dropping his hands and turning to the wall.

Dr. Strudwick motioned for the family to leave the room. "He needs his rest," he whispered.

It was a silent group who sat around the fully-laden breakfast table while the sun rose. Samuel's chair stood empty at the head of the table. No one took a bite as platter after platter made the rounds. Then, with a silent gesture, Jean nodded toward the stairs, where Dr. Strudwick stood. As all rose, he raised his hand, palm facing outward. "Just your mother," was all he said.

THE LOW-HANGING gray clouds and drizzle that had persisted for days were a fitting backdrop for the black-shrouded figures who slowly made their way down the hill to the Mars Hill Cemetery. Francis preceded them to the gravesite, prayer-book in hand. Henry followed with Jean's arm locked through his. Sarah and Susan came next, holding onto one another. Willie and Jane, who had stood inseparable throughout the ordeal, followed next, with Julia leading the other sisters behind them.

Tibitha, John, and Elizabeth followed at a discreet distance with both Susan and Sarah's children. Further behind came Hawkins Stroud with his wife Mary, Cave and Cornelia, and Alfred.

The ceremony was brief. But the little party was, nonetheless, soaked through before returning to the waiting carriages. "I can't imagine life without Father," Sarah sobbed as Henry handed her up to the carriage. "Nothing will be the same again. There'll be no father waiting to greet us when we arrive, no grandfather to ride with the girls. . . Oh, Henry, they'll miss him most of all, I fear. He was so special to them."

"He will always be special—to all of you. Everything he taught you—and them—is a part of each of you. In that way, he'll continue to live through you. Someday the grief will end, and you'll be able to think of him without pain. But it does take time. There's no easy way to face the loss of a parent," Henry added, tears glistening in his own eyes.

"I forgot you lost your mother at such a young age. What it must have been like for you. . .," Sarah cried, looking at Henry with new understanding.

"We endure what we must, Sarah. God never sends us a burden we can't carry. You're strong. You must be there for those who will need to lean on you. But behind you, I'll always be there. When the burden gets too heavy, let me help you carry it—always," he concluded, bending to kiss the lips she turned to him.

CHAPTER SIXTEEN
February 1858

IT WAS A BLEAK February day with a blustery wind. No one had been about all morning, so Sarah was working on the books at the front desk. Hearing buggy wheels, she looked out of the window and watched Colonel Tew's familiar rig pull up before the hotel and the stately gentleman leap out. Pulling his overcoat tightly about him, he ran for the door—head bent against the wind.

"Colonel Tew, I had no idea you were coming in today," Sarah cried, rushing to help him with his coat and usher him to the fire. She poured him a cup of hot cider, which she kept simmering on the sideboard, and watched as he gratefully lifted it to his lips. "Henry never told me. He's across the street in the office. I can send someone for him if you'd like."

"I wouldn't send a dog to fetch anyone in weather like this," Colonel Tew answered, wiping his mouth and placing the cup on the table in front of him. "Besides, he didn't know of my plans," he said. "I believe in giving my news in person, Mrs. Stroud, and I usually don't announce my visits. I prefer to keep the surprise element intact. Good military tactics. Won us the Revolution, I believe. Why, didn't your husband mention that Cornwallis stayed in this very inn? Keeps one in touch with history, it does. I suppose that's one of the reasons you both love the inn so much. Am I right?"

"Actually, the inn is Henry's dream. He's wanted to run it since he was a child. On our first outing, he filled my head with talk of the building's sound architectural design. I should have known then what lay ahead," Sarah confessed with a smile. Pouring herself a cup of cider, she sat down beside him on the sofa, glad of a diversion from the bookkeeping.

"But you've taken that dream as your own and made it happen for him. Not many women would have made the sacrifice you have, Mrs. Stroud," the Colonel added, looking into the fire as he fell silent.

"Have you any family, Colonel Tew? Or is that too personal a question?" Sarah asked. "If it is, forgive me. But I've never heard of a Mrs. Tew."

"Actually, I have no family now. I suppose I was too selfish to give up my dream for someone else. Perhaps I deserved what I have gotten from life."

"I can't imagine you as selfish. I saw what you did for Jane and Willie. You're being too hard on yourself," Sarah said, touching the old man's arm.

"Age mellows us all, my dear," Colonel Tew answered, gazing into the fire.

Uncomfortable with the silence, Sarah was relieved to hear the door open and feel the rush of cold air as Henry strode into the room, stamping his feet and rubbing his hands. Approaching the fire, he stopped suddenly as he noticed the elderly gentleman's dejected figure. "Colonel Tew!" he cried, stripping off his gloves. "I didn't know you were coming. When did you get in? And why didn't you call for me, Sarah?" he asked, turning to his wife.

"She offered to," Colonel Tew admitted. "But I asked her not to. It's not often a man my age gets to be alone with a beautiful woman. We have to take advantage of our opportunities," he added with a sly wink.

"I'm so glad to see you!" Henry beamed. "Does this visit mean you've decided on the academy site?"

"It does. And I have. But if you're trying in your sly way to get the answer out of me, think again, Son. I haven't made my life a study of surprise attack only to be taken down by a young buck like you. Besides, what other fun do I have left in life than to keep young, impatient men like yourself waiting on my every word?" he added, chuckling.

"What I'd chiefly like right now is one of your cook's famous country ham dinners. It's been a long, cold ride, and I could smell those beans simmering from one end of town to the other. Don't suppose I could talk you two into putting business aside for a few hours and joining me—no business talk, though. Just want to catch up on the family," he added. "After dinner, I just might go to the office with you. I assume your brothers are in?"

"Of course. They never miss a workday. And yes, I think Sarah and I both could use an excuse to enjoy some of our establishment's own hospitality. Shall we move to the dining room?" Henry suggested.

Watching her husband from the corner of her eye, Sarah knew why she loved him so. He had never lost that boyish enthusiasm for a new project. It was written all over his face. She saw Colonel Tew's smile as he rose to offer her his arm. She knew the old gentleman's decision, even if Henry didn't.

～ ～ ～

GROUND-BREAKING FOR the new academy was a festive occasion at the most beautiful time of the year in Carolina. The bright

April morning was awash with yellow forsythia and jonquils—against a backdrop of pale-green willows by the river. "If only we could capture this day and keep it forever," Sarah thought wistfully as Henry turned their carriage off the road and parked it beneath the trees near the depot.

Colonel Tew, who had arrived an hour earlier, stood beside the muddy river—his white hair a stark contrast to the burnt-orange clay bank. He was deep in conversation with the former governor, William Graham, whose tall, regal bearing and shock of heavy, dark hair laced with gray made him readily recognizable in any gathering. Graham smiled as he brandished a large pair of scissors that he planned to use to cut the ribbon at the ceremony.

Susan Graham, a slender woman with dark-blond hair pulled smartly beneath a wide brimmed bonnet, stood at the base of the hill, watching several of her children chase a small rabbit. A close friend of Sarah's since girlhood, she waved as she saw the Stroud family approach. Sarah, making her way down the steep bank on Henry's arm, returned the salute and headed off to join her friend.

Smiling at Henry as he left to join the men, Sarah admonished her four immaculate little girls to "stay out of the woods and stay clean" as they scampered off to play. Turning with a sigh, she saw Susan Graham suppressing a grin.

"Oh, Sarah, let them be," Susan answered, taking her friend's arm and walking her to the row of chairs lining the bank. "I gave up long ago trying to keep the children clean at formal affairs. Everyone understands. And no one really minds, you know, as long as they don't interrupt the ceremony.

"Now, do take a minute and tell me all that has been happening in Hillsborough since we left. I did hear about your father, Sarah. I'm so sorry we couldn't have been here for you. He was a wonderful man, and I'm sure you miss him."

"Yes, it was quite a shock. Coming on the eve of Jane's wedding made it even more tragic. This academy has been the one bright spot for Henry this winter. I do hope it comes off well," Sarah said, looking wistfully at her husband, who was deep in conversation with Colonel Tew, William Graham, Alfred, and Cave, who had just arrived.

Seeing Cornelia standing awkwardly beside Cave, Sarah beckoned to her to join them, then turned to Susan. "Do you mind if Cornelia joins us? Cave will be busy with the men, and she knows so few people in town—living as they do so far out on the Stroud property."

"Of course," Susan answered, moving over to make room. "It's a shame we can't involve her more in town functions. I'd like to get to know her better."

"Cave says, 'A woman's place is at home,'" Sarah whispered. "He prefers to keep her there as much as possible."

"Poor thing," Susan whispered back. "Good thing William and Henry aren't so old-fashioned. We two would never stand for it!"

The ceremony was brief. Colonel Tew gave an account of the placement of the buildings against the hillside and announced the parade grounds would be beside the river, where the breeze would keep the cadets cool during drills. He gave a description of the type of boys he would seek for enrollment, ones who would "make Hillsborough proud" in the years to come. Polite applause followed his speech. He then acknowledged Henry, Cave, and Alfred as men "with the great foresight to have chosen this spot so long ago, when the railroad was just a set of tracks in the wilderness."

The speech concluded, William Graham cut the white ribbon with a flourish. A cheer went up from the crowd, and all dispersed to taste the pastries laid out under a small canopy at the base of the hill.

"This academy is going to take a lot of work," Cave said at Sarah's ear as she made her way around the refreshment table. "The project will keep Henry occupied for more than two years, and you know he will personally want to oversee it. Who'll run the hotel in the meantime? Should Alfred and I look for a replacement?"

"I'll run the hotel myself," Sarah replied. "It's functioned all right so far, hasn't it? And I'm perfectly qualified. You and Alfred needn't worry," she added, tossing her head as she returned to her seat.

"I saw Cave talking to you, Sarah. Was there something he needed?" Cornelia asked, looking up as Sarah approached.

"He was only interested in who would run the inn while Henry is involved with the academy," Sarah answered.

"But you run the inn as much as Henry does, and Cave knows that," Cornelia said earnestly, tucking a stray hair beneath her bonnet. "Why, I heard him bragging about you the other night to Alfred. He said you were the only woman he knew who could 'take on a man's work and responsibility and still be every inch a lady.' I envy you, Sarah. You do everything so well."

Uncomfortable with the praise, Sarah turned to the hillside and asked, "Where can the children have gone? I've totally lost track of them."

"Colonel Tew has taken them all on a tour," Susan responded. "He's very good with children. William and I are already looking seriously at the academy, and I suspect many other families will do the same."

"It will be several years before it's finished, though," Sarah said, turning to her friend.

"Not as Colonel Tew tells it," Susan continued. "He expects to enroll the first class in January."

~ ~ ~

HENRY, DID YOU realize Colonel Tew is talking about starting his first class at the academy in January?" Sarah questioned on the way home—over the din of little voices around them.

"Where did you hear that?" Henry gasped, turning to her. "Why, we've just broken ground. There's no way those buildings will be finished in nine months. Eighteen would be more like it. He can't put a class in there before the end of '59—or even '60!"

"Susan Graham says he's already been talking to them about the school for their boys, and he plans to begin with the second semester next year," Sarah answered.

"It's news to me!" Henry responded. "Where'll he put them?"

"I suppose he'll leave that up to you," Sarah said with a sweet smile. "Everyone thinks you can perform miracles, you know. But I do have an idea. The old Caldwell Academy is closed now. It's such a beautiful place. Do you think it's still usable? Colonel Tew could rent it for a year or so while the new academy is being readied."

"Sarah, you're a genius. I never even thought of it! If Colonel Tew is set on starting in January, we can at least look at the options," Henry added, reaching over to hug his wife. "What would I do without you?"

~ ~ ~

THE CALDWELL ACADEMY was indeed available. And after a few minor repairs, the Hillsborough Military Academy opened for business with much fanfare on January 12, 1859. Despite the chilly weather, parents, grandparents, and friends of the new cadets huddled inside the rotunda to watch the first students, visibly uncomfortable in their new woolen uniforms, file into the auditorium, followed by the new administrators and staff.

The ceremony was short as the proud parents were eager to see their offspring settled in the newly-decorated dormitories before beginning the long trip home—to all parts of the state.

After most of the guests had taken their leave, Sarah, Henry, Cave, and Alfred stood in the deserted rotunda to congratulate Colonel Tew on a job well done. Indeed, the venture seemed well received and destined for success.

"How many of these cadets will actually go into the military?" Sarah asked in an offhand manner.

"Sadly, probably all of them, or I miss my guess," Colonel Tew answered as four pairs of eyes turned to him.

"Do you see war as inevitable, then?" Alfred questioned.

"As certain as I'm standing here," the old man answered. Taking a seat in the deserted room, he slumped over and seemed to examine the glass he held in his hand, turning it round and round as if it were a crystal ball where he could read the answer.

For a long moment, no one spoke. Then, slowly, he continued. "You see, I know a lot of things that are not common knowledge in the South. 'Rank has its privileges,' and all that," he said, looking from one to the other with a sad attempt at a smile.

"I left South Carolina because it has become a hot bed of unrest, and I'm not sure I want to be a part of a secessionist movement—not yet, at least. I've been a part of the United States Army for more years than I care to count, and such loyalty would be hard to break. Many things are happening in Charleston that you are not aware of. Did you know that last year more than 15,000 Africans were imported into our country to be sold?"

"But that's illegal!" Henry gasped.

"Nonetheless, it's being done—all in the guise of loyalty to the South. Many people want to re-legalize the slave trade, to allow more slaves to be taken into the territories. They are taking things into their own hands in the absence of legislation, for the docks in Charleston are the site of many a slave-trade at the moment—right under the federal officials' noses.

"In the North, as well, there are many diehard abolitionists who are unwilling to wait for the government to end slavery. They're calling for slave insurrections all over the South. They want to arm the slaves and force a revolt. It's only a matter of time before one of these ill-advised actions leads to a confrontation from which neither side can back down.

"In that event, I see secession as inevitable. It's already common talk in South Carolina, although it scares the life out of me. The Union will not allow everything we have worked for collectively for almost a hundred years to be dissolved by a state legislature. State will be pitted against state, brother against brother, neighbor against neighbor, and war is the inevitable result—a war from which not one of us will be exempt, because it will be fought under our very noses."

"I simply cannot believe what you're saying!" Sarah cried in alarm. "Why, none of us has ever known war. And now you say it's at our very door!"

"I'm sorry to alarm all of you—you, especially, my dear. You know I've grown to love you all, and I wouldn't speak idly about such a monumental issue. But too many of us have hidden our heads in the sand for too long, preferring to think a little tidbit like the Dred Scott decision has solved the problems for the South. I say they are just beginning.

"You can call me an old fool if you wish, but my desire is to train as many young men to fight for North Carolina as I can—whichever direction our state decides to take. That's why I insisted on beginning this school now—instead of waiting for the new buildings to be ready. War waits for no man!

"Now that I've succeeded in alarming all of you and spoiling your day, I fear I must leave you with your thoughts and tend to the good-byes as all of these parents leave me with their pride and joy to train for—they know not what," the old man replied. Sadly shaking his head, he rose and left the auditorium. He had made the best speech of his life—to an audience of four, which was left speechless in his wake.

~ ~ ~

RETURNING TO THE hotel that afternoon, Sarah found the girls gathered around Julia, who sat by the fire in the family quarters brushing Claudia's hair. "Do mine next!" Maria called, bouncing on the sofa.

"It'll be a challenge, but I'll try," Julia answered, assessing Maria's mop of unruly curls.

"Julia, how long have you been here?" Sarah questioned, surprised at seeing her sister at the hotel.

"Long enough to have done three heads of hair," she answered, patting Claudia on the head and lifting her to the floor.

"Did you come by just to do hair, or did you have something to discuss?" Sarah smiled, eyeing her sister across the room. She knew Julia would not have taken the long trip into town without good reason.

"Actually, I have a favor to ask you. But I'd prefer to have Henry here first. I need to ask you both," Julia responded.

"Well, ask away, and I promise I'll say 'Yes,'" Henry grinned as he came through the open door.

"Well, then, you saved me the trouble of asking," Julia smiled coquettishly and started for the door.

"Just a minute, young lady," Henry laughed, catching her arm as she swept past him. "You might at least have the courtesy to tell me what I've just foolishly agreed to."

"If you must know, you and Sarah have just agreed to give me a wedding here at the hotel. And you, dear brother, have just agreed to give me away. There now, that wasn't as difficult as I'd imagined," she laughed, pretending to leave the room.

"Hold on a minute," Henry called after her. "I'm not sure I heard you right. Is this the belle of Hillsborough?"

"The girl who said she never wanted to settle on just one man. . .," Sarah continued for him, laughing at the joke herself.

"Come on, you two, I knew this wasn't going to be easy," Julia said, walking back to the sofa.

"Aunt Julia, are you really going to get married?" Mary Frances asked. "How romantic!"

"Claudia and I are good flower girls," Sudie put in.

"I know you are, Honey, but I was planning a very simple affair," Julia smiled.

"Now I know I'm not hearing right," Sarah replied. "I always had you pegged for the bride of the year."

"Well, things have changed quite a bit in the last several months," Julia continued. "I'm not sure any of us is up for a big wedding again after the last one. And it would be too painful for Mother to have it at the house—too many memories."

"Hold on. Let's back up. I think we're forgetting the most important part," Henry added. "Who is this young man who has captured the heart of the most eligible lady in town?"

"Oh, Henry, I'm hardly that any more," Julia answered, shaking her head. "Why I'm practically an old maid at my age. You don't understand how difficult it was going through mourning all these months. I miss Father as much as anyone. But it was really hard not having any social life for a whole year."

"Julia, I'm sorry. I hadn't realized," Sarah said. "I guess we were all too caught up in our own grief."

"Well, at any rate, Simeon Rogers and I have known each other for years. His father owns the plantation near Mars Hill Church. I offered to help Francis with Sunday School before I went mad from boredom. Simeon was helping too, and. . . Well, he's asked me to marry him. I want to very much, but I didn't want to approach Mother with the idea. I'm not sure she could handle it," Julia concluded.

"So you'd like to have it here? What a wonderful idea. Don't you think so, Henry?" Sarah asked, turning to her husband.

"I guess I do, since I've already agreed to it," Henry grinned. "Quite an idea, little sister, planning a ceremony so you won't have to drive to the honeymoon!"

CHAPTER SEVENTEEN
June 1859

DESPITE COLONEL TEW'S DIRE predictions, the country weathered the remainder of the winter in relative calm, and the Holeman and Stroud families had too much to think about with the wedding only weeks away to worry about political upheavals.

"So much to do and so little time," Sarah complained to Julia one morning when she was visiting the hotel.

"Sarah, it really isn't anything to make such a fuss over. Only a few guests. You serve bigger crowds every night," Julia added, making a sweeping gesture around the dining room, where Sarah was mentally rearranging tables and chairs, pad and pencil in hand.

"It's just that I haven't given a wedding before, and I do so want it to be perfect for you," Sarah answered, hugging her sister. "Do you suppose Mother will come?" she asked, putting her dread into words.

"I don't know. Really I don't. She's being so noncommittal, and I do so want her to be there. . .," Julia's voice trailed off, breaking up.

"Then she will be," Sarah answered. "Count on it. Now, why not go on over to Mrs. Hicks and get your final fitting for your gown over with? We can do this later."

Waiting until Julia was out the back door, Sarah found Henry in the lobby. "I have to go to Mother's for a little while. Can you handle things here?" she asked.

"Want to tell me what this is all about?" Henry questioned.

"Let's just say I'm returning a favor," Sarah said, pulling on her bonnet. "I'll be back shortly."

≈ ≈ ≈

FINDING HER MOTHER on the veranda sewing as she and Tom pulled up, Sarah jumped out to join her, motioning for Tom to wait.

"Sarah, what a nice surprise," Jean said, smiling and reaching out to grasp her daughter's hand.

"Actually, you may not think so when you hear what I have to say," Sarah responded, giving her mother's hand a squeeze.

"Why not? Is something the matter?" Jean cried, setting down her sewing and looking at Sarah.

"Yes, something is very much the matter. You once did me a favor, and now I'm here to do the same for you. Do you remember when I tried to hide from the world after Rebecca died? A very wise lady gave me some sound advice, and I intend to share it with you. I've never forgotten the words you told me. But it seems you have. You said, 'Life is for the living. We can mourn the dead—and there is a time for that. But then we must put that mourning aside and continue to live for the others around us and for ourselves as well.' You told me I had four girls who needed me. So do you. It's April, Mother."

≈ ≈ ≈

THE WEDDING WENT off beautifully. Julia was radiant as she walked down the wide staircase in the Orange Hotel. And Sarah thought Henry had never looked more handsome than he did at her side. "He needed the practice anyway," she whispered to her mother as they sat side by side with the rest of the family and guests.

"Sarah, I never did say 'Thank you,' did I?" Jean responded, looking at her daughter with tears in her eyes.

"Neither did I," Sarah added. "But we didn't need to."

≈ ≈ ≈

SARAH AND HENRY had even more to celebrate than the obvious successes of the new school and Julia's wedding. After the tragedy of losing Rebecca, Sarah had not been sure she wanted to go through the possible heartbreak of another pregnancy. Henry, remembering the family's grief, was also loath to even suggest another child. So it was with complete surprise and total delight that the two of them accepted Dr. Strudwick's diagnosis in late April.

Not ready to take any chances this time, Henry established a routine for Sarah that allowed her free time in the afternoons when the younger children were napping and the older ones in school. "And I mean 'rest'—with no bookkeeping!" Henry ordered, as if he were talking to one of the girls.

On advice from Dr. Strudwick, he also attempted to help Sarah through her pregnancy by keeping her away from any major decisions or controversial discussions. The members of the family and regulars in the hotel were instructed to keep political issues out of any conversation with Sarah. For a time, they did.

≈ ≈ ≈

ONE DAY IN October, when the weather was too bad to be outside, Sarah busied herself with straightening the lobby, where she found a copy of the *Raleigh Register* left by a departing guest. Deciding to read it during her quiet time, she tucked it away for later.

It was a totally distraught Sarah who found Henry late that afternoon at the desk. Waving the paper, she cried, "Colonel Tew was right! Have you seen this, Henry?"

As Henry looked up with a bewildered expression, she went on to explain. "A man named John Brown has led a raid on the federal arsenal at Harpers Ferry, Virginia. He was intending to steal rifles and arm the slaves to start an insurrection. Thank goodness, he was caught. But how many more of these attempts do you think we'll see? What if the slaves in our own state should revolt? I'm so frightened."

"Sarah, remember the baby. You must stay calm," Henry said in a soothing voice, coming around the counter to take her hand and help her onto the sofa. "I haven't seen the article. But I did hear the news last evening in the Tavern Room. It was an isolated incident. He was a fanatic. The United States Army caught him, with Colonel Lee of Virginia leading the troops. The law's on our side. This type of behavior won't be tolerated in the South—or in any part of our country for that matter.

"If anything, Brown's arrest should put an end to further attempts at insurrection. He will most likely go to the gallows as a lesson to any other abolitionist who takes the law into his own hands."

"Oh, I do hope you're right. I just can't help remembering Colonel Tew's words. And now a part of his prediction is coming true. What a tragedy to bring a baby into the world in the midst of a war," Sarah added, her eyes round with fear.

"There's no war as yet. Let's not borrow trouble. The most important thing now is for you to rest and get our baby here safely. Please try to find something less upsetting to read," Henry begged.

≈ ≈ ≈

IT WAS A relief to all the family when baby Pattie arrived in the world a scant month later, hale, hearty, and full of life. She had a head full of brown hair, deep-violet eyes, which gave every indication of turning brown, and a very powerful pair of lungs. Henry laughed that her cry for food could be heard as far away as the Tavern Room, and men had begun to place bets on the time the next scream would be heard.

"They don't really, do they?" Sarah questioned, reddening. "Then I must feed her more often to keep her quiet."

"What, and spoil their wagering?" Henry asked. "We're making money off her, Mrs. Stroud. The men are reluctant to leave until they win, so they stick around for the next scream, spending money all the while."

"You're teasing me," Sarah laughed, secretly glad this birth had been such a happy occasion and that they could smile over it.

The other girls were thrilled with their new sister and spent as much time with her as possible. Claudia had joined her sisters at the Nash-Kollock School that year and had been very good about allowing them to walk her home—until the new baby arrived. After that, each girl seemed to try to outdo the others in being the first to get to the inn to see Pattie.

Maria, who had been feeling left out when the other three went to school each day, now got her chance to play "little mother" while they were away.

Henry was ecstatic with another girl. Friends had stopped asking him when he was going to get his son by this time and started teasing him about his "harem" instead. He took it all good naturedly and loved parading his five daughters to church each Sunday as soon as Sarah and Pattie were strong enough.

As Henry had predicted, John Brown was hung in December of that year. But trouble did not die down. By the time 1860 was ushered in, rumors of insurrection plots were rife throughout North Carolina, and vigilance committees had been formed in many communities.

John Brown's raid had indeed—as Henry Wadsworth Longfellow put it just after the incident—"sown the wind to reap the whirlwind." The only good that the issue had brought was a uniting of minds throughout the state with a single purpose. And the *Raleigh Register* reported that if an anti-slavery man became president, it would signal secession for the South.

The Tavern House was the prime site within Hillsborough for discussion, argument, and rumor. So Henry and Sarah found themselves in the midst of the turmoil gripping the state—and, indeed, the whole South. Even the girls were not kept ignorant of the wave of suspicion and fright sweeping the state—try as their parents might to keep them out of earshot.

$\sim$ $\sim$ $\sim$

RUNNING BREATHLESSLY THROUGH the inn door one January afternoon, Mary Frances appeared at the desk where Sarah was hard at work. Feeling the cold air that heralded the girls' return each afternoon, Sarah replied without looking up from her ledger, "Pattie's asleep, but you can wake her to play after your snack."

"Mother," Mary Frances demanded, hanging her coat and hat on the rack by the fireside and coming to stand at Sarah's elbow. "Is it really true?"

"Is what really true?" Sarah asked, putting down the book and gazing into her eldest's frightened eyes. "Mary Frances, you look as though you've seen a ghost. Come over here, sit down, and let's have a chat," she added, patting the tall stool beside her. "What are you so worried about? And where are your sisters?"

"They're coming. But I wanted to find you first, before they overhear. We wouldn't want to frighten them, too. They're too little. Is it really true what Sally Armstrong said, that the servants are going to get guns and kill us in our beds? Tom, Lucy, and Cook wouldn't do that, would they? I thought they loved us, and we love them," she said, the words tumbling out as she climbed the tall stool beside her mother's and wrapped her feet around the rungs.

"Of course that's not true!" Sarah answered. "Where did Sally ever get that idea?"

"Her brother told her. He's joining a group to fight them when they come," Mary Frances answered.

"Heavens, Mary Frances, Sally's brother is overreacting— along with many other people, I'm afraid. Tom, Lucy, and Cook love you as much as you love them. Each of them would give his own life before he would let anyone hurt one of you. How could you doubt that?"

"But are you worried?" Mary Frances persisted.

With a sigh, Sarah took her daughter's chin in her hands and looked searchingly into her eyes. At thirteen, she was still so young. "I'll be honest with you. I'm very worried about our country right now. I see some things happening that I don't like very much. I'm concerned about the anger and distrust on all sides. But I'm not worried about being attacked by our servants. Throughout my life, I have never had anything but love for them. They're family. We have nothing to fear from them. Does that answer your question?" she asked.

"But will there be a war?" the child persisted.

"I sincerely hope not, Sweetheart. War is a terrible thing. I don't think anybody in our country really wants it. Do you?" Sarah asked.

"No, I guess not. Would it be all right with God if I prayed for him to keep us out of war?" she asked.

"I'm sure yours won't be the first voice he's heard," her mother smiled as the door opened and Sudie and Claudia bounded in.

≈ ≈ ≈

I so HATE to see the children burdened with this terrible crisis that is gripping the country," Sarah said to her husband later that evening as they lay in bed together and she related her conversation with Mary Frances.

"We can't keep everything from them," Henry answered, shaking his head. "They're bound to hear rumors and news at school, in the town, and even from the guests around the hotel. Frankly, we can do nothing but go on living day to day as best we can. A stable home life will do much to erase the worry the children are feeling," Henry tried to reassure Sarah. But he, too, was worried.

Long after Sarah had drifted to sleep, Henry found himself unable to do so. Sitting up in bed, he locked his arms around his bent legs and looked at his wife in the filtered moonlight. He loved her more now than he had ever thought possible—even on his wedding night. And the girls. . . Each was so different—and so precious. His life was so idyllic right now— filled with family, the hotel, and the almost-completed military academy.

He had all he had ever wanted. And he never wanted things to change. But the tensions in Hillsborough and throughout the South were increasing. He knew they would not go away. He'd heard too much—more than he would ever tell Sarah. There didn't seem to be any way to stem the rising tide of anger and distrust—on both sides. And he had no answers, he mused, as he lay down again and watched the moonlight play over the ceiling until dawn.

~ ~ ~

BY APRIL, EVEN Claudia had gotten into the act. Henry rounded the corner from the stable one day to see her marching up and down the courtyard with Susan's little girl, Julia. The cousins were carrying long sticks over their shoulders. "Hello, Daddy," Claudia greeted him. "Julia and I are practicing being soldiers—like at Colonel Tew's—right, Julia?"

The younger girl nodded and continued her marching without a smile. "Am I supposed to 'lower my weapon' yet?" she asked seriously.

"Not 'til I say so," Claudia admonished her. "I'm older!"

"Well, I'm even older," Henry put in. "And I say to put your weapons away and take a break for some of Cook's gingerbread."

"Yea!" the two little girls screamed in unison. Dropping their sticks, they rushed to the kitchen—forgetting their play.

But Henry did not forget. The talk of insurrection and war was too close to home. Something had to be done. Later that evening, as he and Sarah sat on the bench enjoying the heady smell of tulips and hyacinths, he made a decision.

"Did I tell you that I found Claudia and Julia playing soldiers this afternoon?" he began.

"What an imagination the two of them have," Sarah laughed. "Susan and I passed some of the militia drilling on the green this morning when we took the girls into town. I suppose they were imitating them."

"But the children are all so young yet. They shouldn't be worried about insurrection plots and militia drills," he concluded.

"You said yourself that they can't avoid being exposed to what's going on. Living in the midst of the city, they're bound to hear things," Sarah added.

"I've made a decision," Henry announced. "Please hear me out before you say anything. I want you to take the girls to your mother's for the summer—after school is out. Don't say anything. . .," he admonished as Sarah opened her mouth to protest. "I can manage around here. Much as I will miss all of you, I feel it's for the best. I love this place with all my heart, but it's not the place right now for the girls.

"They need to go riding, play in the creek, catch tadpoles, read under the trees, picnic in the woods, and—just smell the earth for a while. They need to get away from this talk of secession and war. Hillsborough is no place for children right now. Your mother will love it, and it will be good for you, too."

"But not without you!" Sarah protested, finally able to get a word in.

"This is no time to think of ourselves," Henry added. "Right now, our family's well being is the only thing we should be concerned with."

≈ ≈ ≈

It was late May when Henry and Tom loaded the children and Sarah into the wagon for the trip to the Holeman plantation. As the cool shade of the dogwood-lined drive descended on them, Henry knew he had been right. Stopping the wagon at the wide front steps, he watched as Aaron—his hair now pure white—exited the large double doors to help with the trunks.

"It's amazing," Henry said to Sarah. "Nothing has changed here since that April day I first saw you in the magnolia tree. You'll have a perfect summer.

"It may be the last for many years, I'm afraid," he told himself later as he and Tom drove back to town.

≈ ≈ ≈

I missed you so," Sarah began on her first night back at the inn when the children were all in bed. "I don't ever want to be away from you again."

"But, Sarah, you agreed yourself this afternoon that this was the best possible summer the girls could have had," Henry replied. "And you see, the hotel and I did survive—didn't we? I'm really glad the summer was so restful and carefree, for I fear the months ahead may prove the bleakest time this nation has endured."

"Are you talking about the presidential election? If Breckinridge loses, do you think there'll be more talk of secession?" Sarah asked, sitting beside her husband on their bed.

"I'm afraid it may be more than talk," he said solemnly. "Many Southerners have made it clear that if someone from a free state is elected they'll favor immediate withdrawal from the Union. I'm certain South Carolina, for one, will secede immediately, and I feel she may take several of the other states—especially those of the deep South—with her."

"What about North Carolina?" Sarah asked.

"Business has been good in our state this year. Planters have taken in bumper crops of tobacco and cotton. Our fledgling manufacturing plants are doing well. Most North Carolinians don't want change. Withdrawing from the Union would hurt us economically by eliminating most of our markets. It also will cost a great deal to set up a new government—as South Carolina proposes. Then there's the very real threat of war if the Union decides to take the states back by force.

"But anger and frustration have caused many wrongs throughout history. I would certainly favor waiting to see what a new administration will do with respect to the South and the slavery question in the territories before we make a regrettable mistake. I can only hope our legislators will do the same."

≈ ≈ ≈

TALK IN THE Tavern Room and in the dining rooms was rife. The big question was, "Union or disunion?" For ten years, Unionist forces in South Carolina had fought to keep their state from seceding. Now, with the possibility of a Republican president, Abraham Lincoln, being elected from a free state, it seemed almost certain that South Carolina would secede immediately—without giving the new administration a chance. Other states of the deep South expressed similar sentiments.

"That's why I left South Carolina," Colonel Tew told Sarah one October evening when the girls were in bed and she had joined him and Henry in front of the fire. "I love my home state. But I love my country more. I could not in good conscience support secession when there is no just cause yet. Even if the Republicans win the election, slavery for us will still be legal. The only difference will be that the Southern states are now a minority and can no longer win an election on a slave issue. That's a bitter pill for many to swallow. But it's hardly a reason to disband a century of loyalty. I had hoped the citizens of North Carolina would prove more levelheaded and give a new administration a chance," he added.

"Do you think they will?" Sarah asked.

"We can only hope, my dear," Colonel Tew said, shaking his head as if to clear the worries of the world off of his shoulders.

They did not have long to wait. When the votes were counted in November, Abraham Lincoln was elected to the White House.

CHAPTER EIGHTEEN
December 1860

CHRISTMAS OF 1860 WAS a sad occasion. As they had since Samuel's death, the entire Holeman family gathered at the Orange Hotel. They were joined this year by Cave and Cornelia and their five children. Tibitha, John, Elizabeth, Alfred, and Colonel Tew had arrived for the evening as well, having attended services down the street. Despite the distractions of Jane's and Julia's new infants and the antics of Pattie, who had picked this occasion to learn to walk, a pall still hung over the little group.

After all the children were finally asleep, Sarah was serving hot cider in the dining room when the door banged open and Susan and Francis entered, fresh from the Mars Hill service. Each carried a sleeping child and tiptoed upstairs to the room they always took.

As they joined the group, Francis spoke. "It was the saddest Christmas service I've ever preached. I tried to call for moderation in this craziness. We need Christian charity and tolerance. But I fear no one is listening," he said sadly, hanging his head.

Susan reached up to rub his neck. "It was a good sermon, Francis. You tried. No one can do more than that."

"I fear we've crested the hill," Colonel Tew's booming voice rang out. "It will be a downhill slide—rather like an avalanche—with several more states following South Carolina."

"Why did they secede so soon?" Willie asked. "Lincoln hasn't even taken office. How do they know what will happen?"

"That possibility has been ripe in South Carolina for more than ten years, Son," Colonel Tew answered. "I've seen it coming."

"How many other states do you think will leave the Union?" Alfred questioned. "What do you think the chances are that North Carolina will follow?"

"Economically speaking," Cave put in, "I can see all the states of the deep South following suit. If they lose the right to slavery, they lose everything. They're running scared since they have nothing but farming to fall back on."

"It's certainly a possibility," Colonel Tew added, shaking his head in despair.

"Then that puts the upper South in a very bad situation, as I see it," John Quackenbush interjected. "If we stay with the Union, we'll be in a very small minority as slave-holding states and will have no support at all in Congress. If we leave to join this Confederacy that South Carolina wants to form, we'll lose the protection of slavery, guaranteed by the U. S. Constitution. If the new administration decides to fight to keep us in the Union and wins, we most assuredly will lose the rights to slavery as a backlash. It appears a no-win situation for us. Don't you agree?" he added, turning to Henry.

"I agree completely," Henry answered. "I also fear military despotism if a civil war occurs. Then we may lose all rights, and our country—as we know it—will be no more."

"What do you think, Colonel Tew?" Alfred asked, eyes wide with disbelief. "What would happen in case of a civil war?"

"Having been in the military all my life, I'd like to defend it. But I must agree with Henry," Colonel Tew responded. "There can be only one commander in a battle zone. Any more would cause mixed signals and lose the campaign. Therefore, Congress and the states would have to defer to the president as the Commander-in-Chief. It could well lead to despotism. So far, we know little of Lincoln, so there's always the possibility of him taking his power too seriously in a national crisis."

"But wouldn't a war ruin the South as certainly as the loss of slavery?" Tibitha asked quietly. "If our men all went to war, there'd be no one to run the farms. And economic ruin would occur just as surely."

"You're right, my dear," Colonel Tew answered. "Moreover, none of us has ever experienced a civil war. Remember, we would be fighting on our own soil, under our very noses. No one would be safe—man, woman, or child. No property would be secure. Cotton and tobacco fields would be turned into battlefields. The Old South as we have known it would be no more."

"And what of those of us who have no men to defend our property?" Jean asked, horrified.

"If this war comes, Mrs. Holeman, there will be no men left to defend any of the properties," Alfred put in. "We'll all be needed to fight."

"But, Cave, would you go to fight, too?" Cornelia questioned, turning to her husband with tears in her eyes. "How would the children and I manage?"

"Fear not, Mrs. Stroud," Cave answered with bravado. "I'm a businessman first and foremost. I have no squabble with the government. I own no slaves, nor does my economic future depend on slavery. I see no reason to go to war for a cause that's not my own."

The silence that followed was deafening, as all eyes turned to Cave. Finally, Henry attempted to clear the air. "Surely you'd go to battle if your state needed you, Cave?"

"On the contrary, Brother. I would stay behind and support you fools who decided to serve. After all, someone has to keep the business intact so you and Alfred will have something to come home to when you've lost the cause," Cave concluded with finality.

BY FEBRUARY 1, 1861 six more states from the deep South had joined with South Carolina in seceding from the Union: Georgia, Alabama, Florida, Mississippi, Louisiana, and Texas. On February 6, delegates from each of these states met in Montgomery, Alabama, to set up a provisional government for the Confederate States of America. Jefferson Davis of Mississippi was elected president. Alexander Stephens of Georgia became vice-president. The new constitution the representatives framed closely followed the Constitution of the United States—with the sovereign status of each state stressed in the preamble.

Governor Ellis of North Carolina—seeing the possibility of a conflict—proposed a statewide volunteer army of 10,000 and strengthened and reorganized the North Carolina militia. He did not want a conflict with the new administration, he said repeatedly. But he insisted that if Lincoln should wage war on any seceded state, the people of North Carolina owed it to themselves to resist him to the end.

Ellis also asked the General Assembly to call a state convention. But the idea was defeated by popular vote. Since state conventions in all seceded states had voted for secession,

North Carolinians—for the most part—were loathe to call one. Relieved that the crisis in their state had been avoided—at least for the time being—all hoped that the new presidency and Lincoln's policies would convince the seceded states to admit their folly and return to the Union.

∾ ∾ ∾

Lincoln's inaugural address on March 4, 1861 was the sole topic of conversation when it appeared in the newspapers the next day. Despite a cold, blustery rain, men gathered on Churton Street at daybreak in front of the office of the town newspaper, the *Hillsborough Recorder*, to get their copy of the day's news. Topcoats drawn against the blowing rain, most then hurried to the hotel to peruse the speech and discuss its ramifications.

Anticipating the rush for tables and talk, Henry and Sarah had been up since before daybreak. "Cook has prepared enough food for an army," Sarah smiled to Henry as she entered the dining room from the kitchen.

"Watch your language!" Henry replied. "I hope this is the closest she ever comes to feeding one."

"Oh, you know what I mean," Sarah sighed, taking a handful of silverware from the nearby breakfront and beginning to set the tables. "Aren't you curious about what President Lincoln had to say? Wouldn't you like a copy of the paper? I can finish things here if you want to go get one."

"I'm sure we'll hear soon enough—judging by the number of people lined up outside," Henry added, walking to the front window and pulling the drapes aside. "And there are sure to be plenty of copies lying around on the tables well before lunch hour. In truth, I'd rather delay the inevitable a little longer, wouldn't you?" he called over his shoulder as he crossed the lobby to unlock the door.

"He's agreed to leave slavery alone and promised he won't send federal officials into the states," Alfred cried, rushing through the open door, his copy of the paper already sodden despite his attempt to shield it under his top-coat. Shaking water from his hair and shoulders, he hung his coat and hat by the door and walked in to take a place at his usual table.

Forgetting his proclamation, Henry followed his brother to the table. "Did he say he would recognize the secession, or does he plan to force the states back into the Union?" he asked.

"According to his speech," Alfred answered, unfolding the damp paper and perusing the columns for the right spot, "Lincoln has refused to recognize the secession of the lower South and vows he will continue to keep control of any federal property there."

"That could mean a great deal of trouble," Cave spoke up as he, too, came to the table, drying his neck with his handkerchief. "He didn't mention force. But how else can he maintain control of federal property? Does he think South Carolina will let him bring troops and munitions right through the Charleston harbor to supply his men who are garrisoned at Fort Sumter? If that's his plan, he's even more naive than we've thought."

"If he attempts it, we join with the Confederacy," Henry sighed. "We're not out of the woods yet!"

"Doesn't he have advisors?" Cave asked. "Surely the Republicans will have told him how foolhardy an invasion of the Confederacy would be. I can't believe he would suggest maintaining control of federal property. Better to let it go—along with the states—and concentrate on keeping the rest of us in the Union. That would seem to me to be the chief concern right now."

"I should think he'll get a lot of pressure to do just that. I'm sure the representatives of our border states will explain the risks," Henry added, getting up from the table to tend to the new guests flocking through the doorway.

It was a sad and disgruntled group of North Carolinians who voiced the same concerns from the mountains to the shore. How could Lincoln risk losing the remainder of the border states over a few former U.S. forts? What did they matter when the whole country's future was at stake?

∽ ∽ ∽

FINALLY, LINCOLN SEEMED to listen. Yielding to border-state pressure several weeks later, he announced that he would pull his federal garrison out of Fort Sumter.

"He's finally come to his senses," said Colonel Tew, who was visiting for the evening. Packing his pipe and pausing to light it before the fire, he continued, "I'm sure he had no idea what he would be risking by bringing federal ships into Charleston Harbor. I could have told him. But he didn't ask me! Why that place is guarded night and day, and the fort has been under a state of siege since January. There's no way a Union ship could get in there and get its men back out alive. Any attempt to reach the fort would be viewed as an act of war."

∽ ∽ ∽

THE MID-APRIL day was warm and almost summery. Sarah sat in the garden mending while Pattie played, waiting for the other girls to come home from school. Sarah had allowed her to pick four jonquils for her sisters, and she was very excited.

"Sarah," Henry yelled, running out the back door, which banged behind him as he took the steps two at a time.

Cringing at the harsh noise, Sarah called, "We're over here." She waved from beneath the magnolia tree.

"Daddy!" Pattie called, running toward her father and grasping him around the knees.

"What's my little pumpkin up to today? Picking flowers, I see. Did Mommy say it was all right?" Henry asked, kneeling beside his petite daughter.

"Uh, huh," Pattie nodded. "Foah my sis-sers," she added proudly.

"They're very lucky to have such a nice sister," Henry smiled, tousling the dark ringlets.

"Uh, huh," Pattie nodded again before running over to peer down the garden path.

"I'd forgotten what a delight they are at that age," Henry said, sitting beside Sarah and putting his arm around her. "How I'd love to spend every day with you and the girls—somewhere far away. . ."

"Has something new happened?" Sarah asked.

"After promising that Major Anderson and his Union garrison would abandon Fort Sumter, Lincoln today sent federal ships in to resupply the fort," Henry answered.

"I'm afraid to ask what happened next," Sarah said.

"As Colonel Tew predicted, fighting broke out as the Confederates at Fort Johnson—on the Charleston mainland—began a bombardment of the fort and the Union fleet. We just got word from Raleigh. I fear it's the fuel to fan our state's fire of secession," Henry added sadly. "It's the last straw."

"Does it mean war?" Sarah persisted.

"The wheels will take time to grind into action. I suppose there will finally be a convention in North Carolina. But it doesn't take a genius to realize that we will now secede and join the Confederacy. What will happen after that is anyone's guess. But if Lincoln persists in trying to supply the fort, I'm afraid the answer is obvious," Henry sighed.

"And in the meantime?" Sarah wondered.

"Why, we tend the hotel as usual," he said with a wry grin. "And if the former bits of news that have come through town are any indication, I'm afraid with this news, we're in for the biggest crowd yet during the next several days."

As HENRY PREDICTED, the crowds came—and waited, and came—and waited, hoping to hear something—be it good or bad. And the news came. A scant two days after fighting had broken out, Lincoln called for 75,000 troops to quell the "rebellion" in the lower South.

"The audacity of Lincoln to ask Governor Ellis for two regiments to fight our own Southern brothers!" Alfred cried, banging his glass on the table.

"Never fear," Cave put in. "Governor Ellis, for all his rhetoric, has been a secessionist all along. Now that Lincoln has 'drawn his sword,' he has just cause for action."

"Ellis has been patient. But he's been shrewd as well," Colonel Tew added, coming in on the tail end of the conversation to take his usual seat. "He's been stockpiling arms and munitions for months. He's also revitalized the militia and established his volunteer army—the best there is. Some of my top cadets have signed on as volunteers as soon as they graduate next month. This state is prepared. The Confederacy will be lucky to have us aboard—if it comes to that."

WITH LINCOLN HAVING committed what was deemed an act of war by violating one of the state's sovereignty, everyone expected the proposed state convention to vote for secession. Young men felt a patriotic duty to offer their services to their state. And groups of volunteers were soon practicing daily on the courthouse green. The young women of the town found more and more reasons to be in the area at drill time.

Maria and Harriett were not immune to the draw and dropped by more and more often "just to visit" Sarah and the children at the hotel. There was something romantic about fighting for a cause. The young men who had tended their plows in the mornings took on the aspect of heroes in the afternoon with muskets over their shoulders, and courtships blossomed.

On the other hand, rumors abounded that Unionists in North Carolina were plotting—now that secession seemed imminent—to unite the slaves and cause insurrections throughout the state. Hillsborough reacted immediately to prevent such an occurrence, passing a law making it illegal for slaves to be about inside the city limits between sunset and sunrise and on Sundays.

"I can't believe people are overreacting so. It's really unfair," Sarah complained to Henry when the children were out of earshot.

"The whole idea is absurd and blown out of proportion. None of the servants I know would consider an insurrection. They are as loyal to the South as the rest of us. My heart bleeds for Tom, Lucy, and our parents' servants. They're being wrongly accused and punished," Henry said. "But people are scared and need some control to hold down the rumors and fright. Mass hysteria, in ecstasy or in anger, is a dangerous thing. I hope never to see it in our town."

HYSTERIA, NONETHELESS, WAS not long in coming. It was a warm May afternoon. Sarah stood alone at the desk looking over the books while Pattie napped and the older girls played in the courtyard. Suddenly, several large "booms" shook the hotel. The courthouse bells began to ring, and church bells throughout the city joined in. Pattie screamed from her bed, terrified.

As Sarah ran to comfort the toddler, Maria rushed in from the courtyard, her little hands covering her ears, eyes wide. "Mommy, what's all the noise about?" she cried.

The other three girls were only a split second behind her, running inside, their eyes round with fear. Clinging to Sarah, the girls watched through the windows as crowds of people flocked into the street. Babies screamed. Children ran in all directions. Dogs howled. Horses whinnied and pulled at their bridles, several managing to break loose. And buggies went careening down the streets, imperiling everyone in their way. Still the bells continued their peeling, and the guns continued to boom.

"Mommy, has the war started?" Mary Frances screamed over the noise. "Oh, where's Father?"

"I don't know, Mary Frances. I haven't seen him. Please help me hold onto Claudia and Sudie. We must be sure they don't get trampled or wander out the door," Sarah cried, distraught herself as she pressed her screaming toddler to her breast and squeezed Maria's hand as tightly as possible while the child continued to cry and gasp for breath.

After what seemed like hours, the noise suddenly stopped, and with it the commotion. Everyone stood in stark terror—waiting. Suddenly, from a good ways down King Street, Sarah heard shouts and the pounding of feet—hundreds of feet. The children clung to their mother's skirt and hid their faces. Suddenly the door burst open. Several young men yelling and waving muskets ran into the lobby and up the stairs—two at a time.

"Mother, stop them!" Sudie cried out in terror.

"How could anyone stop them?" Sarah asked—as much to herself as to her daughter—listening to the feet pounding above their heads.

There was a general shout from collective voices upstairs and in the street, and the pounding of feet resumed, running downstairs this time. When the men reached the landing, the two in front raised the U. S. flag taken from the hotel veranda and, holding it over their heads, ran for the door. Throwing the flag onto the cobblestones in front of the hotel, they motioned to a man with a torch, who soon set it on fire—the fiery tongues licking the air before the inn.

"Long live the Confederacy!" The cry rose with the flames from the burning flag until the whole street was alive with deafening noise and choking smoke.

"Come to that" it had at last as North Carolina's convention in Raleigh passed a secession ordinance on May 20, 1861.

CHAPTER NINETEEN
May 1861

I'M SO SORRY YOU had to go through all the turmoil this afternoon by yourself," Henry told Sarah that evening after the last celebrant had finally left the Tavern Room and they were tidying up.

"It was really a scare," Sarah answered. "I had no idea what was happening. The girls were so frightened, and Pattie wouldn't stop screaming. It was a nightmare. I'll never forget the sound of all those bells and guns going off at the same time. I know I'll hear them in my dreams for years to come."

"I was at the *Hillsborough Recorder* office—along with half of the town, it seemed—waiting for the paper to come out. I tried to get to you—but no one could ever have made it across the street with all the running and loose horses and buggies," Henry added.

"There wasn't much you could have done, anyway," Sarah said. "The mob was too unruly. I just felt so helpless when all those soldiers pushed their way in here and ran upstairs—and Sudie was begging me to 'do something.' I honestly can't think of anything I could have done to protect us or the hotel. I've never known such a helpless feeling," Sarah said, sitting down wearily and shaking her head.

"I hope it's an experience you'll never have to relive. But it was good for business—you can't deny that! All the tables were filled tonight, and they're likely to be each night until this crisis is over," Henry concluded with a sweeping gesture at the disarray.

"The business is too good right now, I'm afraid. If many more things happen around here, we'll never keep up with all the demands. It's so late, and I'm exhausted," Sarah put in.

"Go to bed, Honey. I can handle this. You really do look tired. Are you feeling all right?" Henry asked, lifting her face into the lamp light.

"It's been such an exhausting day with the children, the excitement, and all the customers. I'm sure I'll be fine after a good night's sleep," Sarah responded, refusing to meet his eyes.

"Nonetheless, I want you to see Dr. Strudwick as soon as possible," Henry replied. "We can't have you getting sick. Now go on up. I'll finish here," he concluded, watching her drag herself upstairs with no further protest.

I, FOR ONE, feel we've done the right thing," Henry said the next morning as he took a rare moment to drink a cup of coffee with his brothers before they left for the office. "As you know, I was dead-set against secession from the first. But now I'm proud of our state. We didn't leave when the others did. We waited to give Lincoln and the new administration a chance. No one can say North Carolina seceded from the Union because of Southern sentiment or to protect our 'privileged lifestyle'—such as it is," he grinned, sweeping his hand around the dining room filled with dirty dishes.

"Our state gave Lincoln every chance. We felt we needed 'just cause' to secede, and his decision to make war on the South was that cause. We can do no more than support the other Southern states in repelling this tyranny," Henry concluded.

"I'm glad you feel that way because you may have to sacrifice more than most if it's a lengthy war," Cave answered.

"What do you mean?" Henry asked, puzzled.

"The Confederacy is going to demand a lot of all of us in both money and manpower. We have no treasury to fall back on as the United States does. And it costs money to buy weapons, feed the troops, care for the horses. . . Why, we don't even have any currency at the moment. What are these people paying you with?" he asked.

"I hadn't even thought of that!" Henry said. "I suppose U. S. currency is worthless to us now."

"And the Confederate currency will be even more worthless, with no gold to back it up," Cave continued. "I predict an economic crisis such as we have never seen, and the first place people will cut back is on extras, such as travel and dinner out. This little establishment of yours—full as it is right now—may be empty in just a few months. Then, how will you feed your family? Never counted on that, in your patriotic zeal, did you?"

"But a war—if we have one—won't last long," Alfred said. "No one in the North really wants a war. I don't think they'll sustain Lincoln's little skirmishes for very long."

"We already have a fairly large volunteer army. And with all the states joining together, we should offer quite a good defense," Henry offered.

"I suspect Great Britain will recognize the Confederacy," Alfred added. "They depend too much on our raw cotton for their manufacturing to let us linger over a conflict and leave the fields fallow."

"I wouldn't count on any support but what we can provide ourselves," Cave said, shaking his head. "Great Britain has a lot at stake with the Republic as well. I believe they'll wait to see which way the wind blows before throwing in their hat."

"Well I've thrown mine in!" Colonel Tew commented, joining them at the table. "I've just been down to enlist. They've given me command of the Second Regiment. I leave in two weeks."

"But what about the academy?" Henry asked, his mouth agape. "How will they get on without you?"

"School will be out in two weeks, and I'll have the whole summer. If we can't make old Abe back off by then, we're not worth our stuff. Why, General Robert E. Lee has resigned from the U. S. Army and joined the Confederacy, and men are joining up all over the South.

"I love my school. But I'm a military man first and foremost. When there's fighting to do, I intend to be there. Although, I'll admit, it will be hard to call those familiar blue uniforms the 'enemy.' Hope I can keep things straight!" he chuckled. "How about you three young bucks? Are you joining up? I could use you in my regiment."

"I think you'd better take another look," Alfred laughed. "We may look like 'young bucks' to you, but I'm forty-two years old and Henry and Cave will be forty this fall. Unlike you, we're not military men. And nobody would want to take the time to train us at our age. No, we'll keep the home fires burning and leave the fighting to the younger men. Although I'm willing to do whatever I can here to help the cause."

"Alfred's right. A battle zone is no place for middle-aged men—unless they're commanding," Henry added. "But we wish you all the best. We'll miss you."

"Are you going somewhere, Colonel Tew?" Sarah asked, untying her bonnet as she entered the room.

"I've enlisted, my dear. I'm taking over the command of the Second Regiment of North Carolina. We leave in two weeks," Colonel Tew repeated.

"But. . . so soon? I had no idea they would be enlisting men already for the war. Henry. . .," she gasped, turning to her husband with a stricken look.

"Fear not, fair damsel," Cave grinned. "Your husband and his brothers, young and virile though we may still appear to you, are over the hill as far as the military is concerned. They need young, strong constitutions. And I'm afraid ours have suffered somewhat over the years," he added, patting his midsection.

"Actually, we were wishing Colonel Tew well and promising to keep the home fires going," Henry grinned. "You can't get rid of me that fast!"

"Oh, you gave me such a fright," Sarah added. "I'd hate to try to handle things by myself right now."

"You're right. But Cave predicts a great slowdown in business," Henry laughed, looking at a stream of people arriving with copies of the day's newspaper under their arms. "Business calls, gentlemen. 'Make hay while the sun shines,' a wise man once said. Sarah, it's harvest time."

∼ ∼ ∼

THANK HEAVEN YOU'RE not enlisting," Sarah cried to her husband after the morning crowd had dispersed.

"Is it me you don't want to lose—or is it that you don't want to be left with all the work?" Henry teased.

"I wish you wouldn't joke so at a time like this," Sarah said, lowering her head.

"Time like what?" Henry asked. "Nothing has changed yet. I'm still here. Our hotel's intact. You must stop worrying so about the future."

"I'm only worried about January right now," Sarah said quietly. "I'm going to need some help until then. If you want me to take over after that, I'm sure I can."

"January?" Henry asked.

"That's when our baby's due," Sarah answered, turning to look at her husband's face. "I've just come from Dr. Strudwick."

"Why, that's perfect news!" Henry shouted. "A real little Confederate," he added with a smile, embracing his wife just as the door opened.

"Still celebrating the secession, I see," John said, smirking as he and Tibitha walked in. "Trust Henry to get the most out of every situation!"

"Actually, no," Sarah added, her face coloring as she tidied her hair. "We're thinking a little farther down the road. We're planning to do our part to help populate this new country of ours."

"Another new baby? How wonderful! At least, I think it's wonderful?" Tibitha questioned, looking from one face to the other.

"Tibitha, you goose. Have you ever seen two people more ecstatic in your life? Tell you what, we'll just stroll to the corner or something and come back later so you can finish that celebration you were beginning when we so rudely interrupted. Congratulations, you two," John called out, smiling, propelling his wife back through the door.

"Now, where were we?" Henry began, circling Sarah's waist as she playfully pulled away. "I thought they'd never leave."

≈ ≈ ≈

As HENRY HAD said, the wheels did grind slowly, and little was accomplished by either side throughout the early summer of 1861. Life in Hillsborough returned to normal—except for the militia, which drilled each day in front of the courthouse.

It was a hot day in late July. Sarah was sitting on the shaded bench while Claudia and Maria climbed the magnolia tree and Pattie played beneath it. It was good to feel peaceful again, Sarah thought. It seemed she had worried needlessly about the future.

Things didn't seem to be going too badly in the Confederacy. The new government had levied a tax on the citizens, but that was to be expected. And it was not any more than she and Henry could afford—for the time being.

Several men from the Hillsborough area, including Willie and Simeon, had left town to join garrisons in other cities. Many had gone with Colonel Tew. For the most part, however, the people she knew and loved were still around. No further skirmishes had erupted after the crisis at Fort Sumter, and it seemed Lincoln might allow the South to drift away unmolested.

Feeling a caress on the back of her neck, Sarah opened her eyes and looked up at Henry's smiling face. "I thought you had a lodge meeting," she said, rolling her head and enjoying the neck rub.

"Over," Henry answered, coming to sit beside her. "I stopped at the post office. There's a letter from Colonel Tew. I thought we'd read it together."

"No action," Colonel Tew wrote. "We're at rather a stalemate. I'm champing to get this over with. I have a school to run!"

"How like him," Sarah smiled. "He should be happy there's not much action. Every day without a skirmish brings us closer to a peaceful break, doesn't it?"

"I'd like to think so," Henry nodded. "I'm anxious to have peace again by the time the baby's born—although the state of war so far has posed no real problem."

"Think again!" Cave cried, strolling into the courtyard, waving an afternoon copy of the *Hillsborough Recorder*.

"Has something happened?" Henry asked anxiously, turning to look at his brother as he slowly strode to the bench, enjoying keeping his audience in suspense.

"Only a major battle—or perhaps a stage show, from the paper's description. It seems old Abe got tired of waiting and decided to create his own action by sending Governor Winfield Scott out for some target practice on our brothers at Bull Run, near Washington.

"It was no secret, and our troops were ready. But hundreds of people from the Washington area came out to watch the show. They hoped to watch 'Johnny Reb' run with his tail between his legs," Cave reported.

"And did we run?" Sarah asked.

"On the contrary, my dear," Cave smiled. "Our Rebs sent those Yanks packing. You could see those blue coats on the run all the way to Washington. I hope old Abe is satisfied with his little drama."

"That's wonderful news, isn't it?" Sarah asked, turning to Henry—her eyes alight.

"Sounds good to me! The first major victory, and more to come. At this rate, Colonel Tew may indeed be back for school in September. I'll bet he's sorry he wasn't there," Henry answered.

"Have you heard from him, then?" Cave asked, folding the paper and putting it back under his arm.

"Just received a letter today," Henry announced, handing it to Cave to read. "He's in Sharpsburg—according to the postmark. And he's complaining as usual about not enough action. That old man surely likes to be in the thick of things."

"Better him than me," Cave responded. "I like it as far away from the action as possible."

Henry opened his mouth to respond when he noticed Lucy gesturing to him from behind Sarah's back. He raised an eyebrow at her and quickly excused himself. As he approached the steps, Lucy motioned him inside.

"Mister Henry," she said, head lowered, "I sure am glad you're here. I don't want to disturb Miss Sarah any more than is necessary right now. But we has got a big problem."

"What is it, Lucy, another fire in the kitchen?" Henry asked.

"I wish it was that simple," Lucy replied, shaking her head. "It's the food, Mr. Henry. We've run outa so many things. Why, we don't got no more butter. . . We're down to the end of the last pound!" Lucy answered, eyes round with worry.

"Then we'll just have to order more," Henry said.

"That's just the point," Lucy responded in a low voice, not daring to look Henry in the eye. "When I was down to the market with Miss Sarah today, I heard some talk. There was lots of people askin' for butter. The man there, though, he says they's gonna 'play heck'—those were his words, Mister Henry—they's gonna 'play heck' gettin' any more butter 'cause we can't get no more supplies from up North," Lucy added at last.

"I can't believe that. I never even thought. . . Don't you suppose somebody in the whole Confederacy can make butter?" Henry mused.

"Do you want Cook and me to try?" Lucy asked. "I ain't never done it, Mister Henry, but I can learn."

"Let me ask Cave to try to find out the full story first. If anybody knows what strings to pull to get us some butter, it will be Cave. In the meantime, ask Cook to put strawberry jam out instead," Henry answered, returning to the courtyard.

"Cave," he asked, coming back to the bench. "What do you know about a butter shortage?"

"So it's hit already, has it?" Cave smiled knowingly. "A bit sooner than expected. But it's not surprising."

"You mean you knew there would be a shortage?" Henry bellowed.

"Are we out?" Sarah asked. "Lucy should have told me. I could have gotten some today when we were at the market."

"Lucy says there isn't any to be had. She asked around today," Henry said, turning to his wife.

"Considering that few of you Confederate souls ever deemed it necessary to learn to make butter—or many other commodities as well—when our northern neighbors did it so well, it was to be expected that, once supplies were cut off from the North, we Southerners would have to do without—or learn a new skill," Cave answered.

"I suppose I'll have to take Lucy up on her offer," Henry said grimly, rising to return to the house.

≈ ≈ ≈

SARAH?" MARTHA CALLED as she, Maria, and Harriett banged through the hotel door out of breath. Stopping to wipe her brow, Sarah came out of the dining room where she had been arranging tables for the noon meal. "Are you busy?" Martha asked, thinking better of their hurried entrance. "We can come back. . ."

"Oh, no. I've actually plenty of time. Nobody seems to be in a mood for eating right now, if you understand what I mean," Sarah answered.

"Well, that's good!" Harriett said. Then, blushing as she realized how her statement had sounded, she continued, "It's just that, if you're not busy, maybe you can help us."

"Whatever it is, I'll do my best," Sarah promised, leading the three to seats on the lobby sofa.

"Don't agree too soon, or you may want to bite your tongue," Maria laughed, her large blue eyes alight beneath dark lashes. "It will be a lot of work. Susan Graham and several other women in town are starting a Ladies' Aid Society to feed the soldiers on the trains on their way to Virginia. We thought we could fix them meals and deliver them to the trains while they're waiting to take on more soldiers. Don't you think it's a great idea?"

"It sounds very admirable," Sarah answered. "But how do you plan to get enough food? Where will you prepare it? Do you have any idea how much equipment and preparation time you're talking about? Running this place, I can tell you. . ."

"That's where you come in," Harriett smiled, her deep violet eyes flashing with excitement. She tossed her dark ringlets and looked away for a moment, waiting for Sarah to ask what they wanted.

"All right, I suppose I must ask," Sarah said, smiling at the coyness Harriett displayed. "Although it's a good thing I'm here instead of Henry. He would have turned over the whole hotel to you by now. I declare, Harriett, save your coquetry for the soldiers. Better yet, don't. We can't have them all deserting here in Hillsborough to follow you home," she joked.

"What we really need," Martha continued in a businesslike manner, replacing the pins in her neat bun as she removed her bonnet, "is a place to cook the food. And we all thought that the hotel kitchen would be perfect. We could come in every morning and fix chicken, cornbread, and sandwiches and fill food baskets for the trains."

"We've already gotten permission from the North Carolina Railroad to board the trains at the station," Maria added hastily. "Lots of people have volunteered chicken, ham, vegetables, and corn meal. Say you'll help, Sarah, please. We rather promised Susan Graham."

Sarah laughed. "How is it only the eligible members of the family are so concerned with the soldiers' well-being? What about Mother, Susan, Jane, and Julia? Are they involved in this scheme too?"

"Don't admonish us for being patriotic," Harriett pouted.

"Actually, Mother, Jane, and Julia have formed a sewing circle to make winter clothes for the soldiers in Willie and Simeon's regiment," Martha interrupted. "Mother doesn't get out much, and Jane and Julia could not go to the depot with the children to worry about.

"Susan's helping Francis through the church," she continued. "She's been going door-to-door soliciting blankets, shoes, gloves, and other clothing to send to the soldiers. But we like this idea. We can do something for the soldiers right now to make their sendoff more pleasant. What do you say? You can just supervise and not even go to the station," Martha concluded.

"Well, the kitchen does belong to Cook and Lucy, so we'll have to ask them. But if they don't mind, I'm with you. I know Henry will cooperate. He's already been bringing new recruits in here while they wait for the next troop train," Sarah smiled.

"Well, what are we waiting for? Let's ask them!" Harriett said, jumping up and heading for the door.

~ ~ ~

AFTER THE BATTLE of Bull Run, the Union forces had ceased a lot of activity in Virginia. Now the sparsely-populated and poorly-protected area of coastal North Carolina had become Lincoln's next target. With no large port city, no industry, few inhabitants, and a myriad of swamps and sounds, the coastal area had been all but forgotten by Richmond, as the South concentrated its efforts on Savannah, Charleston, and the James River access to Richmond.

It should not have been a surprise, then, when the news reached Raleigh in October that Fort Hatteras—on the easternmost point of North Carolina—had fallen into Union hands. Any attempt to protect the rest of the area was a case of "too little, too late," as force after force attacked other coastal forts and cities in North Carolina throughout the winter and spring.

Chapter Twenty
January 1862

Henry," Dr. Strudwick called out, opening the door of his small house on the outskirts of town, "what brings you out on such a night?" Pulling his dressing gown tighter around him as the wind whistled into the vestibule, he motioned Henry inside and pulled the door closed.

"It's Sarah, Edmund. She thinks it's time. After her incident with Rebecca, she's rather nervous and wants you there. Can you come?" Henry asked, brushing the snowflakes off his hat and cloak and hanging them by the door.

"As soon as I get dressed and get my bag. I'll only be a moment. But you should be with her. You could have sent Tom and not had to leave her," the old man admonished.

"You're forgetting the law," Henry smiled ruefully. "Servants can't be out after dark. Tom was willing to risk arrest for us. But I wouldn't hear of it."

"Ridiculous law, isn't it? Who would suspect the servants in the families I tend to start an insurrection?" the doctor mused, walking toward his bedroom and shaking his head. "What is this world coming to?"

I HATED TO call you so soon," Sarah apologized when Dr. Strudwick entered the room and nodded to Lucy, sitting in the far corner tending the fire. "It's just that—you know—I want to be sure everything is all right."

"Of course. And you were right to do so," Dr. Strudwick said to cover her obvious embarrassment at being such a nuisance. "With the seventh birth, things can come pretty fast. And the snow is getting deeper. If we'd waited much longer, I might not have been able to come," he concluded.

"I'm sure you have patients who need you more," Sarah added.

"None more important than you," the doctor smiled, opening his bag. "Actually, it's a treat to be in on the advent of a new life. I'm rather tired right now of treating the frostbite cases sent back from Northern Virginia or the many cases of influenza we have daily arriving on the trains.

"I tell you," he said, turning to Henry, "some of these boys aren't ever going to be the same again. There are so few doctors on the front lines, the equipment is so primitive, and the conditions are so unsanitary. You wouldn't believe how many cases of gangrene I'm seeing sent home. By the time I get them, there's little left to do but amputate—fingers, hands, toes, legs. Not many will push a plow again. And what will the South do then? What fools we were to think it would be over in a matter of weeks.

"But on to more pleasant things. . .," the doctor continued, turning back to Sarah. "Not long now, or I miss my guess," he smiled, dropping Sarah's wrist after taking her pulse. "Got a name for this new little miss yet?"

"Do you think it's another girl?" Sarah asked, looking at him in the dim light.

"What else would a Holeman or a Stroud have, I want to know?" the doctor joked. "After thirteen of you women, it would be too much of a shock to see a boy appear."

"But we have both names picked out, just in case," Sarah smiled, then stopped as a contraction gripped her and she grimaced in pain. As the contraction lessened, she continued. "If it's a boy, we want to name him 'Edmund' after you. You've seen us through so much."

"I can't think of a nicer honor. Thank you. But I'm afraid that won't do for a girl," he chuckled.

"If it's a girl," Henry added quietly, "we could use Edmund for a middle name. Don't you think so, Sarah?"

"'Annie Edmund.' Yes, that would be nice. Would that be all right with you?" she asked the doctor.

"Sounds perfect," he said, smiling. "I can't lose either way. Now, let's get this young 'un here before morning."

≈ ≈ ≈

LITTLE ANNIE EDMUND did, indeed, appear before morning, crying lustily and waking the whole household. She was a petite child, but no one could tell it from the size of her lungs, Henry laughed to John and Tibitha when they walked over later in the day. Annie resembled Claudia a great deal, with fair skin and hair. But her scant bit of hair was strawberry blond rather than the flaxen color of Claudia's. She was a lusty howler, and, after only a few nights, the other girls were complaining they could not get any sleep.

≈ ≈ ≈

DURING HER CONVALESCENCE, Sarah's only contacts with the war were tales Henry brought from the Tavern Room, and often she was already asleep when he tiptoed in. "It must be bad when even Colonel Tew is tired of the fighting," Sarah laughed to Henry one April afternoon as they sat in the courtyard reading the old man's letter and watching Annie. "Is it as bad as he makes it sound?"

"Probably worse," Henry answered, shaking his head. "Nobody envisioned the war would last so long. The Confederacy has lost a lot of men, and the number of new volunteers has reduced to a trickle. Just drive past a depot and see the countless pine boxes and stretchers. It's enough to scare any would-be volunteer.

"President Davis and his advisors have realized that and just today issued a Conscription Act, which allows them to draft all men between the ages of sixteen and thirty-five," he added, pausing for his wife's reaction.

"How can they do that? We've never forced people into the military in the entire history of our country. Isn't that the sort of despotism we sought to avoid when we left the Union?" Sarah asked, aghast at the thought of forcing men to fight for the cause.

"Times are different now. We're no longer in the Republic, remember? So our leaders no longer need to play by the rules. And there is a need—there's no denying that," Henry added sadly. "The Union forces have overrun the coastal areas. New Bern and several other cities have fallen. And Wilmington is the only Confederate seaport left in the whole state. We need to shore up the defenses. I suppose conscription is the only way."

"But there are so many men needed at home to run the farms. Will there be exemptions?" Sarah asked.

"Not if we can believe Davis's proclamation. He's threatening to send government agents to enforce his law," Henry sighed. "It's a sad state for all of us."

"What if he still doesn't get enough men with the new law?" Sarah asked, her eyes suddenly wide as she grabbed Henry's arm. "What if he raises the age for drafting men? Would you have to go as well? I'm not sure I could bear it."

"He'd have to raise the age to forty-five to get me. I don't see even Jefferson Davis being so foolish as to expect men my age to fight. Let's not borrow trouble," Henry assured her, patting the hand she had placed on his arm. "Now I'd better see to dinner—in case anyone shows up."

≈ ≈ ≈

AUGUST SAW THE inauguration of a new North Carolina governor, Zebulon Vance. Vance, who had recently fought in Virginia, was young and strong and seemed to have great charisma. The state's spirits ran high in late summer of 1862. But still the war dragged on.

It was a warm September day. Sarah was hard at work, trying to make the books balance. It had been a lean year. The new Confederate taxes had created an additional burden. With the taxes and the food Henry gave away to soldiers passing through town, it was doubtful there would be any profit at all.

Sarah was so hard at work that she did not notice the door open. She started when she looked up to see Alfred leaning on the desk, a newspaper tucked under his arm. "Where's Annie?" Alfred asked solemnly.

"Sleeping, thank goodness," Sarah smiled. "What brings you over? Did you want to see Henry?"

"Both of you, I'm afraid," Alfred answered.

"He's in the kitchen checking supplies with Cook. I'll call him if you like," Sarah offered.

"Could you, please? I'll just wait here," Alfred said.

"Good of you to come by. What can we do for you?" Henry called to his brother as he and Sarah entered the parlor.

"Sit down, Henry. You, too, Sarah. I'm afraid I have bad news," Alfred answered, offering the paper he had placed on his lap. "The Second Regiment was attacked at Sharpsburg. The paper is terming it a massacre. Most of the regiment was killed."

"Colonel Tew?" Sarah asked in alarm, turning to Alfred.

"I'm afraid so," Alfred said. "See for yourself."

Unfolding the paper, Henry read the headline: "Hillsborough's Colonel Tew and Cadets Killed in Sharpsburg Massacre." Handing it over to Sarah, he put his head in his hands and wept. "All he wanted was to help the Confederacy. He didn't even believe in secession. Yet, he enlisted because he believed in the South. And all those fine young men he took with him. . . It's such a waste. Such a waste!" he continued, turning to Sarah, who buried her face in his shoulder.

The three sat in silence for several minutes. "I feel so guilty," Henry said. "Colonel Tew asked us all that evening to join him in his regiment, and we refused. He fought for over a year while we sat here and enjoyed life as usual."

"Henry," Sarah said, raising her head to look at her husband through tear-swollen eyes, "you can't mean that. You have a job to do, just as he did. Colonel Tew was trained in the military. It was right that he should go. He wouldn't have had it any other way. He volunteered himself. At least he died doing what he loved."

"Still, it's hard to sit back and let others do the fighting for us," Henry added.

"But you, Alfred, and Cave have kept Colonel Tew's dream alive by overseeing his academy in his absence. You've been of far more use to him there—and will continue to be—than if you had perished by his side," Sarah reasoned. "Men and women will die. But dreams can live on—if they are entrusted to the right people.

"Colonel Tew once told me he'd never had anyone to share his dream. Then he found you, Henry. You built that academy together, brick by brick. Now it's up to you to keep it going in his memory. The war will end someday. And we owe it to our children and grandchildren to see that something is left of the world we knew and loved. Perhaps we can do more by seeing to that than by fighting. We all must serve in our own way," she concluded, tears streaming down her face.

≈ ≈ ≈

THE MASSACRE'S REPERCUSSIONS went far beyond the death of Colonel Tew and some of the brightest minds of the state—his cadets who perished along with him on that hot September day. After losing so many men, President Davis raised the age of conscription to forty-five, which included all three of the Stroud brothers, as well as John Quackenbush.

"But he has yet to issue us our orders," John said one evening in the Tavern. "And with it being so late in the year, maybe we can make it through the winter before we're impressed."

"There are exemptions we can plead," Cave said.

"On what basis?" John inquired. "'My wife and daughter need me' hardly seems a fitting reason. And with so many men gone in town, we've done little legal work for the last year, so I can hardly plead that. No, I shall go when called and try to serve with honor. I'll trust in God to care for Tibitha and Elizabeth. The women will have each other. They'll survive."

"I suppose with feeding and housing the soldiers who pass through Hillsborough, I could ask for an exemption. But I should hate myself if others had to fight in my place. Besides, Sarah's quite capable of running the hotel alone. Although I shall hate leaving, I, too, will go when called and serve to the best of my ability," Henry answered.

"As will I," Alfred nodded.

"Then I suppose it will be up to me to 'keep the home fires burning,' as they say," Cave said, drawing on his pipe. "For I intend to stay right here."

≈ ≈ ≈

JOHN QUACKENBUSH RECEIVED his wish when victories at Fredericksburg, Virginia, in December and at Chancellorsville,

Virginia, in May buoyed the spirits of the South. The new age was not enforced yet.

Defeats of the Confederate forces at Vicksburg and Gettysburg on the same day—July 4, 1863—changed the tide of the war, however. And Richmond finally issued the order that would bring Alfred, Henry, and John into the war. True to his word, Cave was able to elicit an exemption and remain behind.

~ ~ ~

IT WAS A tearful farewell that summer night of 1863. Henry and Sarah closed the hotel and planned a family dinner to say goodbye to the three men. John would report to the Virginia forces as a captain of a regiment. Alfred and Henry were to stay in North Carolina and help with the coastal defenses. It was a sad time for everyone.

Cook had done her best—with the many food shortages created by the conflict—to provide one of her sumptuous dinners. And Sarah had announced it was to be a celebration—not a wake. She wanted everyone to remember happy times and look forward to the end of the hostilities. Try as they might, however, no one could forget the maimed who hobbled off of the train daily, nor the rows of homemade coffins that lined the sidings after the trains had left. Before the meal, Henry offered a prayer that they would all soon be together again for good—perhaps by Christmas. After the "Amen," there was complete silence as each offered his own prayer for the men's safety and for the families they were leaving behind.

Suddenly, Pattie jumped from her chair and threw herself into Henry's arms. "Don't go, Daddy!" she cried, burying her face into his shoulder. "I don't want you to go."

"Oh, please stay here," Maria burst out. "I'm afraid you won't come home—just like Colonel Tew."

"Of course I'll come home," Henry said, attempting a smile over Pattie's head. "We'll all be home—probably before you even miss us."

"But why do you and Uncle Alfred and Uncle John have to go at all?" Claudia asked. "I thought you were too old to be soldiers."

"Not any more," Alfred smiled, turning to her. "With the battles spread over so many areas, it seems that President Davis needs all of us 'old men,' too, so the war will be over sooner."

"But Uncle Cave doesn't have to go," Sudie put in. "Why doesn't he have to go? It isn't fair."

"Uncle Cave is doing important work here in town. He's serving in his own way," Henry added, glad that Cave had wisely declined the invitation to come tonight.

"Well, isn't what you're doing important, too?" Claudia asked. "Running the hotel and taking in the soldiers seems very important to me. And Uncle Alfred runs the company the same as Uncle Cave. . ."

"Children," Sarah interrupted, "there's a war going on—a very important war. If we lose, everything we know and love will change. You've had your daddy here longer than most children in the South. Now he and Alfred and John are needed to help bring everything to a close. We must let them go so that all the men can get home sooner."

"It doesn't seem fair that anyone should have to go to war," Elizabeth said. "It's such a waste. I knew so many of the cadets in Colonel Tew's regiment. . ."

"It isn't the same, Elizabeth. The older men won't be on the front lines," Tibitha interrupted in an attempt to change the subject. She knew the same thought was racing through every mind at that moment.

"But when will you all be home, Father?" Mary Frances asked. "It won't be the same without all of you."

"I know, Sweetheart. But it won't be for too long. Maybe we can all get home for Christmas. We'll gather right here again as we always do. And we'll have lots to be thankful for," Henry added, guessing her thoughts and trying to be cheerful.

"To Christmas!" John boomed, lifting his tumbler. The other adults, eager to end the sad scene with the children, also lifted their glasses. Finally, one by one, the children did the same.

Annie, not understanding any of the commotion but wanting to get into the act, banged her spoon on her high chair and squealed until everyone burst into laughter—dispelling the gloom.

"At least it won't be dull here," Henry laughed, tousling the child's curls and kissing the wet, sticky little face covered with mashed potatoes.

≈ ≈ ≈

SARAH," HENRY SAID that evening when they were alone in bed and she lay with her head on his shoulder, "I'm pleased that you want to keep the hotel going in my absence. I know you'll do a good job. But I want you to promise me something."

"What is it?" Sarah asked, turning a tear-stained face to her husband.

"I want you to promise me that if the burden ever gets too heavy or the situation too dangerous, you and the children will go to Cave. He'll take care of all of you as if you were his own. I'm glad he's staying behind to look after our interests," he continued, kissing her forehead. "And if something should happen to me. . .," he continued, stopping abruptly when Sarah pulled back to look at him and put her finger over his lips.

"Well," he shrugged, "I just want you to know Cave will take care of everything. I've given him control of all our finances. You're in good hands. Now, may I have that promise?"

"I promise I'll do what I think best. And I'll consider your wishes. Our family's safety and well-being will be my first concern," Sarah said, her eyes filled with tears. "I can't promise more than that. No one knows what life will deal us in the months ahead. I can only do what my reason dictates—no more, no less. If I need Cave, I'll call on him. Does that relieve your mind?"

"I suppose, knowing you, I must be content with that," Henry smiled. "You never were one to obey orders. But it was your spirit that drew me to you all those years ago. And it will see you through all that lies ahead. I know it won't be easy. Caring for the hotel, the children, and your mother's place will be a monumental task. I know, however, that you're up to it. And you—if anyone—will survive this turmoil and be waiting with open arms when I return.

"I'll worry about you and the girls every moment of every day. And I'll write every chance I get. I'll want to know all the news from home—both good and bad. I'm pleased you, at least, will be in familiar surroundings. You'll have so many family members to lean on if you need them. Somehow, though, I feel they will be doing most of the leaning. Don't let it get too burdensome, Sarah. Remember, this war can't last forever. And I will be home as soon as I can. . ." He stopped, tears filling his eyes, and hugged Sarah—as if for the last time.

Chapter Twenty-one
September 1863

Henry's letters were long, frequent, and full of news. He was in charge of a Confederate regiment operating at Kinston in coastal North Carolina. Their job was to protect the city of Wilmington and the Wilmington and Weldon Railroad, which was an important link with the other states of the Confederacy.

Nearby New Bern had fallen to the Union forces in 1862. There were more than 12,000 Union soldiers garrisoned there, and Lincoln had even appointed a Union governor for the region—giving the state, in effect, two governors.

Major General French, the commander of the Confederate forces on the coast, had enough men—with the infusion of those in Henry's regiment—to create a stalemate and hold off the Union forces from further advancement. However, Henry wrote, it did not look likely that they would be able to eject the Union troops or prevent the constant raiding parties, which were plaguing the few residents who remained. Therefore, until Davis sent more troops into the area, there did not seem any likelihood of actual combat.

It eased Sarah's mind to know her husband was not involved in active combat and was relatively close to home. She
was attempting as best she could to keep the hotel running
while waiting for each letter and newspaper.

One warm afternoon in mid-September, Sarah was sitting
in the courtyard with Pattie and Annie waiting for the older
girls to return from school when she heard buggy wheels approach—a rare occurrence these days when so many of the
family buggies had been impressed for military use. Rising
from the bench, she walked slowly around the side of the hotel
where she was surprised to see Aaron helping her mother alight.

"Mother," she called, "the children and I are out back. How
good to see you!"

Hearing her daughter's voice, Jean rounded the side of
the house and caught her daughter in a warm embrace.

"I hope nothing has happened," Sarah whispered, pulling
back to look her mother in the eye. Being so isolated from the
rest of her family, she worried constantly about her sisters'
husbands who were away at war—and her sisters, who had been
left so vulnerable in their various homes.

"Nothing to worry about," Jean smiled. "I just had something to discuss with you and decided this was probably the
best time. Am I right?"

"Perfect timing," Sarah smiled back, relieved. "We're just
waiting for the girls to get home. But I know two others who
will be glad to see you!"

When she saw her grandmother, Pattie ran to her and
jumped into her arms. Hugging the little girl to her, Jean smiled
at Sarah over her head. "It takes only one look at these precious children to understand why our men feel the need to
protect our new country. Although, at such a cost!" she added,
shaking her head as she placed Pattie back on the ground and
watched her run off. Then picking up little Annie, who was

playing on a blanket nearby, she sat down beside Sarah on the bench and put the baby on her lap.

"Speaking of the men, what do you hear from Henry?" Jean asked, looking at Sarah over Annie's head and trying to assess her mood.

"Thankfully, he's still on sentry duty and hasn't seen any action," Sarah smiled. "Things seem to be at a stalemate all over, though. I almost wish for something to break and bring this war to a close. I'm not sure how much longer we can go on. The taxes are eating us up. And you wouldn't believe the number of goods we can't get and the prices on the things we can!

"Flour has doubled in cost during the last year. Bacon—if we can get it—has tripled. Corn meal has quadrupled. And ham is almost unavailable. There you have our standard menu—shot through with as many holes as if it had been before a Union firing squad! You're lucky to have your own farm. At least you and the girls won't starve," Sarah concluded, turning to her mother.

"Actually, that's what I've come to tell you. I've made a decision. After the fall harvest is in, I intend to close the plantation. It's too much for me to handle. And with Henry gone now, the burden will fall to you. You have so much to do here that I can't ask you to do more. No, let me finish," she interjected as Sarah began to protest. "I've given it a lot of thought. I'll close up the house for the time being and not plant for next year. It will do the soil good to lie fallow for a while, anyway. The servants will stay on. They have nowhere else to go. When the war is over, if I decide to, I'll move back," Jean announced.

"Where will you go?" Sarah asked. "Do you want to come here?"

"Jane's asked the girls and me to live with her. She has room. And her small farm will be much easier to manage. It will supply all the food we need. I may even bring one or two of our hands over to help out with Willie gone. It's far enough from town to give the girls a stable atmosphere," Jean concluded.

"Well, if your mind's made up. . . I'm sure Jane will enjoy the company. I've worried about her being so alone out there. Is there anything you'd like me to look out for at the plantation?" Sarah asked.

"Aaron will come for you if there's a need. And you'll send for me, I trust?" Jean asked. "Who knows? By this time next year, the war may be over and the men may be back. Now, I've lots to do, so I must get going," she said, placing a kiss on Annie's head and handing her back to Sarah as she rose. "Come to us, if you need us. Bring the children if things get dangerous here. We'll make the room. Promise me."

"I must stay here as long as I can. I promised Henry to keep things going. And I can't in good conscience leave the inn empty. But I'll come if I feel the need," Sarah promised, walking her mother to the buggy where Aaron waited.

～ ～ ～

SARAH SAT BY the fire in the lobby, watching the rain pound against the window and wondering if Henry were warm and safe. Suddenly, the door opened and Tibitha entered—wet leaves whirling around her as she quickly closed the door and brushed off her skirt.

"Letter for you, Sarah," she beamed. "Nothing from John. But I didn't expect it. His unit is in the thick of things right now, and I'm sure writing letters is the least of his priorities. But maybe you'll share Henry's news."

"Of course. Would you like some tea, Tibitha? I wouldn't palm Lucy's new 'corn coffee' off on anyone I cared about," Sarah laughed, pouring her sister-in-law a cup.

"Now, let's see what Henry has to say," Sarah began, tearing open the letter—which was a single piece of paper, folded over into an envelope.

"He says he'll be home for Christmas! What wonderful news! With no real action expected until spring, it seems that they are allowing three-day furloughs to many of the men. What fun! Wait until the girls hear. It will be a wonderful Christmas after all," she smiled. "You and Elizabeth must plan to be with us," Sarah added, placing her hand on her sister-in-law's arm.

"Thank you, Sarah. I don't know what Elizabeth and I would do without your family," Tibitha smiled. "I'm so happy for you and the girls. They'll be so excited."

"Perhaps John will come home, too," Sarah offered.

"I rather doubt it," Tibitha said ruefully. "His unit is quite involved right now. And he's much farther away. I can only pray that he stays safe and well."

JOHN DID GET to come home—well before Christmas. But it was not in the way Tibitha had hoped. She received a letter from his commanding officer in November informing her that John had been injured in action when a bullet passed through his leg, shattering the bone. He was one of the lucky ones, however, for the wound was clean and had not caused gangrene. His leg was safe. But the break was a bad one. He would probably lose a great deal of mobility—enough to earn him an honorable discharge.

On a blustery day in late November, Tibitha and Elizabeth rode with Tom in the hotel wagon to meet John's train at the Hillsborough station. Tom and Tibitha managed to get him awkwardly into the wagon, as Elizabeth settled him somewhat comfortably with pillows and blankets for the short ride home.

Although he was clearly in a lot of pain, John was ecstatic to see his family again. Never mind that he would be lame now. The war was behind him, and he was home and safe.

As HENRY STEPPED off the train, he was mobbed by six eager little girls, who ran past all the other soldiers, tripping over valises and shoes in their hurry.

"Whoa, there, Pumpkin!" one young private laughed as Pattie plunged into his leg. "Where are you headed in such a hurry?"

"My daddy just got off the train," she shouted, pulling away to head through the crowd.

"Looks like you're going to need some help getting to him," the private answered. As he spoke, he lifted her on his shoulders and, jogging like a pony, managed to break through the ranks and deposit her giggling into her father's arms.

Grabbing Henry's neck and giving him a big kiss, she looked down to gloat at all her sisters, who were just arriving.

"Thanks for the help," Henry called after the private.

"Any time, Sir," he answered with a salute. "Any man with that many women needs all the help he can get."

Henry's knapsack was bulging with mysterious packages. And Pattie and Maria couldn't help trying to peek. "Now, no looking," Henry ordered, swinging each one up onto the wagon and depositing the knapsack beside them. "I'm trusting you while my back is turned," he called, grabbing Sarah playfully around the waist as all the girls giggled.

"Henry, the children!" Sarah cried, trying to catch her bonnet before it slipped.

"I don't care if the whole town is watching. Come here, Wife," he ordered, sweeping her into his arms.

∼ ∼ ∼

CHRISTMAS DAY WAS meager in gifts, but warmer than ever in love. No one could get enough of Henry, and the girls seldom left his side. "Oh, for a moment alone," he said in an aside as he seated Sarah for breakfast.

"Later," Sarah smiled, "when your adoring public has left."

After breakfast, the parents brought out presents. There were so few this year that each opening took on a special meaning. When the few under the tree had been opened, Henry turned to the family. "Now, I have some things made by the men in my regiment. Maria, would you get my knapsack?" He smiled, remembering how much she had wanted to peek the afternoon before.

Everyone gathered around as Henry presented each package. Sarah, Mary Frances, and Sudie received beautiful keepsake boxes made of cedar. Maria and Claudia got a complete set of doll-house furniture, beautifully carved. Pattie had a cradle large enough for her favorite doll. And Annie received a set of wooden rings on a spindle. All were thrilled with the gifts.

"Oh, Henry, the presents are perfect," Sarah remarked. "How kind your men must be."

"They didn't want me to go home for Christmas empty-handed. We do a lot of waiting, so the projects helped pass the time. I guess I talk about you all the time, so they feel they know you, too. I wish you could meet them someday," Henry smiled wistfully.

"Maybe we will. I'd like that very much," Sarah added.

"There are a lot of good men out there, fighting for a cause we all believe in," Henry said. We do have a lot to be thankful for. We must remember that."

SARAH HAD GOOD cause to remember Henry's words in the weeks to come as food became scarcer and scarcer and the price of available items skyrocketed. Salt was extremely scarce, so pork could not be preserved. This meant that the ham dishes, for which the inn had been so famous, had to be scratched from the menu. Beef, too, became unavailable after military occupations cut off the inland Southern states. Fish and fowl were the only meats left. And Cook and Lucy constantly tried to find new recipes for each.

Other commodities were totally unavailable. Candles, which were needed for each room in the hotel, had to be made from pan dripping, which Cook managed to save in large containers in the kitchen. Soap had to be made with meat scraps, bones, skin, and lye, which were boiled with ashes for bonding. This mixture did remove dirt. But it also smelled awful and drew flies.

Feeding and clothing the girls had become almost a full-time job. Hand-me-downs came for Mary Frances from Harriett. Mary Frances, in turn, passed her clothes down to the other girls. Still, there were the necessary alterations and repairs. When buttons were missing, anything that would hold in a button hole was used—from beans to nuts. Leather was so scarce that when shoes were outgrown and replacements could not be found, the girls had to make do with a new variety of shoes produced in Raleigh that had leather uppers and wooden soles. The clattering of little feet on the wooden stairs became thundering, and Sarah had to hold her ears when the children ran by.

By February, Sarah was so tired she could barely drag herself out of bed. Her head pounded, and her stomach churned. "I don't know when I've felt so ill," she confided to Tibitha, who arrived one afternoon for a visit.

"Why not close the hotel for a few days?" Tibitha suggested. "There are few travelers this time of year anyway. And with the bad weather and the economy, you surely don't expect many townspeople to come in to eat."

"You don't know how tempting that idea is. But there are still the food baskets to be prepared and the soldiers to house," Sarah answered. "I couldn't turn my back on that."

"Then give me Pattie and Annie for the morning tomorrow while the other girls are in school. I have nothing planned, and John would love to see them. That should free you up to see Dr. Strudwick. Maybe he can prescribe something to help you feel better. You know Henry would order you to go if he were here," Tibitha pleaded.

Dropping the girls off the following morning, Sarah sought out Dr. Strudwick at his office. "I'm sure you have many more serious problems than mine," she apologized. "But I just can't seem to shake this. I really must get well to tend the hotel."

"Sarah," Dr. Strudwick said solemnly after giving her an examination. "I'm surprised at you."

"I don't understand," Sarah said.

"How many Strouds have I delivered?" Dr. Strudwick asked, scratching his head. "Seven by my count. . ."

"But I can't be expecting. I'm forty-one years old!" Sarah gasped. "And Henry's been at war since last fall."

"If the Lord decides to send a new life, He does it. And Henry was home at Christmas, wasn't he?" Dr. Strudwick added, trying to conceal a smile.

"But Henry. . .," Sarah began.

"Will be pleased as punch, I'll warrant. Maybe at last he'll have that boy," Dr. Strudwick finished for her. "Now, why not go home and write him the good news and leave my office for people who really need me? And, when you become one of them, I'll be here for you."

I'M THRILLED TO hear of the new baby," Henry wrote. "I hope you'll forgive me, but I couldn't keep it to myself. I think I've told everyone within earshot. The odds around here are on for a boy. I, myself, would be thrilled with another girl. But my men are betting otherwise. If it's a boy, they've promised a twenty-one-gun salute. So you must keep us informed.

"If it's a boy, I'd be honored if he held my name. If it's another girl, I can think of no more fitting name than 'Octavia,' which means 'the eighth.' I'm telling you my choices now—in case I can't get home," Henry wrote, not saying what they both knew he meant.

≈ ≈ ≈

THE EYES OF the whole South that summer of 1864 were drawn collectively to General William Tecumseh Sherman, a Union general with a new battle plan. His idea was to cut the South in two, destroy everything in his wake, demoralize the people, and prompt the soldiers to desert to protect their loved ones. It was a bold plan, but Sherman was determined.

Fresh from victory in Chattanooga, he marched his troops into Georgia. Despite a decided Confederate victory at Kenesaw Mountain in north Georgia, where nearly 2,000 Union soldiers died, Sherman's troops marched on. By July they had surrounded Atlanta. Doing his best to hold off the siege, Confederate General J.B. Hood saw his supplies cut off and his manpower dwindle in some of the costliest battles of the war. By September, Hood had no choice but to evacuate what men he still had left and leave the city of Atlanta open to Sherman's attack. Sherman's "Bummers," as they were called, proceeded to loot the city and burn everything of value, striking a totally demoralizing blow to the heart of the South.

Into the midst of the heartbreak of the loss of Atlanta came little Octavia Stroud on September 24. She was a sturdy child with the characteristic dark hair of most of the Stroud and Holeman women and a pleasant disposition—apparent almost from the first. Despite her age, Sarah had no problems with the delivery. And she sent an immediate letter to Henry announcing yet another girl.

"You can't imagine how happy I was to learn of little Octavia's birth," Henry wrote upon hearing the news. "Everyone in the barracks was excited as well, despite their hope for a boy—which I assure you was not my sentiment. All my men decided, however, that any man who could father eight girls was still worthy of a salute. Consequently, you may tell little Octavia one day that a twenty-one-gun salute was given by my men in her honor on the day we received your letter.

"I long for the time when I can get home to see you, dear Sarah, and to meet my new little girl. Under normal circumstances, I would have been allowed time off for the birth. But with the threat of Sherman ever present, not one of us can be spared. No one knows his plans after destroying Atlanta. Some say he'll proceed to Savannah. Others feel he'll head north through the Carolinas to meet with Grant near Richmond. We're on constant alert to be ready when he comes.

"Be assured my thoughts and prayers are with you constantly, and I'll return with open arms when this turmoil is over," Henry concluded.

Sarah, too, was thrilled. Octavia was a beautiful child. She was the one bright spot in the past dark year, and Sarah clung to her as if to a life-line, for she was the promise of a future that was yet to come—when the war would finally be over.

CHAPTER TWENTY-TWO
November 1864

EVEN THREE YEARS AFTER the skirmishes started, the war seemed far removed from Hillsborough. After all, Grant was in Petersburg, Virginia, and Sherman was in Georgia—both miles away. Yet worry over Sherman's next move sent men and women scurrying for each day's edition of the newspaper. And people began to flock to town once again to discuss the news and the ramifications of his march.

Finally, after Sherman's army had looted and burned most of Atlanta, troops began to move again on November 10. There was much speculation that Sherman would head north, and Sarah was worried that Henry would have to face the "Bummers" himself.

Sarah and the rest of the town felt great relief, then, when Sherman surprised everyone and headed southeast toward Savannah. It was being called the "March to the Sea," with the obvious attempt to divide the Confederacy—north from south. Everyone knew Sherman would eventually turn north again and head through the Carolinas. But any reprieve was welcomed. And people looked forward, at least, to a peaceful Christmas in the state. It was obvious, however, that there would be no holiday leaves this year.

It was a dreary day in early December, with dark clouds threatening rain. Sarah had placed Octavia's cradle near the fire in the lobby and was watching Annie play nearby when the door opened and Cave came in. Sensing Sarah's feelings— and, indeed, those of the whole family—towards him since he had claimed his exemption, he'd been a rather infrequent visitor for the past year. Sarah was startled, therefore, when she saw him.

"What brings you out on such a miserable afternoon?" she asked. "Is there any more news on Sherman's progress?"

"Not that I'm aware of," Cave answered. "Can't a body check on his favorite sister-in-law without a reason?" he smiled, walking to the desk and looking at Sarah across the wide, wooden top. "How've you been, Sarah? Are the children all right?"

"We're all well," Sarah nodded, putting her ledger aside and circling the desk to invite Cave to the settee. "Octavia's a good baby and is little trouble. Even the hotel seems to be doing better now—strange as it might seem. I think more people have been in town lately with the news over Sherman's March."

"You're looking tired, though. Has it been too much for you?" Cave asked. She wasn't sure if his voice betrayed concern or pleasure.

"We're doing all right. Of course, it's been a strain with a new baby and the war and the many substitutions we must make to keep the hotel going. But we'll manage. I only wish Henry were coming home for the holidays. It will be lonely without him. And the girls are so disappointed. They had so hoped to have him with us, if only for a few days," Sarah added.

"I should think you'd be relieved, or do you want another one of those?" he questioned, pointing to the cradle. "Seems the best thing my brother does is keep you with child. Perhaps that's his way of keeping you safe from the roues of Hillsborough and the passing soldiers," Cave said, raising an eyebrow.

"Henry and I both wanted a large family. I hardly think he has to worry about another man at my age," Sarah laughed.

"Are you so sure?" Cave asked. "You're still a very beautiful woman. But I expect you know that."

"I'm forty-two years old," Sarah replied, moving to the cradle and picking Octavia up to put her between them.

"Are you still frightened of me after all these years?" Cave laughed. "Very well. I'll pay you no more compliments and bore you with my company no longer," he added, starting to rise.

"I'm glad to see you, Cave, really I am. I don't want you to leave. I'm sorry," Sarah apologized, reaching out to touch his arm. "I guess it's been so long since I've had a compliment, I don't know how to receive one."

"Well, actually you were right when I first came in," he continued, sitting back down. "I did have another reason for coming by." Reaching into his breast pocket, he withdrew a letter. "I was at the post office when this came for you. I thought it might be important. It's from Henry's division. But it's not his handwriting," he said, handing her the letter. "Mind if I stick around and see what the news is? I'm sure the rest of the family will be interested, too."

"Of course," Sarah waved absentmindedly, placing Octavia back in her cradle and tearing open the letter.

My dear Mrs. Stroud,

I'm writing to inform you that your husband, Henry Stroud, has been in the infirmary at our post for the past several weeks suffering from influenza. Now, with the possible advent of a conflict as Sherman returns north, I'm taking the liberty of sending him home on unlimited sick leave until he feels strong enough to return to his regiment.

You can expect him on the December 22 train.

Sincerely,

Dr. Aaron Curtis

"He's coming home!" Sarah screamed. "Henry will be home in only a few days."

"But why?" Cave asked, taking the letter from her hand. "Sarah, he's ill," he said, scanning the short note. "It must be serious, or they wouldn't be sending him home."

"How serious can a case of flu be? Henry's strong. A Christmas at home will be the best medicine he could have. He'll be well in no time. Goodness, I have so much to do," Sarah said, rising and extending her hand. "I'm sure you'll excuse me. Thank you for bringing the letter over. We'll contact you when Henry gets home. I know he'll want to see you."

~ ~ ~

SINCE THE COLD, overcast morning promised snow or sleet, Sarah forbade the girls to come to the depot. "Your father's been sick, and too much excitement will not be good for him. Besides, it's much too cold for Octavia, and some of you will be needed here to watch her. Tom and I will go to the station with the wagon and bring your father back as soon as possible. It'll be a warmer greeting here."

There were many protests. But in the end, Sarah won out. As Tom brought the wagon to the front door, Sarah—clutching several lap robes to protect Henry from the elements—climbed onto the seat beside him and waved back to the children gathered at the front windows.

The trip to the depot was a difficult one at best. Sleet had begun in earnest by now, and Tom winced as he stared forward into the face of the storm. The horse shied several times as its hide was pelted with the small ice pellets. Sarah, however, seemed to notice nothing as she faced forward, peering through the grayness to catch sight of the depot. Henry was coming in, was her only thought.

Parking the wagon as near the depot as possible, Tom took a blanket from under the seat, planning to hold it over Sarah to protect her from the elements until the train arrived. Not to be kept down, however, Sarah jumped from the wagon before Tom could say a word. Running alongside the tracks to the platform, she watched as person after person ran by her, obviously in as much of a hurry as she.

Within moments, she heard the whistle in the distance and soon saw the train pulling slowly into the station. Pushing her way through the large crowd, Sarah was annoyed that so many people were blocking her way. She couldn't understand why they were there until a man standing in the open doorway at the front of the train handed out a stack of newspapers from Raleigh. The papers were snatched up as soon as they hit the platform, and Sarah could only glance briefly at the headline, which read:

"Sherman occupies Savannah."

A gasp went up from the crowd as others read the news. Atlanta and now Savannah had fallen to Union forces. Sherman had succeeded in doing what everyone had thought impossible: He had invaded the heart of the Confederacy and cut it virtually in half. If those cities were gone, where would he turn next? Would he now head north? Would his route take him through North Carolina?

The babble of voices surrounded Sarah as she sought in vain for Henry. The war didn't matter. Sherman didn't matter. Atlanta and Savannah were hundreds of miles away, and they didn't matter, either. All that mattered at that moment was that her beloved Henry was coming home at last. Nothing else could hurt her. They would weather whatever came— together. If only she could find him.

By this time, Tom was worried as well. He could see Sarah being buffeted by the wind, the sleet, and the large crowd. But he couldn't see Henry. As passenger after passenger alighted, and there was still no sign of his master, he pushed his way to the front of the platform and caught the conductor by the door. "Are there more soldiers on board?" Tom asked.

Turning to him with an annoyed look, the conductor waved toward the last car on the train. "Only those on stretchers in the last car," he announced. "It's only the ones who are of no use to them now they're sending home this Christmas. Didn't you see the headlines, man? The 'Bummers' are coming this way!"

Not waiting for any more conversation, Tom pushed his way toward Sarah. "In the last car," he yelled over the din of the station and the wind. "Come on!"

Sarah turned and ran past the departing passengers toward the end of the train, holding her skirt in one hand and clutching her bonnet with the other. Her hair came loose and fell in wisps across her face. The sleet stung her face, and twice she slipped on the ice crystals that had formed on the platform.

The crowd thinned as the last passengers descended and met their loved ones. But still Sarah ran, faster now, since she sensed the train was ready to depart. Her breath came in gasps, and she felt a pain in her side. But the thought of finding Henry drove her on. Finally, reaching the last car, she found her way blocked by an unrelenting row of pine boxes.

Stopping, she gasped, afraid of her thoughts. "But Henry was only sick," Sarah said to herself. "He can't be. . ."

"Sarah," came a weak voice beside her elbow. "Sarah, over here."

Turning her head to the side, she saw nothing until she heard a groan. Finally, she looked down at a stretcher wedged between two rows of boxes and dropped to her knees just as Tom approached. "Henry," she said, "my dear Henry!"

Tears stung her eyes, and she struggled to hold them back. This was not the Henry who had strode away so gallantly just a year ago. The man who looked back at her from the stretcher—so carelessly placed by the boxes of Confederate dead—looked at least ten years older. His eyes were sunken, his skin sallow, his once-golden hair lifeless. But his smile— his smile—Sarah thought, was as genuine as ever as he reached up his arms to enfold his wife.

"Miss Sarah," Tom whispered at her ear, "we gotta get Mister Henry outa this weather right now. I'll go get the wagon as quick as I can. You wait here," he added, taking charge.

The train moved off, slowly at first, then faster and faster as it picked up speed. Soon there were only Sarah and Henry— and the endless row of pine boxes left on the platform. Tom was right. Despite the cover over the platform, the cold and blowing sleet still penetrated everything. It was no place for a sick man. Sarah looked around for someone to help or, at least, someone at whom to rail for Henry's plight. But there was no one. It was wartime, she reminded herself.

Unable to move Henry, Sarah sat beside him on the cold, wet platform holding his hand and attempting to shield him with her own body. Patiently, she answered all the questions he asked with his eyes, while searching for Tom with her own.

Finally, after what seemed like ages, Tom appeared with the wagon, the wheels crunching over the icy roadway. A young boy sat beside him, peering through the blowing sleet and then pointing toward Sarah. As Tom stopped beside the platform, he and the boy jumped from the wagon. "We'll take him now, Miss Sarah," Tom said gently, touching her on the shoulder.

Sarah turned glazed eyes to Tom. Not fully comprehending, but willing to let him take charge, she stood up and moved away as Tom and the boy lifted the stretcher and placed it in the back of the wagon. The boy jumped from the wagon and, lifting his hand in a salute, ran back toward the train terminal.

Without a word, Tom grasped Sarah's hand and helped her to climb up beside her husband. He handed Sarah the blankets from under the seat, and she wrapped Henry as best she could. "Stay with me," Henry gasped, as he lapsed into a coughing fit.

"I'll never leave you, Henry," Sarah answered, rubbing his brow. She hoped the stinging sleet and rain would disguise the tears streaming down her face.

≈ ≈ ≈

As T<small>OM</small> <small>TURNED</small> the wagon onto King Street, she could see the inn ahead. The wreath the girls had made so lovingly looked forlorn in the gray light. But the smoke from the chimneys echoed the warmth waiting inside.

"Sarah," Henry whispered, lifting his head and smiling as Tom drew up before the steps. "I want to walk through the front door. The girls mustn't see me like this. It will frighten them."

"I'm not sure. . .," Sarah began, looking around for the best means of getting her husband down.

As she spoke, a figure approached the wagon hesitantly, hat over his face. "Henry, Old Man, need a hand?" came a cheerful greeting. "I swear I can't tell you how good it is to see you again. I don't mind telling you how difficult it is to be the only man around here. And all those young ladies in there asking for their daddy. . .," John said, continuing to talk as if nothing were wrong as he helped Tom lift Henry from the wagon and carry him to the door.

Alighting from the wagon herself, Sarah wept anew to see John, stumbling on his bad leg, doing his best to hold his ill friend upright, and dear Tom supporting the dead weight of his master against his own body.

They had no sooner stood Henry on his feet than the door burst open and six little girls rushed out. Tibitha and Elizabeth stood in the background. Henry, faltering as he stood upright, attempted a grin and opened his arms.

Mary Frances and Sudie, noticing the change in their father, reacted immediately, allowing him to lean on their shoulders and leading him to the sofa, where they removed his wet top-coat and boots. Sarah produced new quilts, while Mary Frances, exchanging a worried glance with Sudie, went for pillows.

The younger girls seemed to notice nothing, however, except that their beloved father was home—as each climbed up beside him for a hug.

Elizabeth placed Octavia beside Henry on the sofa, and the love in his eyes grew to tears as he saw his new daughter. "God has been good to me," Henry whispered, stroking the soft hair and placing his finger in her tiny grasp. "I never thought to see her!"

"God's been good to all of us," Sarah said, drawing a chair beside her husband. "He's sent you back to us. You have nothing to do now but get your strength back," she added, as a silent prayer tore itself from the depths of her heart.

Pulling his hat over his eyes, Tom uttered his own prayer as he turned the horse back toward town. "Please, God," he begged, "just let me get to Dr. Strudwick's before the darkness or the authorities catch up with me, and I'll never ask for nothin' else."

CHAPTER TWENTY-THREE
December 1864

DR. STRUDWICK CAME IMMEDIATELY, riding up front on the wagon with Tom, his bag clutched under his arm. Tom's description of Henry's condition sounded very serious, and he wanted to lose no time. As everyone else in town, Edmund Strudwick loved the quiet, gentle Henry and would have done anything for him.

Entering the hotel, the doctor—even with Tom's preparation—did a double-take at the change that had come over Henry. It was clear the influenza was only the most recent manifestation of the deprivations his gaunt body had undergone in the past year.

"Hello, Henry," Edmund called, concealing his alarm at his friend's condition. "Had to come home to see that perfect little young 'un Sarah and I brought into the world, did you? Well, what do you think? Isn't she as beautiful as all the others? Eight—my, my, you certainly know how to produce them!"

"Edmund!" Henry called weakly from the sofa. "How good of you to come. I would stand and greet you properly. But

I'm afraid this cold I've had and the long trip home have left me a little weak. Come over here and sit by the fire and tell me all the news, if you have time."

"I'll be happy to fill you in on everything. But first let's have a look at you and see what we can do to get rid of that 'cold,'" Dr. Strudwick answered as Sarah hustled the children off to the family quarters.

≈ ≈ ≈

I WON'T MINCE words with you, Sarah," Dr. Strudwick said quietly as he sought her out in the dining room where she was preparing a cup of tea for Henry. "You're a strong woman. And you need to know what you're up against. Henry's a very sick man. But I'm sure you've guessed that. He's been suffering from malnutrition, bordering on starvation, for several months. The insect bites and cuts he received in their maneuvers in the swamps have not healed properly. It has all put a severe strain on his body. The influenza was devastating in his weakened condition. And the effects of the cold in the infirmary tent and the train ride home have left their mark as well.

"I can't tell you if he'll survive this. Good food, warmth, and lots of love often can do wonders. But I'm not sure they can produce miracles. Only God can do that. The only thing I can tell you is that Henry Stroud will never again be the same man he was when he left here. He may recover—I pray that he does. But even then, his body will be a living memorial to all that he's suffered.

"You'll need help around here. You can't run a hotel, mother six girls and a new baby, and nurse an ailing husband. And Henry will be of little use to you for quite some time, I'm afraid. Would you like me to try to find you a nurse for him to take at least that much off your mind?" the doctor offered.

"Thank you, Edmund. I appreciate your honesty. But the girls and I will care for Henry. If love can cure him, you can be assured he'll recover dramatically," Sarah answered.

Henry did seem to improve. By Christmas Eve, he felt well enough to sit in a chair by the fire and watch the family as they decorated the house. Tibitha and Elizabeth came for the children and met John for the church service, leaving Sarah at home with Henry and Octavia. Afterwards the whole family gathered around the tree, which Tom had cut in the nearby countryside.

After the tree was decorated, Mary Frances played the piano and everyone sang Christmas carols. The family tried, for Henry's sake, to pretend that everything was normal and make it a joyous occasion. And it seemed to work—for Henry at least. If he noticed the tears in her eyes when Tibitha looked at her favorite brother, or the shake of his head when John caught her eye, he gave no indication. As Claudia sat beside Sarah, she whispered, "We prayed for Daddy this evening, Mommy—the whole congregation. Do you think God heard us?"

"I'm sure he did, Sweetheart," Sarah answered, not adding that her voice had preceded theirs, though she had not been at church.

CHRISTMAS AFTERNOON, CAVE and Cornelia arrived with their boisterous family. Sarah could have shot Cave for his bluntness as he remarked on removing his coat, "You look a little worse for the wear, Brother. Guess the war didn't agree with you as much as you thought. I tried to advise you to get an exemption, as I did."

"I did what I had to, Cave. We may listen to others. But we have to answer to our own inner voice. No man can do otherwise. I don't regret it," Henry answered. "I was part of a wonderful group of dedicated men, all fighting for a cause we believe in. None of us would change that fact—no matter what the outcome."

"That cause is all but worthless now," Cave added. "With Atlanta and Savannah in Union hands and Sherman poised to march through the Carolinas, there will be precious little to salvage of the old South. If you're an example of the men left on the coast, Sherman will cut through the Confederates like a knife through butter, and the cause will be history by spring."

"Be that as it may," Henry answered sadly, "we did what we had to. And my men and the others in the field will meet Sherman head on when he comes. I only hope I'm well enough to be with them then. Nothing would give me greater pleasure than to face that man eye-to-eye. We have our pride, Cave. We still have that."

"That stubborn Southern pride will be the death of us all," Cave remarked. "It's lucky I, at least, never felt the need to prove my loyalty and so have kept things going for you and Alfred."

"Have you heard from Alfred?" Henry asked, suddenly turning with interest. "I lost track of him after I was stationed near New Bern. I understood he went on to Wilmington."

"At last account he was waiting—as were you—for that devil Sherman to show his face on his way north. Ah, my patriotic brothers!" Cave said with a mock sigh.

$$\sim \quad \sim \quad \sim$$

BY NEW YEAR'S EVE, word spread that Sherman and his army were again on the move. Rumor had it that they would head straight up through both South and North Carolina toward a union with Grant's forces. Day after day, the newspapers reported the destruction as the troops made their way north through South Carolina.

Sherman had more than 60,000 men in his army—wagons, ambulances, and supplies. His customary march was in groups of at least four, each traveling different roads. Foraging parties of approximately one hundred men often preceded the bulk of the army by a day or more. These groups were ordered to destroy anything of military value for the South—including wagons, horses, tools, ammunition, and even foodstuffs. Nothing in the homes, farms, or businesses was sacred to the Union soldiers.

Silver, heirlooms, china, furniture, bedding, clothing, and livestock were confiscated or destroyed before their owners' eyes, leaving the people with only the clothes on their backs. The bulk of the army followed, finishing the job the scouts had begun—often burning towns, houses, barns, and crops in their wake to complete the destruction.

Word of the atrocities flowed into the city of Hillsborough daily as both newspapers and travelers arrived at the depot outside of town. Injured soldiers returning home brought tales of the horrors they had seen and heard in Georgia and South Carolina. And relatives of Hillsborough residents fleeing northward brought eyewitness accounts. The Orange Hotel was filled again with men—and women—discussing each day's news and the prospects for the rest of the South, their loved ones in battle, and their beloved city.

Cave came to the hotel daily now to bring Henry news of the fighting and the paper, oblivious to his brother's frail health. Sarah tried several times to tell Cave that Henry was too ill to be disturbed. But somehow Henry always knew when Cave was about and asked to see him. After such visits, Henry was visibly shaken. He worried most about his own regiment now that he was gone. It was clear they would finally see action, and he longed to be with them.

Henry's condition did not improve. Despite Dr. Strudwick's care and the constant attention of Sarah and the rest of the family, he continued to lose weight and become weaker. By the middle of January, he could not even stand with assistance, and his voice seemed to emanate from a giant chasm within his emaciated body. Yet Henry did not complain as he continued to plan for the day when he would be well and back with his unit—in time for Sherman's arrival.

≈ ≈ ≈

IT WAS A bleak day in early February. The older girls were in school. Octavia was napping. And Annie and Pattie were baking cookies with Cook. Sarah, being relieved of her numerous duties for the moment, sneaked into the darkened bedroom to check on Henry. She had long since moved out herself, not wanting to disturb his rest.

The smell of camphor filled her nostrils as she entered. And the room, in the gray dawn of early morning, seemed unfamiliar to her. The bedside table was covered with medicine bottles, cups, and plates. The shades were drawn against the light, which hurt Henry's sensitive eyes. Piles of blankets and quilts used to stem Henry's chills stood stacked on the dresser.

She could not tell if Henry was asleep or awake and hesitated at the threshold. "Sarah?" She heard his harsh whisper across the room. "Come and talk to me," Henry implored.

"I don't want to tire you, Henry. But I'd love to spend some time with you," Sarah answered, sitting in the chair beside the bed and taking her husband's hand.

"We need to talk," Henry said, attempting to pull himself up in the bed. He accepted Sarah's help as she raised the pillows behind him. When he was comfortable, he began, "I wanted nothing more than to see this war to a close and to come home to you and the girls and our hotel. Now it seems the war is finally drawing to a close. But I'm afraid I won't see it. My men must fight without me. And you and the girls, I'm afraid, must carry on with the hotel without me. I wish it were otherwise. . ."

"Don't talk like that!" Sarah interrupted.

"I must," Henry continued. "We both know I'm not getting any better, and it's just a matter of time. The Lord knows I don't want to leave you, especially at this critical time. But He seems to have other plans for me.

"You're strong. You've always been stronger than me. You've endured childbirth eight times and have run this hotel singlehandedly for the last year and a half. You can survive. I'm counting on you to keep this hotel going for you and our girls. It's their home and your livelihood. We did realize our dream, Sarah. We did accomplish that much. And we did it together. This hotel will always be a lasting memorial to our love. . .," he added.

"Cave has a list of all my investments and properties. He knows what to do to look after them. And he'll make sure you and the girls can continue to live here. I trust him. He's my twin. I know we're different. And I also know that for some reason you have never liked him much. . ."

"Henry, I. . .," Sarah began, but Henry waved her away weakly.

"Your feelings are your business. I won't ask you about them. But please, for our family's sake, let him help you. He won't fail you. Promise me, Sarah, so I may be at peace," Henry concluded, collapsing in a coughing fit.

"I promise—whatever you ask. I'll turn to Cave and ask his help if the need arises," Sarah sobbed, tears streaming down her cheeks as she looked at her stricken husband. "Now, please, don't talk about the future any more. I only want to hold you now, to enjoy this moment. You will get better. We just need to be patient. Spring will be here soon. It will be a time of healing—for you, and for the South. You'll see.

"Rest now, Honey. Don't talk any more. You need your strength," she continued, rising to ease her husband back down into the bed and cover him further.

"Stay with me!" Henry pleaded, patting the bed beside him. "Don't leave me, Sarah!"

"I'll stay, Henry. I'll be here as long as you need me—always," Sarah promised, lying beside him on the bed and cradling his head on her chest—as he had so often done for her.

≈ ≈ ≈

IT WAS THERE Dr. Strudwick found them two hours later as he let himself quietly into the room. "Sarah," the doctor said, touching her arm. "Sarah," he whispered louder, getting no response.

The wan light sliding under the shutters fell across her face. He could see her eyes were opened wide. But no recognition showed. Tears stood in their wells and rolled down her cheeks, soaking the fair head still cradled on her chest.

"Sarah," Dr. Strudwick whispered again, trying to rouse the forlorn figure. "You must let me see to him. Please."

Finally acknowledging his presence, Sarah turned her eyes to the kindly ones of the doctor—her friend who had seen her through so much. Slowly, she began to stir, gently laying the head of her beloved Henry on the pillow beside her and stepping out of the doctor's way.

Dr. Strudwick felt for pulse in the hand hanging so loosely from the covers. Laying the hand back on the bed, he gently closed Henry's translucent eyelids. Then, turning to Sarah and taking her gently into his arms, he murmured, "There's nothing more I can do. The Lord must take over from here. He put up a gallant fight. He will be sorely missed and never forgotten by those of us who loved him.

"You and the girls were blessed to have him, Sarah. Remember the good times, if you can. Henry would not want you to grieve. Now why not let me call Tom and Lucy to take over from here? Your family will need you."

"Dr. Strudwick. . . Edmund," Sarah faltered, "you've been a true friend all my life. I'm glad it was you who was with me. Thank you for all you've done. But I alone will see to my husband. Could you tell Tom and Lucy for me, though? I'll need them later."

~ ~ ~

IT WAS A gloomy gathering at the Old Town Cemetery on Churton Street. The new grave stood open beneath the spreading magnolia tree, steam from the newly-turned earth rising into the still, morning air. The swirling mist hung like a curtain around the graveyard, giving an eerie stillness and otherworldliness to the stately headstones, some dating back almost a century and including some of Hillsborough's most prestigious men.

The pallbearers, Cave, John, Francis, and Dr. Strudwick, walked carefully up the stone stairs to set Henry's coffin beside the gaping hole. Then six little girls dressed in ill-fitting black dresses—borrowed from trunks and attics all over town— formed a semicircle around the large box.

Sarah, holding little Octavia in her arms, walked in a trance, her head bowed and her eyes on the ground. Her black veil blending with her dark hair and black dress, gave Sarah the appearance of a specter. Behind the forlorn family stood Tibitha and Elizabeth, Cornelia, and Sarah's mother and sisters. Tears flowed freely as each suffered her own loss. Years of memories played through each mind.

With a glance at the mourners, Reverend Dodson opened his Bible and began, "In Ecclesiastes 3, the Bible reminds us that 'For everything there is a season, and a time for every matter under heaven.' The verse goes on to tell us there is 'A time to be born, and a time to die,'" the minister recited in a solemn voice. "There is no set time allotted to any of us on this earth. God makes no promises, nor does He see fit to explain His actions to us. While it may seem that Henry Stroud's work on Earth was far from done, God has proclaimed otherwise. We can do no more than accept that.

"The 'time to weep' and the 'time to mourn' the Lord allows us. Then he expects each of us to carry on. In the years to come, those of us gathered here will remember Henry Stroud—each in his own way—as the remarkable man he was. And each of you will be proud to say he was part of your life," the minister concluded.

As the graveside ceremony ended, Cave took Sarah's arm while the others gathered the children by the hands and led them down the wide, stone steps to Churton Street and on toward King Street and the hotel—where Lucy and Cook had worked for two days to provide food for the mourners.

No one spoke. Merchants along the busy Churton Street left their businesses to bow their heads as the little procession filtered by. Passerby after passerby stopped to pay homage to their grief, some grasping Sarah by the hand with a mournful expression—for everyone in town had known and loved Henry Stroud. War, deprivation, hunger, fear all were forgotten as the loss hung heavy in the air of Hillsborough.

It seemed to Sarah that she had suffered the worst. Nothing more could happen to her. She had lost a father, a daughter, and now her beloved Henry. There was little more that could be taken from her, she thought, until she passed the office of the *Hillsborough Recorder*, where the day's paper was displayed. Sarah riveted on the headline: "Columbia in Flames; Sherman turns to North Carolina."

CHAPTER TWENTY-FOUR
March 1865

WITH EACH PASSING DAY, Sherman's "Bummers" came closer. The headlines rang with news of their destruction. Wadesboro, Rockingham, Fayetteville—still the "Bummers" came, looting, vandalizing, pillaging, killing, and burning the cities in their wake. By March it was clear they were heading for Raleigh to destroy North Carolina's capital city.

It was one of those rare, warm days in March when the promise of spring was just out of reach. Though the trees were still bare, the hint of green hung on every branch, so that one had to squint to be sure he had seen correctly. The crocuses were up, however. And even the daffodils sported swollen, yellow buds.

Sarah had so much to do. But she couldn't bear to be inside another minute. The family quarters, which had not been aired because of the inclement weather and a reluctance on Sarah's part to enter the master bedroom, still smelled like a hospital. And the whole hotel seemed musty and dark. Taking Octavia's pram into the courtyard, Sarah returned to re-

trieve Pattie and Annie, who ran immediately to the old magnolia tree to examine the newly-sprouting bulbs.

Sarah seated herself on the bench, where she and Henry
had so often sat together. The ache for him was still too much
to bear. But she was tired, bone-tired. Since no one was ven-
turing far from home these days until they knew Sherman's
plans, she, Lucy, and Mary Frances had begun spring cleaning
in the empty hotel rooms. Every muscle ached. But at least
she'd had a diversion for a time.

Hunger gnawed at her stomach as it had for months.
There was so little food, and the girls needed it worse than
she. She barely had enough milk for poor Octavia, who had
been extremely restless the past month—a reflection of her
mother's state of mind.

Looking down, she saw that the dress she had worn when
her father died and now wore in mourning for Henry hung
on her as if it had been placed on a broomstick. "What does it
matter?" she asked herself, fingering a pleat of the soft, black
silk, which was now worn almost threadbare. "What does anything matter? This accursed war has taken everything I ever
held dear."

Slowly, checking to see that the girls were occupied, she
lay her head back on the bench and closed her eyes, letting
the warm sun wipe out the memories that were too painful to
bear. The sound of the girls' laughter faded into the distance,
and she dozed.

Suddenly, two hands gripped Sarah's shoulders, knead-
ing away the ache. "Henry," she murmured contentedly. Slowly
opening her eyes, she looked upward at the face above her. A
shock of blond hair, highlighted by the bright sunlight, formed
a halo around the head, throwing the face into shadow. Confused, Sarah shook the sleep from her eyes and looked again.

"I'm so sorry, Sarah. It seems I can never be who you want me to be," Cave's voice said sadly.

"Cave!" Sarah called, coming instantly back to reality as she felt a blush rise up her neck.

She was saved any further reply when Pattie and Annie, hearing the familiar voice, jumped up from their play and ran to Cave calling, "Daddy! Daddy!"

"Looks like I'm disappointing all the Stroud women today," Cave added ruefully, bending to tousle Annie's bright curls.

"Girls, it's Uncle Cave," Sarah said quietly. "I think he fooled all of us."

"Uncle Cave, you looked just like Daddy," Pattie said. "But I forgot. Daddy's not coming back."

"That's right, Pattie," Sarah answered. "Why don't you each give Uncle Cave a kiss and then maybe you can check Octavia for me while Uncle Cave and I talk."

Cave bent down for the two wet kisses and patted each head absently as the girls ran back to their play.

"You did come to talk, didn't you?" Sarah asked, moving over on the bench to give Cave room.

"I've waited a month to talk to you about finances, Sarah. I know it's still too soon, and I'm sorry. I would have waited longer. . . But with Sherman so close, I really feel it's imperative to straighten your affairs out while we can and while the Confederacy still exists. Who knows what will happen if Sherman comes through here. If he leaves Hillsborough as he has every other town, everything will be lost. There will be nothing of worth left to any of us," Cave said resignedly.

"What do you mean? Henry said you had everything under control and that he had left us well taken care of. Is there some problem?" Sarah asked, looking squarely at Cave, her dark brown eyes studying his opaque gray ones. She never could read Cave's eyes as she could Henry's. And she was frightened with what she saw.

"Henry thought you were well taken care of," Cave began slowly. "Actually you were—at the start of the war. But like the rest of us, he failed to take the war into account. The taxes the Confederacy has required have taken a big chunk from every household—yours especially because of all the properties Henry owned. . ."

"Owned?" Sarah questioned, brows raised.

"Let me finish," Cave went on, raising his hand to stop her and ignoring her question. "The price of food, as you know, has skyrocketed. It has cost an absolute fortune to keep this hotel going—particularly since the majority of the guests for the past four years have been nonpaying. But Henry always did have a soft spot for the downtrodden that overruled his business sense."

"That's unfair, Cave. They were hungry and needed a bed. How could we have turned any of the soldiers away?" Sarah asked, afraid of what she would hear next.

"At any rate, what's done is done. You need to understand this, Sarah, and not become defensive. Colonel Tew's academy, which started off with such prospects, has fallen on the same hard times that have hit us all. The Confederate Army is now taking the young men before they could possibly finish the academy. So even families who could afford to send their sons have stopped doing so, seeing no purpose in it.

"Then there's the matter of your own girls. The tuition for four children at the Nash-Kollock School the past four years has not been cheap. The bill for uniforms in the face of the fabric shortage has been exorbitant. I'm afraid what it boils down to is that you are flat broke. I've taken the liberty of selling your part of the academy and all of Henry's properties—including your house near Mars Hill. . .," Cave said, pausing.

"My house!" Sarah screamed. "That land was part of my father's property. He deeded it to Henry and me to keep it in the family. How could you sell it?"

"I had no choice, Sarah. And neither did you. What livelihood could you reap so far from town? I've saved the hotel for you—for the time being at least. After the war, perhaps it will earn enough money for your family to live on," Cave answered.

"I did what I thought best. I've looked after you as Henry asked. I'm sorry to have acted so hastily. But I fear the end of the war is coming, and it will not be pretty. At least, acting now, I could find buyers in the South for each of Henry's holdings. Hopefully you can realize enough profit to pay off some of your debts before the U. S. government repossesses everything. And maybe the new owners will be able to hold onto the property and keep it from falling into the hands of some get-rich-quick Yankees, who will take advantage of the South's poverty when the war is over.

"I really am sorry, Sarah. Please believe me. I would have given anything to have spared you all this," Cave concluded, reaching out for her hand.

"I'm sure you did what you had to," Sarah replied icily, drawing her hand away and averting her face so he would not see the pain and anger in her eyes. "The girls and I will be all right. We've survived worse than poverty. When the war is over, this hotel will prove itself anew. It will be the best in the state. You'll see," she said, rising and beckoning to the girls.

How dare he? How dare he sell all that belonged to her without even asking? Henry had never made a move without consulting her. And now she had nothing left in the world but the Orange Hotel. The only consolation was that she owed him nothing and need not ever see Cave Stroud again, she decided, pushing the pram into the hotel and ushering her girls inside.

Tears stung Sarah's eyes. But she vowed she would not shed them. Already there had been enough tears for a lifetime. There would be a time to cry—later. Someday, when this accursed war was over and the world was right again, there would be time for that luxury.

CHAPTER TWENTY-FIVE
April 1865

IT HAD BEEN A month since Cave's visit. On April 13, the Confederate forces had moved out of Raleigh and Governor Vance had left the city, opening it to Sherman's forces. Sherman arrived the next morning. Finding the city deserted, he set up his headquarters in the governor's mansion and drew up plans to pursue the fleeing General Johnston and his Confederate troops along the rail-lines—right through Hillsborough.

The silence was almost as unbearable as the waiting, Sarah decided, rising from her chair and pulling the curtains aside. No sign of life emanated from any of the houses down King Street—as far as she could see. Craning her neck, she felt a knot in her stomach when she saw the gate to John and Tibitha's home swaying in the breeze. They must have forgotten to close it in their haste to leave last evening.

She remembered how John had beaten on her door after supper and announced breathlessly that he was taking Tibitha, Elizabeth, and their valuables to the Stroud homestead outside of Hillsborough to wait out the Yankees' arrival. He had pleaded with Sarah to come with them. But she had been resolute. Perhaps she should have relented and at least sent the girls along. But it was too late for hindsight now.

Sarah thought with a pang how much she already missed the little family, who had been her lifeline these last few unbearable months. They would all be sitting on the large veranda right now waiting to see the smoke of the burning Hillsborough, saddened, but out of harm's reach. She could only pray her family's safety would not cause them undue worry. She knew how angry Henry would have been with her for not seeking his family's protection.

But Sarah knew why she had stayed behind—why she'd refused even to send the children with Tibitha and John. Yes, Henry had asked her to protect their family. But he had also asked her to keep the hotel going for herself and the girls. He had loved this old inn so. . . And now it was all her little family had. Henry had trusted her to keep it alive so that she and her children would always have a home. She'd lost so much. . .

Surely, God would allow her this one, small victory, Sarah reasoned. For she would rather face Sherman and his whole army than to ever show Cave any weakness. Clenching her fist in defiance, Sarah swore out loud in the empty room, "I will never let him see me beg for his protection, so help me, God!"

As the door banged shut behind her, Sarah jumped as if she had been shot. "Yankees" was her only thought.

"Don't let me startle you, Miss Sarah," Tom apologized, coming forward with his hat in his hand. "But Lucy and me just noticed smoke to the east. There may be Yankees here within the hour. Sherman always sends a scouting party ahead, I hear. We didn't want you to be unprepared."

"Thank you, Tom. I'm as prepared as I can be. I can never tell you and Lucy how much your loyalty and friendship have meant to me over the years. You two do what you can, as I know you will. But if all else fails, save yourselves. Promise me. The Yankees say they are fighting to free you. Let them do it. They won't hurt you two if you don't resist. Let me feel a part of our effort was not in vain. The girls and I will be all right," Sarah added, attempting a reassuring smile.

"Miss Sarah, Lucy and I ain't never goin' to leave you and those babies. Why, we done raised 'em the same as you. And you folks are all the family we've got. We don't want to go with no Yankee soldiers after what they've done to folks all over the South. You can count on that. Lucy and I will go down fightin', same as you. There ain't nothin' you can say to make us do different," Tom answered, shaking his head as he walked back to the door.

As Sarah returned to the settee, she felt rather than heard a faint throbbing in the distance toward Churton Street. It was the unmistakable beat of a drum, and the high, plaintive notes of a fife suddenly joined it. Sarah felt the hair stand up on her neck. Glancing toward the back door, she caught Tom's eye, and he nodded solemnly.

Within minutes, the cobblestones echoed with the pounding of feet as Sherman's scouting party turned onto King Street and entered the various shops. Walking to the window, Sarah pulled back the drapes and watched astounded as groups of men entered the Hillsborough Improvement Company. Returning time and again with furniture and other valuables, they piled them in the street or placed them in wagons, which rumbled along behind their brigade.

The Masonic Hall was next. With her heart beating wildly in her chest, Sarah saw men moving like shadows across the large, upstairs windows—rummaging through desks and papers and carrying out ceremonial equipment and flags.

The inn would be next, Sarah knew. Slowly making her way to the desk, she stood in readiness—her knees shaking so badly she had to lean on the counter to support herself. She had only seconds to wait as two young men in blue uniforms suddenly pushed their way through the door, which Sarah had left unlatched—knowing they would break in if not admitted.

Mustering all her courage, Sarah stood her ground by the desk. "Good afternoon, gentlemen," she said as pleasantly as possible, praying they would not notice her quaking knees. "Do you want a room or a meal?"

"Lord! There's a real, live woman in this town, Jed!" one of the soldiers said, turning in confusion to his companion.

"Nice establishment," said the man named Jed, removing his hat and wiping his damp brow. "Bet with such a nice outside, you got lots o' good stuff inside."

"Actually, I have nothing of value left," Sarah said, opening her arms wide to show her threadbare dress and the simple cross she wore. "I have had to sell all I had to keep food on the table the last few years. But you're welcome to look," she answered, thinking how young both boys looked. They couldn't be any older than nineteen—Mary Frances's age. "Oh, Lord," she prayed silently, fearing for Mary Frances, Sudie, Claudia, and Maria, who were hiding in the attic. "Please let the girls remain quiet."

"How many folk live here?" the first soldier asked.

"As you can see, gentlemen," Sarah replied, indicating her black dress, "I'm a widow."

"Husband die in the Confederacy?" Jed questioned, looking at her sideways under his sandy hair and chewing on a straw.

"Actually, he died in bed of influenza," Sarah answered truthfully. "He was the owner of this hotel. I'm trying to keep it going for my children."

"How many children you got?" Jed persisted.

"Those are my daughters playing in the courtyard with their nurse," Sarah responded, pointing to Pattie, Annie, and Octavia—while not revealing the actual number of daughters.

"Didn't you think to get them away before we got here?" the first soldier continued as an evil leer spread over his dark countenance. "I hear tell most of you Rebs is afeared of us 'count of what we've been doing."

"We have nowhere to go," Sarah answered truthfully. "I haven't heard of you harming children. And I'm no threat to you. Go ahead and do as you must."

"Come on, Dave," Jed growled impatiently. "Let's get what we come for. Lots of places still to cover in this town. Can't let the others get away with more than we find!

"Afternoon, Ma'am," Jed said, pretending to tip his hat and pulling Dave with him up the stairs.

Sarah held her breath as she heard footsteps in the room above her head—the room behind which Mary Frances, Sudie, Claudia, and Maria were hiding. She knew after hearing Dave's exchange what would happen if they were found. As she strained her ears, two more soldiers rushed in through the open door, not even acknowledging her presence as they raced upstairs.

Within minutes, Dave and Jed were back downstairs carrying china cups, candlesticks, and washbasins stolen from each room. The two new arrivals followed carrying bedding and towels. Sarah stifled a cry when she saw the hand towels Mary Frances had made the last Christmas wadded up in one of the soldiers' fists. "What's the matter, Lady?" he asked. "This stuff ain't gonna do you no good. When we get through with this place, there ain't gonna be nothing left but ashes," he added with a throaty laugh, pushing the door open with his hip and throwing the goods on the nearest wagon.

"You fellows finish upstairs," Jed said, coming back inside and taking charge. "I'll see what they might be hiding out back."

"There's nothing but the kitchen and an empty stable," Sarah answered. "There's no food in the kitchen. And I had to sell the horses to make payments on the hotel after my husband died," she lied.

"Maybe you is tellin' the truth. Maybe you ain't," Jed said. "Mind if I find out for myself?"

"As I said before, gentlemen, help yourselves," Sarah added, turning resignedly to sit back down on the settee, hoping the solid weight beneath her would stop her quaking knees.

"That's some fine piece of furniture," Dave said. "'Fraid we're goin' to have to ask you to move, Ma'am, so we can get this out the door. Come on, Bill, help me," he added, grabbing one end of the settee.

Sarah stood and moved aside quickly, bumping into the fourth soldier, who was exiting the family wing loaded with Sarah's few dresses. "Thank heaven Tom suggested we move the older girls' clothing to the attic so we wouldn't give away their presence," Sarah thought, blessing Tom even more for his clear thinking.

She could hear the stable door opening. But she knew Jed would not remain long when he encountered only straw. Tom had done a good job, she was sure, of ridding the stables of all signs of recent occupation.

It seemed hours to Sarah that she sat on the stool behind the desk watching the Yankees carry out her beloved possessions. She, Tom, and Lucy had, had such hopes that their plan would work. But her hopes had now gone up in smoke. And she was beginning to fear the hotel soon would, too.

Two soldiers were exiting the front door with a large, carved chest when an older man entered, shoving them aside. "Who owns this hotel?" he asked one of the men.

Holding the chest with both hands, the young man lifted his chin in Sarah's direction, then continued on his way.

"Ma'am, I'm Sergeant Aycock," said the dark-haired man with the silver-streaked moustache. "Do you own this inn?"

"The hotel belonged to my husband, Henry Stroud, who is recently deceased," Sarah answered. "He died of influenza here just two months ago. And I have been attempting to keep his business running for him—and my children."

"Was your husband a Mason, Mrs. Stroud?" the sergeant asked.

"As a matter of fact, he was the grand master of the lodge across the street," Sarah answered, nodding toward the window.

"Were you aware when you hung the Masonic apron from your flagpole that you had issued the Masonic distress signal?" Sergeant Aycock continued.

"I learned that by accident several years ago," Sarah replied, attempting to hide a smile. The apron she'd hung in place of the Confederate flag had at least provided the attention she'd hoped for. "I certainly think the situation warrants a 'distress' signal. Or hadn't you noticed all my worldly goods exiting my home, leaving my poor babies and me with nothing?" she added, gesturing toward the little girls playing in the yard. Lucy had done her job well, she noted. Nothing had been disturbed in the courtyard.

"A thousand apologies, Mrs. Stroud," Sergeant Aycock said, grabbing Sarah's hand to shake it. "I, too, am a Mason. I'm sworn by my vow to honor the needs of a fellow Mason, alive or dead. Since you've displayed the distress signal, I must make it my duty to protect your husband's property—including his widow and children.

"Here, men," he called to the two soldiers who had just carried out the chest and were entering for more. "Return that chest you just took out. And return the other goods you've stripped from this lady's home. I want to see that wagon empty and everything back in order when I return within the hour."

"Yes, Sir!" the two men answered in unison, turning puzzled looks on each other.

"Ho, there, Soldier," he called to Jed, who was just cross-ing the courtyard. "Help these men return all of Mrs. Stroud's goods. When you've finished, you and your buddy," he said, gesturing to Dave, who was just descending the stairs with one last load, "will stand guard by the front door of her inn to protect it from harm while our troops are in town. Do you understand? No looting! And above all, no torching. That's an order, Soldier!"

"Yes, Sir!" Jed answered. "Dave, put that stuff back where you found it and help get the rest of those things back in here," Jed said with a superior tone as the sergeant walked over to Sarah.

"Sorry to have put you through this, Ma'am," the sergeant said, bowing low. "If you have any further trouble, just send one of my men for me. You're a courageous woman, Mrs. Stroud. I salute you," he added, clicking his heels and raising his hand to his hat as he left the hotel.

Sarah watched the sergeant's retreating back. Then, with an air of authority, she walked to the back door. "Lucy, you may bring the girls in for a nap now," she called as, unseen by the men, she winked at both Lucy and Tom, who followed the children inside.

"By the way, Tom," she added smiling, "would you please see to that loose slab on Henry's desk? We really must get on with our spring chores. It's April."

Epilogue

Less than a week later, on April 15, Abraham Lincoln was shot and killed as he sat in a box in Ford's Theater in Washington, D.C. His more lenient plans for the reconstruction of the South died with him. The war in North Carolina was over three days after that, on April 18, when General Joseph E. Johnston surrendered his forces to General Sherman at Bennett Place, a small homestead between Hillsborough and Durham, North Carolina.

By April 26, President Davis had fled, and the Confederate forces had surrendered. The "accursed" war was over at last, though its aftermath offered little relief to the suffering the South had endured for so many months.

Thousands of threadbare, hungry, disillusioned, ill, and wounded soldiers—the "pride of the South"—finally made their way slowly back home, many through Hillsborough. Those who ventured down King Street in the months to come soon found a warm welcome and a hot meal, meager as it was, at the Orange Hotel.

Clarissa Thomasson, Sarah Stroud's great-great granddaughter, received her BA in English literature from Duke University and her Master's degree in English literature from the University of Florida. She taught English literature, creative writing, and journalism in Montgomery County, Maryland, before moving to Nags Head, North Carolina, with her husband to pursue her writing career. *Defending Hillsborough* is her first novel.